The Management Secrets
of
T. John Dick

The Management Secrets of
T. John Dick Guarantee

"The Management Secrets of T. John Dick" will teach you nothing of any value. It will not make you a better manager. It will not provide a valuable insight into anything. We guarantee it.

If this book should provide an insight of any kind or prove to to be a source of inspiration in any way, please contact the the publisher immediately with full details.

AUGUSTUS GUMP

The Management Secrets
of
T. John Dick

Mainland Press

Hickory, North Carolina, USA
Edinburgh, Scotland

Published 2001

Published by Mainland Press, P.O Box 3895, Hickory, NC 28603, USA
www.mainlandpress.com

This is a work of fiction. All characters and events depicted are fictitious. Any
resemblance to actual people, living or dead, or actual events is entirely coincidental.

Cataloging-in-Publication Data
Gump, Augustus
The Management Secrets of T. John Dick / by Augustus Gump
     p.   cm.
ISBN 0-9708746-9-3
1. Management—Fiction 2. Wit and Humor—Fiction I. Title
PR6057.U83M21   2001
823'.92-dc21   2001088297

ISBN 0-9708746-9-3
Library of Congress Control Number: 2001088297
Manufactured in the United States of America .

ACKNOWLEDGEMENTS

Grateful thanks are due to all the boneheads I have had to work with; men (mostly) whose cheerful and single-minded dedication to incompetence is an inspiration to us all.

Thanks also to Elayne, Niamh and Aoife for their forebearance and to Elizabeth Glynn, an empress amongst editors.

For My Father

FOREWORD

By Ronald Byrd
Vice President of Finance, Pumpex-SuperPumps

The reader of this book is almost certain to find himself confronted by a very fundamental question. Why would anyone consign to paper a series of events which reveal him to be one of the most monumental jackasses in the history of American business? As one who was close to those events and who knows the author well, I feel I am as well placed as anyone to attempt an answer to this perplexing question. The editor of this book is of similar mind, which is why she looked me up and asked if I wouldn't mind contributing some sort of an explanation in the form of a foreword. I leapt at the chance. I have always had a special place in my heart for my old friend and colleague T. John Dick.

I am consistently struck by a sense of awe in the presence of absolute purity, and it is with a sizable helping of this awe that I have always beheld T. J. There is something magnificent about incompetence so totally unsullied by common sense. In the same way, you have to be moved by the spectacle of someone so supremely confident of his own abilities—abilities of which the most careful observer would have a hard time catching even a fleeting glimpse.

Returning to the fundamental question outlined above, I think that there are two main motives which impelled T. John Dick to pick up the pen and proceed to make of himself one of the foremost fatheads on the contemporary business scene. The first of these reasons is simple enough: T. J. believes that his account of the goings on at Pumpex-

SuperPumps will offer valuable insights into the workings of a top class company in a highly competitive industry and the vital role of a dynamic marketing professional within that organization. He simply doesn't see the jackass bit at all.

The second reason arises out of a party held about a year ago at the house of the Vice President of Engineering at Pumpex-SuperPumps, Peter Braithwaite. I remember I was talking to Peter in the kitchen, where we had gone to liberate two of his distinctive English beers from the refrigerator, when I heard the familiar braying laughter that told me that my old friend and colleague T. J. had arrived. It had been some considerable time since I had seen the old goat and we had a lot of catching up to do, so I happily seized the opportunity to reminisce about the old days and the singular goings on at Pumpex-SuperPumps that fateful summer. I remember that our memories differed somewhat in their perspective. As I recalled the events, T. J.'s role was very much that of chief knucklehead, on occasion to a dangerous or even fatal degree, while, not surprisingly, he saw his part in the proceedings in a completely different light. It was then that I uttered the words to which I believe this book owes its conception:

"You know, T. J.," I said, "someone ought to write a book about it. There's enough material to fill a whole library. Maybe I'll write one."

I think perhaps for a fleeting moment I might have seriously considered the idea. That beer of Braithwaite's is powerful stuff and more than enough to make the most scatterbrained schemes seem not only feasible but a damned good idea, at least for a few seconds. I may even have mentioned a few choice episodes which I believed would entertain and inform the reader. T. J., I recall, got quite hot under the collar. His glasses steamed up, and he kept on muttering things like: "No, it wasn't like that at all" and "It was quite obvious that I was in no way to blame for the incident in the hotel bathroom."

Of course, by the next morning I had completely forgotten the whole episode, so I was surprised when, a few weeks later, T. J. called me at the office. I knew something had to be on his mind because he rarely calls me. To be honest I think he finds a conversation with me a bit of a chore. He has nothing to gain by it, and I am not compelled by line of authority even to pretend to take him seriously. He has always been prone to indulge in impatient grunting noises when forced into a discussion with me. Anyway, he started off by asking about some sort of figures he said he needed for a report, but I could tell that that wasn't the real reason for his call. After a few minutes of this sham, he came to the point. I could be sure that this was the real point of the call by the casual note he attempted to sound in asking the question.

"Oh, by the way, how's the book coming along?"

"Oh fine," I said. I had no idea what he was talking about.

"I see."

It was only after I had put the phone down that I remembered our conversation at Peter's party. The bonehead really thought that I was writing a book. After that I got a phone call about once every month or so. They always started off the same way, asking for some figures he needed for a report. I always promised to send them, but never bothered to—I knew he didn't really need them. Then he would casually ask about the book and I would come up with some nonsense, like "I'm about half way through it" or "I'm glad you called. I wanted to ask you something about that incident with the projector at the Sales Meeting. I want to make sure I've got it right." It was a silly little game, I suppose, but it amused me. Life in the Accounts Department can be a bit dull at times and we have to seize whatever chances of diversion present themselves.

I had no idea of the fateful consequences of my little game with T. J. The poor sap was so worried that my book might present him in an unfavorable light that he decided to nip it in the bud and write his own account of events. In the end the joke was on me. His real book mirrored my imaginary one, so that by the time I told him mine was at the publishers, his really was. You've got to hand it to him. I have no idea how long it normally takes to write a book, but my imaginary writing moved along at a cracking pace and he must have worked furiously to keep up.

So you can see how I justify taking some credit for the book you are now holding. Of course I had to come up with an explanation for my own work's failure to appear. This, as it turned out, was not difficult. I simply told T. J. that my book had not been able to arouse the interest of any of the publishers to whom I had submitted it. I was obviously not as good a writer as he. This was an explanation he had no difficulty in accepting.

When the editor asked me to write this foreword, she suggested I might like to set the scene a little. T. J., you see, has a tendency to leap right into things. This is in keeping with his view of himself as a man of action, but it does tend to leave the reader a bit short of background against which to set the events of the story.

SuperPumps was founded in 1982 in Falling Rock, North Carolina as a manufacturer of various kinds of pumps. Very good pumps they were too, because the company grew to a strong position in the specialty pump market, making founder and owner Gaither T. Bumbarger very rich in the process. Of course, it was only a matter of time before SuperPumps drew the attention of the big names in the pump industry, and in 2000 it was taken over by Boston-based multinational giant Pumpex Corporation. Gaither was persuaded to take thirty million dollars and put his feet up for a while on a lavishly equipped yacht in the Caribbean, while his erstwhile employees wondered what changes the new regime would bring down from Boston. What they got was a whole new management team: a new President, a new VP of Finance (me) and a new Head of Marketing—T. John Dick.

So there you have it. The scene is set. I will now hand you over to the incomparable Mr. Dick.

Oh yes, one more thing. A few people who have read the manuscript have asked another fundamental question—how does a bonehead like T. J. get to be a senior executive in a major corporation in the first place? These people, I hardly need tell you, have never worked for a major corporation.

Chapter 1

"The Marketing Department is the Beating Heart of a Forward-Looking Company"

In my opinion, there can be few sterner tests of a Senior Executive's caliber than a lengthy meeting with the President of the company with a bladder brim full of coffee. I had occasion to reflect on this fact, as I noticed by the clock on Rich's desk that our "little chat" had now lasted over an hour. I crossed my legs, changed my mind and uncrossed them again. It was an unwise move. Previous experience in similar situations had proved beyond doubt that the most effective technique was to remain immobile as far as possible. By rigorous application of this method, a powerful mind can erect a barrier between itself and the bladder, enabling it to focus on the matters under discussion. I got a grip of myself. I had to. Rich had finished speaking and was looking at me in a way that invited a response.

"The trouble with Harvey," I said, "is that he still seems to think he's working for a small-time company." I removed my glasses and wiped them with my handkerchief, a gesture which, though completely natural of course, always tends to reinforce the insightful intelligence of my remarks.

"Mm, I know." Rich took a sip of his coffee. "They all do. All these SuperPumps people. It's inevitable I suppose. A small outfit, doing well enough in its way. Then along comes a corporation like us with a big company structure. These people don't find it easy to come to terms with our professionalism." He sipped his coffee again.

"Yes Rich, that's it exactly. People like Harvey have to realize that there comes a time in a company's life cycle when it, you know, reaches a size, a complexity where the old management style just won't hack it. That's when they need people like us, with our uh...you know...."

Despite my best efforts, my attention was straying to my bladder again. It seemed to happen each time Rich took a sip of coffee.

"Professionalism, T. J. Yes you're right. It's up to us to bring the same level of corporate discipline to SuperPumps as you find up at Corporate. In a way I suppose you could call us missionaries." Rich leaned back in his big leather chair. His head struck the frame of one of the modern art prints on his office wall, and he leaned forward again quickly, rubbing his distinguished, silvery gray head. His hair was gray, of course, not his actual head.

"Missionaries, Rich. Exactly." I removed my glasses again, not because of the insightful intelligence thing this time, but to pick off a large piece of lint from my handkerchief, which had inexplicably become stuck to the inside of the left lens.

Rich continued: "It's our job to make everyone at SuperPumps realize that they're part of the Pumpex family. And that means doing things the Pumpex way. By the way, how are you coming along with that New Product Development Procedure? It needs to be.... Where are you?"

"Right here, Rich," I said, rising from under the desk, where I was engaged in retrieving my glasses. "It'll be ready for the meeting on the seventeenth, as promised."

"Good. Well, if there's nothing else, I have to get to my three o'clock meeting with Ken and the people from Pumps-R-Us."

"Right. No. Nothing else. I've got a three o'clock myself. Got to try and knock some discipline into the PX-3 project team."

The Executive Rest Room was directly across the corridor from Rich's office. I had been able to see it from where I was sitting in front of Rich's desk and, during our conversation, had imagined many times the relief I now experienced. I had even calculated the number of steps it would require to reach the point where I now stood, surrounded by the plush carpet, marble finish and padded seat covers. Of course, I could have interrupted my meeting with Rich at any time and strolled across the hall to the rest room. I am not the kind of man to be in any way inhibited by a meeting with the Company President. It was just that Rich depended on me to be there to listen and give advice. And once he had got started, I hated to interrupt his flow. Although I could not now recall precisely what he had been talking about toward the end of the meeting, it had been important and he had valued my contribution.

Now that my mind was clear and incisive again, I used my time in the rest room for some strategic thinking. It had been a year since the Pumpex takeover of SuperPumps, although I myself had only recently made the move down to North Carolina from Boston. It had not been easy managing the Marketing Department from a distance of a thousand miles. Perhaps now that I was here as Rich's right hand man, we would have more success in instilling the kind of professionalism a top class company needs to survive in the highly competitive pump market. My thoughts turned to Rich's meeting with Pumps-R-Us.

Pumps-R-Us, SuperPumps' largest customer, had been complaining that our standard of service had declined since the take-over by Pumpex. In fact, they were threatening to take their business elsewhere. The owner, Clayton Sipe, and his Purchasing Manager had come up from Greenville, South Carolina to "get a few things straight." I had never met Clayton, but I understood he was one of those gruff blustering types, who liked to shoot from the hip. So this meeting with Rich and Ken, our VP of Sales, was important to smooth things over.

Just then, the door opened and Ken walked in.

"Oh, hi T. J." he said, as he took up position beside me.

"Hi Ken. Ready for your meeting with Pumps-R-Us?"

"Oh, I don't think they'll be any problem, T. J.," he smiled.

I understood exactly what he meant. Ken was a Pumpex man like Rich and me and a real "mover and shaker." He exuded professionalism, with never a shiny black hair out of place and a fine collection of ties which I had always admired. He was tall and imposing and never failed to make a powerful impression on customers with one of the firmest handshakes and finest eye contact techniques in the business. He would soon make Pumps-R-Us understand the benefits of our new quality-oriented customer service procedures. After all, for someone who had handled the International Pumps account at Pumpex, a small-time distributor from South Carolina like Pumps-R-Us should not be too difficult to deal with. As I washed my hands, I smiled confidently at my reflection in the large wood framed mirror above the sink. I glanced at

Ken, who nodded to me from where he still stood at the urinal. There was no doubt about it. Once the Pumps-R-Us people got a look at our "big guns," they would feel a whole lot better about everything. I checked my glasses for lint, straightened my red silk tie, swung open the door and made my way back along the corridor toward the Marketing Department.

As I walked, I reflected on the signs of change since the take-over. Not just the new Pumpex purple paint on the walls, but the impressive modern prints which informed visitor and worker alike that he was entering the up-to-the minute state-of-the-art facility of a top class company. The changes really were striking. Plush new carpet in the corridors extended into the executive offices. Even the Executive Restroom I had just left had been upgraded with the same plush carpet and stylish new faucets.

The Marketing Department is the beating heart of any forward-looking company, so it was entirely appropriate for it to be right next to Rich's office. It was a bit disappointing, therefore, that it was in fact so far away. To get to it, you had to go past the Accounts Department and Personnel, as well as Ken's office. Rich had explained to me that it had to do with the inefficient layout of the SuperPumps building. SuperPumps had not been a forward-looking company and had not even had a Marketing Department *per se*. All the marketing functions had been handled by Harvey, a Product Manager reporting to the VP of *Sales*, of all people. I shook my head sadly, as I reflected on this absurdity. A company without a proper appreciation of the unique and vital role of Marketing is a company destined for failure. I was sure that, as the effect of my department came to be felt, Rich would want to do a bit of modification to the lay-out of the building and give Marketing its proper place at the heart of things.

Organization is one of my greatest strengths, and anyone entering my office is bound to be immediately aware of the kind of person he is dealing with. "Everything in its place" is an important maxim in my book. On my arrival I had insisted on the replacement of the desk with a larger oak model, which allowed me adequate space to keep the organization of the office running smoothly. One of the secrets behind my management success is to keep a very tidy desk. I always emphasize the importance of this to my team and make sure to set an example with my own desk. Half an hour each morning and evening arranging papers, writing utensils, calculator etc. is time well spent in my opinion, and American business would run more smoothly and efficiently if more people realized the value of a tidy desk. "It may not be in the business text books," I often remark humorously to friends and colleagues, "but it certainly ought to be! How much business has been snapped up by the Japanese, while American management was looking for its stapler?"

I was therefore rather surprised not to find the papers I needed for the PX-3 meeting in the *Meetings* tray on the left edge of the desk. I went over to the filing cabinet and looked in the *PX-3* file, but they weren't there either. I concluded that my secretary, Jill, must have misfiled them. I had made it perfectly clear to her that papers concerning the PX-3 project in general should be placed in the *PX-3* file in the filing cabinet, while those pertaining to the PX-3 team meetings in particular should be kept in the *Meetings* tray on the left edge of the desk. I liked Jill and was willing to believe that she tried her best, but she was not the kind of secretary I had been used to up at Corporate. She seemed to have difficulty keeping her mind focused on the job. I had just resolved to go out to her desk and have a word with her about her concentration span and the need to remain focused, when I happened to notice that the plant on top of the filing cabinet seemed to be wilting a little. I picked up my coffee cup and set off for the Executive Rest Room to get some water. When I returned, Jill was standing at the door to my office.

"Ah Jill," I said. "I want to talk to you about something."

"Yes, T. J."

"I believe I have explained quite clearly several times where the papers for the PX-3 meetings should be filed, have I not?"

"Yes, T. J."

"And where should they be filed, Jill?"

"In the *Meetings* tray."

"Exactly. Well they're not in the *Meetings* tray."

"I know. They're here." She held out a pile of papers. "You left them in Rich's office. Debbie just dropped them by a couple of minutes ago."

I looked at the papers. They appeared to be in order. I handed them back to Jill.

"Well you know where to put them Jill."

"Oh yes, T. J. I know exactly where to put them."

"Excellent."

One of the first things I had done since coming down from Boston to take on the Marketing Manager's position at SuperPumps was to institute a proper procedure for reserving the two meeting rooms, known at the time as the "Fishbowl" and "The Blue Meeting Room." Of course I had changed the names to Meeting Room A and Meeting Room B. This was easier for everyone, when it came to filling out the forms. These forms were then handed to Jill, who entered the reservation in the book. I had a few minutes to spare before my meeting, so I took the opportunity to stop at Jill's desk and check the book.

"Excellent, Jill." I noticed that Jill had filled in my 3 o'clock in the Meeting Room A column. "You seem to be getting the hang of it. Nobody else having any meetings?" This last remark was in my famous ironic tone, perhaps a little too much so, since it was hardly Jill's fault if nobody else was using the procedure. I arched my eyebrows humorously to put her at her ease. Man-management has always been one of my greatest strengths. Or woman-management. Person-management. Anyway, I am sure that this was one of the leadership qualities Rich had recognized in me when he picked me for the Marketing Manager's slot at SuperPumps.

"Nobody else has handed in any forms."

"Yes Jill, I'm sure that otherwise you would have entered them in the book, as per the procedure." I looked at my watch and started toward the meeting room door, which was directly opposite Jill's desk. "Well, I'd better get in there. Is the team assembled, Jill, ready for action?" I said 'ready for action' in a dramatic voice, like in the movies and arched my eyebrows again. Jill didn't smile. I was beginning to think that she wasn't much of a one for office humor. A pity; I always think a little humor is a good thing in the office, so long as it doesn't get out of hand.

"Well they're there, all right. But the thing is, they're not *in there*." She gestured toward the door to Meeting Room A, which I was on the point of opening.

"There, but not *in there*, Jill?" This time I gave her my quizzical half-smile, that says "I'm very busy, but I always try to be patient with my people."

"The thing is, The Fish...Meeting Room A was occupied, so they went to Meeting Room B instead. Harvey said to tell you that's where they'd gone."

"Occupied? I don't recall seeing anything in the book! We'll soon see about this!" I opened the door and strode in, not too fast, and my voice was angry but controlled as I said, "Right. This meeting's now officially over. If you people can't follow a simple procedure...."

I still believe that Rich's reaction was unjustified. After all, if he had followed the meeting room reservation procedure, the whole embarrassing episode could have been avoided. It was indeed unfortunate that the negotiations with Pumps-R-Us were not going well and were just then at such a delicate stage. Still, I believe that calling a fellow senior executive, even a subordinate, a bonehead in front of customers is unprofessional and can only make a negative impression on the customer. It was particularly unjustified since it was my quick thinking that went some way toward retrieving the situation created by *his* failure to follow the procedure. As soon as I saw Rich, Ken and the people from Pumps-R-Us sitting round the table, I turned and looked out the door to where Harvey was passing, thus skillfully creating the impression that my earlier outburst had been directed at him. I continued in the same tone, turning the situation to our advantage by showing Clayton Sipe and his Purchasing Manager that the new regime at SuperPumps were not the kind to take any nonsense from their subordinates. "Next time, Harvey, follow the procedure, OK? No more screw-ups!" Then turning to Rich, I said "Sorry about that Rich," and, handing him my notes for the PX-3 meeting, "Here are those papers you have to sign." I then turned toward the Pumps-R-Us people and smiled at them in a way that said "Sorry about this, but these papers are important. Won't be a minute." Then I took the papers back, smiled at everyone in the room, and left briskly and efficiently. Or I would have left briskly and efficiently if Harvey hadn't still been standing in the doorway holding a cup of hot coffee. He failed to get out of the way, so that the coffee spilled over both of us, scalding me quite badly. Another man might have let out a far louder scream than I did. It was at this point that Rich uttered the words which I considered unjustified and unprofessional.

"Get out, you bonehead!"

I turned to Harvey. "Yes, get out Harvey! What are you still standing there for?"

"I thought you might still need to shout at me," he said.

I shot him one of my 'You're skating on thin ice, my boy' looks, which he seemed to miss completely. He set off along the corridor in the direction of the other meeting room. I strode over to Jill's desk and said, "Jill, please get out the book and change my three o'clock to Meeting Room B."

Chapter 2

"A Total Commitment to Making the Customer Number One"

The PX-3 meeting began ten minutes late in meeting room B. Besides Harvey, there were a couple of engineers and manufacturing people, and a representative from Accounting, who together made up the Project Team. I don't usually attend meetings of this kind, preferring to delegate them to my Product Managers, leaving me free to concentrate on the big picture. However, every so often you have to put in an appearance for the sake of morale, and to make sure that everything is proceeding as it should. As this was the first meeting of the team I had attended since my arrival, I thought it appropriate for me to say a few words at the start. I kept it brief—I always believe in being concise and to the point— assuring the team that Pumpex intended to build on the success of SuperPumps and, by applying the resources of a world class organization like Pumpex, SuperPumps could soon become a professionally organized outfit. I could see that everyone appreciated the encouragement. I then turned the meeting over to Harvey, who was the Product Manager for the project. At Pumpex we believe in empowerment, in letting our people run with the ball. Harvey had been the team leader in the SuperPumps days, and I thought it important not to rock the boat yet. Managing change has always been one of my strengths. There would be plenty of time to make changes later, and I could see from the way the meeting proceeded that changes would indeed be needed. The PX-3 project was nearing completion, and as far as I could see, there was hardly any documentation. When I asked to see the Project Justification

Form, Harvey told me that they didn't have anything with that name, but I was welcome to look at his figures after the meeting. "Look at his figures!" I noted with a mixture of sadness and satisfaction, how badly the PX-3 team needed my New Product Development Procedure.

For the duration of the meeting, I said little, contenting myself with impressing the team with my manner. Certainly my presence, as a member of Senior Management must have imposed some discipline on the troops, because the meeting seemed to move along quite briskly. I decided to overlook the lack of a formal structure to the proceedings and merely adopted the attitude of one who could certainly have run things better, but thought it important that Harvey should have a shot at it. I think the team appreciated this.

I also made a mental note to hold all my meetings in Meeting Room A in future, as it had a window, while Meeting Room B was dependent entirely on artificial light, which made it hard for me to stay awake.

That night Ken and I took the Pumps-R-Us people out for dinner. Rich was unable to make it, so he naturally left it in our hands. Before leaving to pick them up at their hotel, I stopped by Ken's office to discuss our strategy for the dinner. I immediately noticed a certain coolness toward me on Ken's part (I believe that sensitivity and an ability to pick up on my colleagues feelings has played a big part in my success at Pumpex). I guessed that he in some way blamed me for Rich's earlier "screw-up" in failing to follow the correct procedure for reserving the meeting room, thus leading to an unnecessarily embarrassing situation. I considered this most unfair, since it was my quick thinking that had saved the day, but I said nothing. I have always believed that loyalty is vital to an organization's success, even when the boss makes mistakes.

"The important thing," said Ken, getting straight to the point with the kind of directness which had always so impressed the people at International Pumps, "is to impress the hell out of these people. Show them what a big organization like Pumpex can bring to the party. Convince them that by getting into bed with us they can hit the ground running."

I nodded eagerly. Ken's hard-edged dynamism came through strongly and fired me up. "You bet, Ken!"

"So I think it's best if you don't say too much."

I immediately saw the sense of this. The thing was to let Ken bond with these people. In their minds Ken should be Pumpex, and Pumpex should be Ken. He would be their contact man, their champion at Pumpex-SuperPumps. Injecting another strong personality into the mix would only tend to blur the relationship. We couldn't have them coming running to me every time there was a problem that Ken couldn't fix. No, it was better to let Ken be the point man on this one.

"You got it, Ken!" I said.

"Right. Let's go catch us a fish!"

"What was that, Ken?"

"A fish. Let's go reel him in!"

"Oh. Right, yes."

Dinner was at Chez François, the only quality restaurant in Falling Rock, North Carolina. It wasn't the kind of place that we would have taken visitors to Corporate in Boston. But, as I light-heartedly pointed out over pre-dinner drinks, it was the best you were going to find in a one horse town out here in the sticks. This opened up the conversation quite nicely, as Clayton Sipe, President and founder of Pumps-R-Us, turned out to have been born and brought up right there in Falling Rock!

"Really," I said. "I bet you like grits then. Can't get used to them myself. Taste like shredded cardboard." I gave a little laugh and arched my eyebrows in my most humorous expression. It has often struck me how people in the South lack our Yankee sense of humor. Clayton didn't smile. I wondered whether he was feeling well. He was a big red faced man, but his face seemed to have turned somewhat redder. He turned to Ken and said "Who is this guy talking to us about grits?"

It was then that I realized that Ken hadn't even introduced me. "T. John Dick," I said, reaching my hand over the table. "Marketing Manager." Clayton was just at that moment lifting his glass, while scratching his ear with his other hand. Having no free hand, he was of course unable to shake mine. I smiled to show that I understood, and continued to break the ice by introducing myself to Clayton's Purchasing Manager, Rajiv Singh, a dark, slightly built young man who had been very quiet until now. "Are you from round here too, then Rajiv?"

"No, I'm from Bombay."

"Yes, I thought you spoke a bit fast for a good ol' boy. Have you learnt to say 'you all' yet?"

One of the negative aspects of Ken's direct "go get 'em" personality is that he tends to interrupt. He was totally unable to sense how I was drawing Rajiv out of his shell and making him feel at ease. The relationship with a customer's Purchasing Manager is always vital, as Ken, as VP of Sales, should have known. Instead, he butted in with a question to Clayton.

"You'll have noticed a few changes since your last visit to the factory, Clayton?"

"I certainly have."

"Once our new Total Quality Control procedures are in place," Ken continued, "you'll notice even more of a difference. We're going to take this company and move it into a whole new philosophy in which quality is number one. You saw those signs in the factory *Quality is Number 1*? Well, that's only the start. We're getting T-shirts made."

"What?" said Clayton.

"With *Quality is Number 1* printed on them. Yes, with the benefits of Pumpex expertise, quality problems are going to be a thing of the past."

"But we never had any quality problems with SuperPumps in the past." said Clayton. "In fact they were our best supplier."

"Well, now we're going to be even better. With a total commitment to making the customer number one.….."

"I thought that quality was number one."

I laughed, showing that we Pumpex people can appreciate a joke at our own expense. Clayton looked at me, and though his face was partially obscured by his glass of Jack Daniel's, I was almost sure that it was one of those mutual respect kind of looks that self-made men reserve for people they warm to. "Here," it seemed to say, "is someone I can do business with." By the time that he turned his head a little toward Ken however, at the same time lowering his glass, I was able to see, with some dismay, that his face wore a look closer to disdain. Obviously Ken was not making a good impression. In fact, Clayton looked downright angry. He slammed his glass down on the table and shouted:

"Look, you stupid sons of bitches. I've been here all day, listening to your bullshit about total quality management and making the customer number one, but when my people call up about a whole bunch of PX-2s that don't even work, they get the runaround from you guys. What I want to know is what the hell you're going to do about it. We never had these problems before you damn' Yankees came in and started messin' with SuperPumps. Fired half the people we were used to dealin' with and brought in a bunch of slimeballs. Nobody knows what they're doin' anymore. Tell us we have to follow a new returns procedure that they don't even understand themselves. You guys are just full of shit."

I nodded, showing that we were taking his comments on board. At Pumpex we take customers' feelings seriously. Ken unfortunately was at a loss, so I took the lead.

"We're taking your comments on board." I said. This gave Ken time to recover.

"We see where you're coming from." he added.

"Oh for Chrissakes!" said Clayton throwing down his napkin.

Ken went on, "Once our Total Quality Management philosophy has been fully absorbed by the Customer Service organization at SuperPumps......"

It was at this point that Rajiv, taking everyone by surprise, hit Ken firmly on the nose, forcing him to pause in his explanation. Looking back, I think that was the most unfortunate aspect of the whole evening. If Ken had only had a chance to explain the TQM procedure as it related to Customer Service, I'm sure the situation could have been saved. As it was, Clayton and Rajiv got up from the table and walked toward the exit. Rajiv was saying: "Very sorry, Mr. Sipe. Since I am in America, I never hear such a big bullshit."

Clayton put his arm round his shoulder as he said, "That's OK, Rajiv. It's lucky for that asshole that you hit him before I had a chance to. I'd have broken his damn' nose."

I looked at Ken, who was holding a napkin to his face to staunch the bleeding. At that point I noticed the slim elegant figure of François, owner of Chez François, standing at my side. Quietly he whispered in my ear: "If y'all ain't out of here in two minutes, I'm callin' the law."

Chapter 3

"A Willingness to Reward a Job Well Done"

Driving home from the emergency room in my new Ford Explorer, I was consoled by the thought that at least Ken's injuries weren't serious. Severe bruising, the doctor had said, nothing broken. Ken was made of tough stuff. He had played a bit of football in his day and was used to harder knocks than this. Of course, I had offered to drive Ken home, but he had refused. He seemed to harbor some bitterness toward me, as if I were in some way responsible for the evening's events. I sometimes think Ken has a problem with facing a situation head on, and saying "OK, I goofed." People would think more highly of him, if he would admit to an honest mistake. A willingness to admit to mistakes has always been one of my strengths.

I was absorbed in these thoughts as I passed the "Someplace Else Saloon," where I was surprised to see a familiar car. Wasn't that Harvey's old Chevrolet in the parking lot? "The trouble with Harvey," I thought, "is that he has no class. There's absolutely nothing of the executive about him." That car in the parking lot of that place said it all. "He certainly wouldn't fit in here," I smiled to myself, as I swung into the entrance to Regal Pointe. It was early, and old George at the gatehouse was still awake. I gave him a friendly wave (I don't believe that even a wide gap in social status need stand in the way of civility.) He raised his cigarette in salute.

I drove past Rich's house by the lake, turned right and then left up a steep hill. Regal Pointe was certainly a neighborhood with tone. Each of the houses was a fine example of executive taste. All had brick façades and many had quite sizable white pillars. As I pulled into my driveway, I noticed my neighbor Ralph standing on his lawn, squinting at the ground in the fading light. Ralph, an orthopedic surgeon, was typical of the class of person you would find in Regal Pointe.

"Hi Ralph!" I said.

"Oh. Hi!" said Ralph. We had always had an easy and uninhibited relationship.

"Lost something?"

"No. I'm just looking at my lawn. I'd swear I saw some grass yesterday."

I got out of my car and joined Ralph in his search. Many potential residents of Regal Pointe were put off by what they considered its starkness. The fact that all the lawns were for the moment bare earth, together with the complete absence of trees tended to dissuade the superficial type of home buyer in search of what such people call "character." (Whatever that is!) The presence of the bulldozers still at work in many locations, including directly across the street from my home kept out the impatient type. These people probably wouldn't have fitted in here anyway. What they failed to appreciate was that if Regal Pointe wasn't the most desirable neighborhood in Falling Rock, you wouldn't have found people like Ralph or Rich or me living there, would you? And the price of a house there wouldn't have been so high.

We didn't find any actual grass on the lawn, although we did find some beginning to grow through a crack in Ralph's driveway, which suggested we should see some developments on the lawn before too long. On this upbeat note I wished Ralph a good evening and entered my house.

Grace, my wife, was waiting to greet me in the hall—a pleasant surprise. She was wearing her bathrobe and dripping onto the parquet flooring.

"Hello honey." I said. "E. R. finished already?"

"What? Oh, no. I don't know. You're home early."

"Are you OK, honey?" I said, letting her see the caring concern that I always try to bring to my marriage, despite the stresses of being a top executive at Pumpex. Just then the door to the bathroom at the top of the stairs opened and a man I vaguely recognized emerged. When he saw me, he stopped and just stood there gaping. I noticed that his hair was wet.

My wife spoke, breaking the awkward silence: "Did you fix it then, Dwight?"

This man was obviously not too bright. He just stood there and dripped. It was then that I recognized him as one of the construction workers from across the street. I suppose brains are not too important in that line of work.

"The shower. Did you manage to fix it?"

"Oh yes. Fix it. Yes I did. Fixed it. Yes." The man was obviously a cretin.

"Dwight was kind enough to come over and fix our shower for us."

"What was wrong with it?" I asked.

"Well it was fine and then suddenly it came on scalding hot. I screamed and Dwight heard the scream and came running over to see what was wrong. When I told him, he was kind enough to stay and fix it."

"Yes that's right. It's fixed now," said the cretin. "I'll be going now Mrs. Dick. If you need any more work on your plumbing, just you give me a holler." He was grinning now, which made him look even more of an idiot.

"Not so fast, Dwight!" I said, intercepting him before he could reach the door. "What do you take me for?"

I squeezed twenty dollars into his hand. One of my greatest strengths has always been a willingness to reward a job well done.

Chapter 4

"A Relaxed, Informal Relationship with my People"

I wasn't looking forward to Rich's weekly staff meeting the following morning. Although I was not to blame for the events of the previous evening, the loss of the company's major customer was certain to create an unpleasant atmosphere, and in those kinds of circumstances recriminations tend to be distributed at random with little regard to who is really to blame. I was also sure that Bill and Ronnie were bound to seize this opportunity to take some cheap shots at me. Although I myself have always abhorred office politics, they were a fact of life at Pumpex-SuperPumps and you just had to learn to live with them.

Ronnie was the Vice President of Finance, a Pumpex man like Rich, Ken and me. Altogether too full of himself for someone who looked like an ostrich, with his skinny neck and bald head and those silly round spectacles balanced on the end of his nose. I had heard some of his people refer to him openly as "the Ostrich." If I suspected for a moment a similar lack of respect amongst my own people, I would know what to do, but Ronnie seemed to find it amusing. I suppose that in the slow moving world of the bean-counters such laxity is less serious than in the fast-paced field of marketing. It was obvious to anyone that Ronnie resented my position of influence within the company, and in particular with Rich. I don't think he had ever forgotten my victory in having the new coffee machine placed in the corridor outside the Marketing Department instead of beside the photocopier in Finance. This victory was of course more than a symbolic indication of the unofficial pecking order at Pumpex-SuperPumps. It also meant that I could see when Rich was on his way to get a coffee and, if I happened to want one just then, time my arrival at the machine to coincide with his. This gave us many opportunities for those coffee machine chats which are so useful in creating office camaraderie. Obviously as Rich got to know me better, he would become even more aware of my capabilities, and I suppose it was hardly surprising that the Ostrich, in his rather childish way, felt threatened. His childishness extended to counting my trips to the executive restroom, which was next to his office, and calling out remarks as I passed, such as:

"Fifth time this morning T. J! You ought to cut down on that coffee. Haven't seen Rich yet today. He must have a bladder like a basketball."

He made no attempt to suppress his comments in the presence of his subordinates or other executives. In fact, he would make a point of bellowing them even louder. Hardly the kind of behavior you'd expect from a Pumpex man.

Bill, the Production Manager, was the only senior staff member left over from the SuperPumps days. He brought with him much of the unprofessional management style of the old regime. At the time of the last big lay-off, for instance, he had shown a complete lack of the professional detachment required of a leader. Instead he had reacted childishly, totally failing to see the big picture. He had implied that if Sales and Marketing were doing their job properly, lay-offs could be avoided, a completely unjustified assertion of course. He had even gone so far as to suggest to Rich that if the senior staff didn't pay itself such "bloated salaries" we wouldn't have to let so many people go. This was a totally unrealistic point of view. If you want to attract top caliber executive talent, you have to pay us competitive salaries. I considered Bill's attitude to be dangerously close to communism and suggested he might want to move to China and see how it liked it there.

Bill was obviously having major difficulties in adjusting to the new professionalism of the Pumpex regime. In the last staff meeting, for instance, he had been extremely scathing about my proposal for increased efficiency in Manufacturing. He had rather unwisely told me that in the area of manufacturing I "didn't know my ass from a hole in the ground," that it was none of my damned business anyway and that I should take a good look at the shambles in my own department before sticking my nose into his. I had let him finish his diatribe, calmly maintaining my composure, and then taken the opportunity to remark that I was sorry he felt that way, that at Pumpex we were used to working as a team and sharing ideas, and that nobody who had seen our latest advertisements featuring the runner-up in the Miss North Carolina Pageant holding a PX-2 compression unit would refer to the Marketing Department as a shambles. I think Rich could see who was the real team player, and who was the embittered has-been, who just wasn't shaping up to the challenge of a top class organization. Significantly it was me, and not Bill, that he had entrusted with the creation of the New Product Development Procedure. This was the explanation for the note from Rich that I had happened to catch sight of on Ken's desk: "Let's give T. J. the New Product Development thing. Surely he can't screw this up." The implication being, of course, that Bill could.

This morning Bill had already made several childish references to the swollen state of Ken's nose, referring to Ken as Coco the Clown, and seeming to find himself very funny. The Ostrich had joined in this puerile amusement, as might be expected.

The meeting was in Rich's office, which meant that there was no need to reserve either of the two meeting rooms. Rich liked to keep these affairs informal. Just the key staff sitting around the table and bringing up any important matters for discussion. In view of the negative attitude of Bill and Ronnie and their well-known habit of making opportunistic attacks on those of us who are really trying to make a difference at Pumpex-SuperPumps, I had come in early and prepared an analysis of how our over-dependence on Pumps-R-Us had actually been bad for the company. My analysis showed that if the Marketing Department were allowed to increase its promotion in the specialty pump market, we could recoup the lost sales in a matter of 7.8 months with a 1.2% increase in margin. Deciding that attack was the best form of defense, I struck at the very start of the meeting, as soon as everyone had settled into their chairs.

"I've been looking at some figures regarding Pumps-R-Us, and you know it's funny but it looks like we'd actually be....."

"I'm glad you brought up Pumps-R-Us," Rich interrupted. "I had a phone call from Clayton Sipe first thing this morning. What the hell happened last night?"

"Dad man is dodally unreasonable," said Ken, "and as for de budcher of Bombay...."

"I also had a call from François. Apparently you're not welcome in his restaurant any more."

"Well dat's no loss. De damned soup was always cold anyway."

"According to my figures, Pumps-R-Us...."

"Nobody wants to know about your friggin' figures," said Bill. "They're always garbage anyway. Plucked out of thin air. That so called manufacturing analysis you did was nothin' but a pile of...."

"Actually, Bill," my calm riposte was an impressive contrast to his torrent of spite, "I think Rich might be interested in...."

"Perhaps later, T. J.," said Rich in a voice that suggested he was indeed intrigued, which I'm sure Bill must have found extremely galling. Once again he had been bested by T. John Dick. Rich went on, "Anyway, it seems Clayton is willing to give us one more chance. After they left you, he and Rajiv went for a drink and calmed down a bit."

"Probably had a chance do dink over what I was exblaining about Dodal Quality Management."

"I expect so," said Rich. "Oh by the way, T. J., Clayton had a message for Harvey. He said: "Tell Harvey not to forget he owes me twenty bucks.""

After the meeting, I summoned Harvey to my office. I intended to give him a good dressing down about borrowing money from our customers. This time he had overstepped the mark.

"Ah, Harvey," I said in my gravest voice. "Sit down." I was not surprised to see that he had entirely missed the gravity of my tone and had already sat down, looking quite relaxed. The trouble with Harvey is that he is altogether too relaxed. Nobody could accuse me of being a stickler for hierarchy. A relaxed, informal relationship with my people, in tune with the latest management theories, is one of my greatest strengths. I count it as one of the qualities that marks me as an effective leader. But Harvey's attitude seemed to hint at a failure to appreciate the level of respect due to Senior Management. I had touched on this at his last performance review, and he had promised to improve. I remembered his exact words: "I promise I'll try hard to respect you more." Since then there had been precious little sign of an improvement. I was beginning to wonder whether we really needed someone like Harvey at Pumpex-

SuperPumps. Now that I had straightened out the meeting room situation and almost completed my New Product Development Procedure, I saw little reason why I shouldn't myself take over Harvey's leadership of the PX-3 team. With my experience at Pumpex, I could surely bring stronger leadership to the team than someone like Harvey, who was in his late thirties and had never made it past Product Manager in a small time outfit like SuperPumps.

"I have to tell you that we have had a complaint about you from a customer."

That took the wind out of his sails, though he tried to hide it.

"Really? Who?"

"Clayton Sipe of Pumps-R-Us"

"Old Bubba Sipe? He seemed OK last night."

I gave him a stern look. He missed it of course. "Are you telling me you saw Clayton last night?"

"Sure. He was at 'Someplace Else.' I recognized him when I came in. Bubba and I go way back. I handled his account when I was in Customer Service. He had his new Purchasing Manager with him. I didn't catch his real name; Bubba kept calling him Rocky. Anyway, he seemed a bit upset at first. Said something about having to deal with complete morons. He didn't want to talk about it though. So we had a few drinks and I let him beat me at pool. Cost me twenty bucks. I didn't have it on me, so I said I'd give it to him next time I saw him. I'm afraid Bubba had quite a lot to drink. He kept putting his arm around me and telling me I was the best damned friend he had in the business. 'As long as you're at SuperPumps, you can count on my business,' he said. When he started to fall off his bar stool I took him back to his hotel."

I fixed him with my most penetrating stare, which would, I'm sure, have been more effective, if I had been able to think of any appropriate words with which to accompany it. Harvey looked at me strangely. I almost thought I saw a hint of a most inappropriate smile on his face. At last he said, "Now, what was that complaint?"

"Get out, Harvey," I said, "We'll say no more about this." As he was leaving, I added. "But don't let it happen again."

Chapter 5

"Balance the Stresses of a Fast-Paced Career with a Fulfilling Home Life"

The beauty of my New Product Development Procedure was its simplicity. I was explaining this to Grace on the deck of our prestigious executive home with the lake view in sought-after Regal Pointe. It was Saturday morning, the sun was shining and Grace and I were sharing a family moment. It is vital for an executive to balance the stresses of his fast-paced career with a fulfilling home life, and I made a point of doing so on Saturday mornings.

"You see, it all starts with a New Product Proposal form, which anyone can submit to the Marketing Department."

"Is that Ralph's boy Roger on one of those jet-ski things?" Grace asked. I could barely hear her, as she was at the other end of the deck, leaning out over the rail so that she could see the lake past the house in front of us, which belonged to Steve Taylor, the owner of Taylor Chrysler-Plymouth-Dodge. It was a large house of pink stucco with a kind of tower thing at one end and, when it was finished, it would make a stunning view from our deck. Unfortunately the automobile business had been in a bit of a slump recently and it had stood in its half-finished state for the better part of a year.

"I review this form and pass it on to one of the Product Managers, who is responsible for originating the New Product Opportunity Analysis Form or NPOA. I then review this, point out any changes required, sign it and present it at the next meeting of the New Product Review

Committee, the NPRC." I thoughtfully shouted my explanation so that Grace could hear me at the other end of the deck over the noise of the bulldozer working on the lot next to us, which had recently been purchased by one of Falling Rock's top dentists. "After getting the OK from the committee," I yelled, "the NPOA is then returned to the Product Manager, who goes to the next stage by preparing five copies of the New Product Justification form."

Grace had returned to my end of the deck, picking up her half-finished margarita on the way. I lowered my voice to its normal level.

"The NPJ should include sales and gross margin projections, as well as the projected cost for each stage of the project. One copy of the NPJ remains with me, while the others are circulated for signature by the other members of the NPRC, Rich, Ken, Ronnie and Bill."

"Isn't he the one they call the Ostrich?"

"Ronnie is, yes."

"Then who's Bill? Is he the fat one?"

"He is big, yes. Production Manager from the old SuperPumps days. Not really the kind of man who can…"

"That *is* Roger on the jet-ski. He must be home from college for the weekend. He's turning into a fine-looking boy."

I continued with my explanation. It is important for a husband to share things with his wife, ask her advice, make her feel part of the team. I often think that managing a marriage is a lot like managing a department in a top-flight company like Pumpex.

"Only when all the senior staff signatures have been obtained can we move to the next stage. The Product Manger submits a Development Schedule or DS, which includes inputs from all the departments, Marketing, Sales, Engineering.…."

"Do you think that's his girlfriend?"

"Whose?" I asked. It can sometimes be hard work making Grace feel part of the team. Nevertheless, I concealed my irritation. In my home life, as well as at Pumpex, patience has always been one of my greatest strengths.

"Roger's. Shit, he could do better than that! Skinny as a rake." Grace had her binoculars trained on the lake. One of the things that made our home in Regal Pointe so desirable was that if you leaned out over the end of the deck with a pair of binoculars the view was really quite stunning. Some care was needed not to lean too far, however. On one occasion, I had over-stretched a little and finished up in the azalea bushes below.

"Once the DS has been duly filled in and signed by the NPRC, I take that, together with the NPJ and the NPOA with me to HQ to get the OK from Ray at the Quarterly Operations Review."

"The QOR?"

"Precisely." I was gratified by Grace's level of attention.

"I didn't think that you got to go to those meetings. I thought it was only Rich, Ronnie and Ken. I remember last time you went on and on about how you...."

"Yes, but now I'm the key player in the New Product Development Procedure. They'll need me at the QOR now."

"My God, will you look at that swimsuit she's wearing? Looks like she cut up a pair of old curtains."

"Anyway, once we have the official OK from Ray, the Product Manager prepares....." My voice was drowned out by an airplane coming in to land at the municipal airport at the other side of the lake. I paused to let the noise die down. Grace stood there, sniffing the air and screwing up her face. Over the noise of the airplane she shouted to me:

"My God! The wind's changed again. I really wish you'd found out about that damned sewage plant before you bought this frigging place!" She turned and walked off into the house. As she went I couldn't help noticing the sulky attitude which is one of her least attractive features.

Alone on the deck, I picked up the binoculars from where Grace had thrown them and knelt down in the corner where I could point them through the railings at just the right angle. From here I could see Rich's house down on the water. It was 10 o'clock, and that meant that Rich would soon be leaving for his Saturday game of golf. Sure enough, after a few minutes he emerged from his back door, carrying his clubs. And sure enough, just as I had suspected, there was the Ostrich. He had a big grin on his silly bald head and was laughing and joking. As I watched, he even went so far as to punch Rich on the shoulder in that kind of fake jovial way typical of the corporate crawler. If there's one aspect of corporate life that I find truly obnoxious, it is the kind of crawling that seems to come so naturally to brown-nosing, baldy morons like Ronnie. I sometimes regret that I am by nature unable to lower myself to such behavior. It seems to work for insects like the Ostrich, who would certainly never have made it to senior management level on the strength of their ability. As I watched, he looked up in the direction of my house and seemed to wave, as if he had seen someone he knew. I swung my binoculars around in a wide sweep, but I couldn't see anyone.

Chapter 6

"The Unique Contribution Women Can Make to an Organization"

On Monday morning I handed my New Product Development Pro cedure to Jill for typing.

"Can you have that on my desk by tomorrow, please Jill?", I said in my firm but friendly voice, the one that sounds like I am asking a favor, while making it clear that it is in fact an order from the boss. I have always had a way with secretaries. Betty at Pumpex Corporate was devoted to me, quite distraught when I took the position down at SuperPumps, although she did an admirable job of keeping up an appearance of unconcerned efficiency, poor girl.

"Well, yes," said Jill. "Only I've got this letter from Harvey that has to go to Clayton Sipe about his problems with the PX-2. He said it was urgent."

"Well, do it as soon as you finish my New Product Development Procedure. I want to look at it tomorrow and make any changes before the meeting on Thursday."

"Well, if you say so. Only Harvey said....."

"Never mind what Harvey said, Jill. This is important. Top level stuff."

I went into my office, a little annoyed. The trouble with Jill was that she had no idea of priorities.

Now that the New Product Development Procedure was in typing, I had time to reflect, review what I'd done so far at SuperPumps and do some planning. I had plenty to be pleased about. The Meeting Room Reservation System was in place. The New Product Development Procedure, once accepted by top management, promised to make a real impact on efficiency. My department had issued the advertisement with a picture of the runner-up in the Miss North Carolina Pageant holding a PX-2 compression unit. I reflected on these achievements for about half an hour, until I saw Rich go past my door on his way to the coffee machine. Feeling a bit thirsty myself, I decided to go and get some coffee too.

"Hi Rich," I said. I think that one of the reasons that Rich likes and respects me so much is that I am able to talk to him in a casual way, subordinate to him in the organization but his equal as a man, as it were. I think he regards me more as a trusted friend and advisor than as one of his staff. Leadership can be lonely, and it's important for men in Rich's position to have a right-hand man they can rely on.

"Oh, hi T. J. Did you have a good weekend?" Rich's voice was cheery. He enjoyed our little coffee machine chats.

"Yes thanks, Rich. How about you?"

"Oh, pretty good."

"At least the weather stayed nice."

"Yes."

"I hope it stays nice tonight."

"Why's that, T. J?"

"Oh, I thought I might take a trip over to the driving range. Hit a few balls." I moved my arms in a golf swing motion.

"I didn't know you played golf, T. J."

"What, me? Love the game."

"Oh."

"Yes, love to get out there." I executed another perfect golf swing.

"Good. Well, must get on. I've got a 9:30 with Ronnie about the budget."

Obviously, my timing was not good. The budget was very much on Rich's mind. Sipping my coffee, I went back to my office. I checked my voice mail. Nothing. I played my own message back a couple of times, just to check the way it sounded. "You have reached the desk of T. John Dick…" The Ostrich had once left a message in which he childishly pretended that he thought he was actually talking to my desk, and made some stupid remark about being able to see my drawers. I had considered changing my message, but decided against it. You can't let people like the Ostrich think they're getting to you. Besides, it was a good message, delivered in a steady authoritative tone. "I'm not able to take your call right now. Please leave a brief message and I will return your call at my earliest convenience." Satisfied with the voice mail situation, I decided to go and check the Meeting Room Reservation Book. It was most disappointing. There were no entries, and yet I could see through the window of Meeting Room A that there was a meeting in progress. It was Bill and his Manufacturing team. I made a mental note to talk to Rich later about the incident.

I decided to go on a little tour of the department. These little tours are a very important part of my management style. Not only do they inspire my people and keep them on their toes, but they also give them a chance to talk to me informally, ask for advice and see that I care. One of my greatest strengths as a manager is that I always have my finger on the pulse of the department.

I started with Mike, Product Manager for the PZ line. Mike, a smart youngster of twenty-eight, was the newest of the Product Managers and the only member of my team that I had recruited, rather than inherited from the old SuperPumps organization. Although he had only been there a month, he was already showing promise and a natural leadership. Pretty much what you'd expect from a man with an MBA from Northern University, my old Alma Mater, and a background in Corporate Planning at Universal Technologies. His brand of professionalism, honed in the Planning Department of one of the biggest companies in the world was just the shot in the arm that the SuperPumps organization needed. We had been lucky to get him, even at a salary forty percent higher than the other Product Managers. In fact, I sometimes asked myself why he left a company like Universal to come to Pumpex-SuperPumps. Whatever the reason, their loss was our gain.

I was pleased to see that Mike was hard at work at his computer. I'm not much of a computer expert myself, more of a thinker and strategist than a number cruncher, but, although I couldn't see the screen, I could see that whatever Mike was occupied with, he was giving it his full attention. He was moving his mouse around at breakneck speed, every so often crying "Gotcha!" It was awesome to watch Mike in action, totally absorbed in his work, man and machine in perfect synergy, completely committed to the task. If only some of the others, like Harvey for instance, would pick up on this enthusiasm and go get 'em spirit! I decided not to disturb Mike and risk breaking his concentration. As I moved away from his office, I heard him cry "Shit!" and saw him throw up his hands. Whatever had gone wrong with his calculation though, it didn't deter Mike for long. He grabbed his mouse again and got right back into it.

In view of Mike's computer skills and need to work undisturbed, I had allocated him the corner office, moving Harvey to a cubicle between Jill's desk and the entrance to the department. This was not without its problems however, as for some reason Harvey's desk was always surrounded by people from other departments, asking him questions or getting him to look at some drawing or other. This was the case now, for instance, as an engineer called Keith or Kevin or something and some guy I had seen hanging around in Manufacturing were crammed into the space between Harvey's desk and the door, waving some sort of mechanical objects about and saying, "What do we do about these Harvey?"

"Well, let's call the supplier and tell him we'll accept them this time, since we don't have any choice. They'll work in the PX-1 although the tolerances are too wide for the PX-2, so keep them separate from the others. I'll call Pumptrol and tell them they'll get their PX-1 order this week and ask them to hang on until next week for the PX-2."

I shook my head sadly. The trouble with Harvey was that he couldn't see the big picture. Always caught up in the details. He obviously didn't have a strategic mind. I noticed that his desk was untidy again, with papers and pump parts all over it—in stark contrast to Mike's neat and spotless office. I made a mental note to write Harvey a memo about this.

I moved on to Rachel, the Marketing Communications Manager. I thought it important to stop by her desk as often as I could for a chat. She had been a little irrational in her reaction to my idea for the PX-2 advertisement featuring the runner-up in the Miss North Carolina Pageant. In fact she had been decidedly frosty about the whole thing. I had tried to explain that there was nothing sexist or exploitative about using a beautiful woman in a bikini to advertise a product that is bought mostly by men. After all, nobody was forcing her to do it. Some women don't seem able to grasp this kind of argument and have a tendency to react with an unnecessary emotionalism. In my experience, this is often more pronounced in slightly overweight women. I think that perhaps in this case, hormones may have had a lot to do with it. I've noticed a pattern of these outbursts at particular times of the month. It was about the same time as her objection the previous month to Mike's new *Big 'n' Busty* calendar, which ended with me asking Mike to take it down in the interests of office harmony. One of my greatest strengths as a manager in the modern workplace is a willingness to respond with sensitivity and understanding to even the silliest concerns of the female members of my department. Nevertheless, I did wonder whether her reaction to the Miss North Carolina ad might not have been more positive, had she been a bit better looking herself. Unfortunately, I may have mentioned this to a few people over an after work drink a couple of weeks previously, and I rather feared it might have got back to her.

"Everything OK, Rachel?" I asked breezily.

She didn't look up from her work, which seemed to consist of putting together some photographs and text on a page. There is no doubt that women are better at this kind of finicky work than men, who always need to be doing something more challenging and important. I have always had a keen understanding of the unique contribution women can make to an organization. I glanced at the papers on her desk. It looked like some sort of a catalog.

"Is this some sort of a catalog then, Rachel?"

"Yes."

I waited for her to say more, but she was obviously too absorbed in her work. Probably at one of those critical points where you can't afford to take your mind off it or your hand might slip and ruin the whole thing.

"Great," I said. "Carry on then." I said this in my most encouraging and appreciative voice and moved on.

Randy, the other Product Manager was not at his desk. I wondered where he was. He could hardly be at a meeting as there was nothing about any meeting in the book.

"Where's Randy?" I asked Jill.

"At the dentist."

"Ah yes."

I vaguely recalled Randy telling me he would be in late again, as he was having some work done on a troublesome molar. My tour of inspection finished, I walked back to my office. I checked my voice mail again. Nothing. I noticed that the earpiece of my telephone was dirty, and cleaned it with my handkerchief. I looked at my watch. Still an hour to lunch. The mouthpiece, I noticed, was also dirty, so I cleaned that too. Satisfied with the condition of the telephone receiver, I checked my voice mail again. Still nothing. Then Rich walked by and I realized my coffee cup was empty.

Chapter 7

"Obtaining Vital Synergies in an Integrated yet Flexible Market-Oriented Management Structure"

I managed to snag Rich for lunch that day. One in the eye for Ronnie, who attaches great importance to these things. This was the third time this month, which by my reckoning was one more than Ronnie or Ken and, significantly, two more than Bill. I saw Ronnie in the parking lot, as we made our way to Rich's Ford Explorer. He pointed to his ass and made an obscene kissing gesture, which he seemed to find very funny. I sometimes wonder how someone like the Ostrich ended up in a top-flight professional organization like Pumpex.

We went to The Imperial Dragon Chinese restaurant, where they do a lunchtime buffet that isn't too gruesome. I have a delicate stomach, so I steered clear of the spicy shrimp and loaded my plate up with sesame chicken and sweet and sour pork. As we sat down at our table, I noticed with some satisfaction that Harvey was in the restaurant, having lunch with some engineers or manufacturing people or something. It is good for my people to see that I have a close relationship with the President of the company. Excellent for department morale.

I had hoped to steer the conversation round to golf. However, somehow, just as I was leading up to the subject, Rich always swung the discussion back to business.

"You know that Ray is coming down in a couple of weeks?" he said.

I didn't know that.

"No, I didn't know that," I said.

"Oh. Well he is."

Ray Hacker was the President of the Pumpex Group of North America, responsible for all six companies in the group and reporting directly to the Board. Many found him a difficult man. Grace, who had met him at a company function when I was still based at Corporate in Boston, had gone so far as to call him an "ugly, obnoxious bastard." Her opinion was based on a failure to grasp the essence of the man. He could be abrasive, it was true, but with strong leaders like Ray, the important thing was to earn his respect, and the way to do this was to show you were a tough fighter yourself. This was a theory that I had put into practice with great success in the matter of Pumpy the Possum.

Pumpy the Possum was a fine example of the creativity that makes an exceptional marketing talent stand out from the crowd, and a brief account of the episode will give you a valuable insight into both my uncanny knack for the winning concept and the interpersonal and intra-organizational skills for which I am known. Pumpy was an engaging little cartoon character whose pump-related adventures were at the center of a strikingly original advertising campaign that I had put together with the cutting edge ad agency Makem, Paimore & Lovett to illustrate the virtues of the SuperPumps line. The concept was brilliant in the freshness of its approach to the stuffy and conservative pump market and would certainly have been a great success, had it ever been given a proper chance. The first ad ran in the leading trade magazines, *The Pump Gazette*, *Pump Distribution and Marketing* and *Pump Dealer* shortly after I moved down to Falling Rock. It took the form of an amusing cartoon strip which showed Pumpy, a muscular possum in a cape and costume with a large letter P on the front, coming to the rescue of a pump engineer called Hydraulic Harry. Harry's pump (a non-Pumpex-SuperPumps model) was at a standstill, due to a broken grommet. Pumpy had solved Harry's problem by turning up with a PX-1B, whose grommetless design proved to be the answer to Harry's prayers.

This was to have been the first of several similar advertisements, but shortly after it appeared I received a call from Rich asking me to come to his office immediately, as he wanted to talk to me about our advertising strategy. I naturally assumed that he wanted to congratulate me on the Possum concept and discuss how we might maximize its impact, perhaps with a bigger budget to provide Pumpy with greater exposure. Nothing had prepared me for what happened.

"Listen to this," Rich said, before I even had a chance to sit down, pressing a button on his telephone:

"This is Ray Hacker. Are you all stark raving mad down there? I open my copy of Pump Gazette this morning and am confronted by a damned rat in fancy dress, waving a SuperPumps pump around the place. We'll be the laughing stock of the industry. Kill the rat. And while you're at it kill the damned idiot who came up with the idea. What a moron! I ought to come down there and...."

Rich switched the machine off at that point. I was shocked. How could someone of Ray Hacker's leadership caliber have so completely missed the point? It was very unfair.

"Well, what do you have to say?" Rich asked.

"He's not a rat."

"What?"

"He's a..."

"A possum! I know he's a darned possum!"

"No, not a possum," I said calmly. "Well, he is a possum, of course, but that's not the point. He's a concept."

For some reason, Rich clasped his hands to his head, muttering "Pumpy the Concept. Not Pumpy the Possum. Oh no, Pumpy the damned Concept!" I admire Rich greatly, but I have occasionally noticed that coolness under pressure is not one of his greatest strengths.

"I feel sure," I suggested, "that if I just had a chance to explain to Ray the whole Pumpy concept...."

"I really don't think that's a very good idea," Rich said, interrupting me with unaccustomed rudeness. Before I had a chance to argue my case further, he asked me firmly to leave, so that he could think about how to clear up the mess that I and my damned Pumpy the Concept had gotten us into.

Back in my office, I needed a few minutes to collect my thoughts. How could anyone, let alone an executive of Ray Hacker's brilliance, so completely miss the potent marketing message of the Pumpy the Possum campaign? Had he failed to appreciate its freshness and originality? Had he lost touch, under the pressure of managing the whole Pumpex Group, with the latest marketing theories? It would have been understandable. Marketing is a dynamic and very demanding field. Even I didn't find it easy to keep up with all the advances, now that managing my department demanded so much of my time. That was why I had called on the very best marketing talents in the form of Makem, Paimore & Lovett. Pumpy the Possum had not come cheap. There was no point in skimping on something as vital as advertising, and the extra expenses of hiring a New York agency and paying for the frequent but vital brainstorming sessions and concept presentations in New York and Falling Rock had been an essential cost of generating a winning campaign like Pumpy the Possum, and not, as the Ostrich had stupidly suggested, "The Mother of all Boondoggles."

In the circumstances, I resolved, there was only one thing to do. I picked up my pen and wrote "Memo to Ray Hacker, Group President."

In my memo I succinctly explained the thinking behind the Pumpy concept. I devoted a few sentences to the staleness of the advertising in the pump industry trade press and then went on to explain the theoretical basis for a fresh approach, such as Pumpy the Possum. It would, I wrote, create a whole new image for the SuperPumps brand. Marketeers are, of course, masters of communication, and, reading through what I had written, I felt sure that it could not fail to make Ray see things differently.

When I had finished, I got Jill to type it up and hurried round to Rich's office. One of the qualities that made me such a valued member of Rich's staff was that I was every inch a team player. I was anxious that Rich should see the memo before I sent it to Corporate. When I got there, however, I found that Rich had left for the day. I therefore left the memo on Debbie's desk with a little note asking her to make a copy for Rich and put the original in the intra-company mail.

As it turned out, Rich was out for two days with Ken meeting a client in Chicago. When he returned, I called him first thing.

"Hi Rich. Good trip?"

"Oh, hi T. J. Yes, great actually. I think we clinched the deal." He sounded in a buoyant mood.

"Did you read my memo?"

"Just reading it now. It's um...interesting."

"Yes, I think it ought to convince Ray on the Pumpy concept. Make sure Debbie drops it in the mail, will you? If she doesn't mind."

"Hmm." It sounded like my memo had certainly given Rich a lot to think about. My memos often have that effect. "Well, I'll make sure it gets where it needs to go."

"Do you think I ought to call him? After he's had a chance to read the memo?"

"No, no!"

"You think I should leave it at the memo?"

"Definitely."

"I suppose he is very busy. Doesn't need me to call him up to explain what's already clear from the memo."

"Yes, T. J., something like that."

I never heard back from Ray Hacker, so I could only imagine his reaction to my explanation of the Pumpy concept. At any rate, I was sure that he could not have failed to appreciate one thing—that T. John Dick was a man who was not afraid to speak his mind, argue his case respectfully but firmly, stand his ground for the good of the Corporation. I didn't continue with the Pumpy the Possum campaign however. Not because of any doubts about having convinced Ray of its merits, but because in a series of brainstorming sessions over after-dinner cognacs with the troops from Makem, Paimore & Lovett, we came up with the idea of using the runner-up in the Miss North Carolina Pageant, a charming and intelligent young woman who had joined us for dinner on a couple of occasions, to advertise the SuperPumps line.

Rich put down his fork and dabbed his mouth with his napkin.

"Ray wants to have a look around," he said. "See the changes since the take-over."

"Well, I'm sure we can put on quite a show for him," I said through a mouthful of noodles.

"What was that T. J.?"

"I'm sure we can put on quite a show for him."

"Hmm. Yes," said Rich, and he looked at me in a way that suggested he would be expecting great things of me during Ray's visit.

On the way back to the office, Rich talked some more about Ray's plans. I don't remember everything he said, as I was having some difficulty suppressing a build-up of gas caused by an excess of monosodium glutamate in the sweet and sour pork. I did catch something about the New Product Review Procedure, which Ray would no doubt want to take a look at, and something about the importance of making sure that my department was tidy.

At last, Rich paused long enough for me turn on the radio without cutting him off in mid-flow.

"You don't mind if I turn the radio on for a moment do you?"

Rich looked at me in surprise. "No, of course not. Are you OK T. J.? You look as if you're about to explode."

"What? No, I'm fine, Rich."

I flicked through the stations until I came to one that was just a very loud hissing noise. I held it on that station for just long enough to do what I had to do. The gas made a slight rasping sound, as it exited, reverberating against the vinyl of the Explorer's seat. I looked at Rich. He had his eyes fixed firmly on the road. I was pretty sure he hadn't noticed anything. I rolled down my window.

"Are you hot, T. J.?" asked Rich with obviously genuine concern.

"Nothing good on," I said, as I turned off the radio. "Yes, just a little."

"Oh. I didn't realize it was that hot."

He must have changed his mind though, because after a few seconds, he wound down his window too and we drove back to the office with a cool breeze in our faces.

Back in the office, I gave some thought to Ray's upcoming visit. He would no doubt be impressed with the new Meeting Room Reservation Procedure. I would have to make sure that there was a meeting in progress during his visit, which would give me an opportunity to explain the procedure to him. I decided to call a Marketing Team Meeting to coincide with his visit. The New Product Development Procedure was bound to go down well too. But I needed something more. Something that showed vision and leadership, something that would make him remember T. John Dick when he was sitting in his plush office up in Boston with its Van Gogh reproductions and view of the Charles River (as an "insider" during my days at Corporate, I had once been in his office). It was then that I hit on the idea of the Mission Statement.

There was no doubt that SuperPumps needed a Mission Statement. Under the old management, the company had been content with rapid growth, high margins and speedy introduction of new products. There was no overall guiding philosophy, no clear statement of strategic goals.

The impact of this fuzziness and "fly by the seat of the pants" attitude was becoming apparent now that, despite the firing of most of the previous regime and its replacement by a top class professional management team, sales were beginning to drop alarmingly and several projects were disturbingly behind schedule. Yes, a Mission Statement was just what the company needed. It would show Ray that with people of vision like me at the helm, SuperPumps would soon be on the right track.

My thoughts were interrupted by the sight of Jill at the door to my office.

"Come in Jill," I smiled. "My door is always open. You know that." This was a part of my management style that inspired great affection and loyalty in my people.

"It's about that Pumps-R-Us letter. Harvey says that Clayton Sipe desperately needs the information today."

"I'm sorry Jill but it will just have to wait until you've finished my New Product Development Procedure." I make a point of not changing my mind. Decisiveness is one of the hallmarks of a leader and one of my greatest strengths.

"You're the boss," said Jill. This was undoubtedly true.

"In fact I might have something else for you this afternoon," I said, thinking of my Mission Statement.

"OK, but Harvey says the customer really needs........."

"I think I have a little more expertise than Harvey in setting priorities Jill." My voice was firm and made it quite clear that I wished to hear no more about the Pumps-R-Us letter.

When Jill was gone, I turned my mind once more to the Mission Statement. I picked up my pen, wrote "Mission Statement" at the top of the page and began:

At Pumpex-SuperPumps, the customer is Number One.

A Mission Statement is a vital document. It defines a company's very *raison d'être*, its aims and the way it will achieve them. It is just the kind of big picture strategic thinking at which I excel. I wanted to set precise goals that would shape the company's destiny, while at the same time allowing latitude for creativity and providing an inspiring document that all in the company could get behind. And I wanted to get it finished by half past two, so that I could get to the garage and pick up my car from its oil change and service. So I set to work and pretty soon had it finished. I read it over with considerable satisfaction. It was certainly a job well done.

Pumpex-SuperPumps Mission Statement

At Pumpex-SuperPumps, the customer is Number One. By meeting and exceeding the very highest standards of customer service, and obtaining vital synergies in an integrated yet flexible market-oriented management structure, we will meet the company objectives of maximizing growth and earnings, while maintaining the highest business and ethical standards .

Pumpex-SuperPumps will maintain and expand its position in the general and specialized pump markets by innovation in product design, uncompromising quality in manufacture and a dynamic approach to marketing.

In Pumpex-SuperPumps' empowerment-focused work environment, everyone is important, from the ordinary associate to the highly skilled policy-making executive. At Pumpex-SuperPumps we work as a team. **_Together we can_**.

It was certainly inspiring. Like any well thought out Mission Statement, it included the words "synergies" and "dynamic approach." I underlined the last sentence again, to make sure that Jill would know to print it in bold type. I saw Rich walk past. I looked at my watch. Just time for a quick coffee before I left to pick up my car.

Chapter 8

"You Can Tell a Lot from a Man's Handshake"

On Tuesday I was in a particularly good mood as I arrived at the office on the stroke of 8 o'clock. I had much to look forward to. Not only did I have my Mission Statement to lay before Rich, but today I got to interview one of the candidates for the vacant position of Vice President of Engineering. The previous VP had been a friend of mine, Hal Patterson, who had been fired owing to a mix-up arising from his frequent trips back and forward between the SuperPumps facility in North Carolina and Corporate back in Boston. The trouble was it had always been difficult to put your finger on exactly where he was. When we assumed that he was up at Corporate, they were often under the impression that he was with us in Falling Rock and vice versa. It all came to a head several months after the take-over when Ray Hacker ran into him on a golf course in Myrtle Beach on a day when Hal was supposed to be heading a new technology meeting in Falling Rock. It was a pity. Hal was a brilliant man and would be difficult to replace.

Rich liked to get input from all the Department Heads, when considering an important appointment like this one. I enjoy interviewing people, and I would certainly say that my interviewing technique is one of my strengths. During my MBA studies, I had sat in on some of the Human Resources classes, feeling that someone destined for a top management role owed it to himself and his future employers to become expert in the matter of selecting his people.

At my desk, I went through the contents of my in-tray. There were the weekly sales figures. These were disappointing again. I had expected to see an improvement since the appearance of the advertisement with the runner-up in the Miss North Carolina Pageant holding a PX-2 compression unit. My eyes strayed to the framed copy of the ad that adorned my wall, next to a reproduction of Pumpy the Possum which had been presented to me by Makem, Paimore & Lovett. The Miss North Carolina runner-up ad was a beauty all right! A young lady in a red bikini held a long cylindrical object, glistening with oil, a few inches from her face. Her eyes were dreamy and her mouth open, as if about to speak of the advantages of the PX-2. Under the picture appeared the text: "*When I need a good pump............Pumpex.*" I couldn't understand why the ad wasn't producing results. I made a mental note to speak to Rachel about it, when she was in a more responsive frame of mind. In the meantime, I had better ask Mike to come up with a detailed plan for increasing sales.

I laid the sales figures aside for Jill to file and picked up the next paper from my in-tray. It was a memo from Rich:

T. J.

Next week we are in line to pass two million safe work hours. The State is having a big drive to cut down on workplace accidents and they want to reward us with a plaque. This presentation is next Tuesday, during Ray's visit. The press and TV will be here, so it's a big chance for us to get some favorable publicity. I want you to organize the event so we make a big splash.

Rich

This was great news. As Rich was obviously aware, organization is one of my greatest strengths, and this was an opportunity to show Ray Hacker what I could do. I had already started planning when my phone rang. Normally I let Jill screen my calls but, being in such a good mood, I decided to answer it myself.

"Hi T. J., Rich here."

"Hi Rich, this is T. J."

"Yes, I know. Look, I got this fax this morning from Clayton Sipe. I'll read it to you.

Dear Losers,

All day yesterday I waited for information about the PX-2. What did I get? Zip! If it wasn't for the fact that your competition's a bunch of damned Japs, I'd be faxing them orders right now instead of wasting my time with you morons. Either I get my answers this morning or I go elsewhere, even to a bunch of slants, and I don't come back."

"Strong stuff," I said. "Harvey was supposed to be handling this. I'll find out what happened, get right onto it."

"There's more, T. J.: *'And don't go blaming Harvey. He's the only one out of the lot of you who's worth a damn. Fax me today, boneheads, or it's Sayonara.'"*

"I'll handle it personally, Rich. There'll be no more screw-ups."

I put down the phone and went over to Jill's desk.

"Have you finished that fax to Clayton Sipe yet Jill?"

"Just finished it right now. I had to do your New Product Development thing first and....."

"Yes, yes. Let me see."

I looked at what Harvey had written. Something about specifications of a gasket for linking a PX-2 to some other kind of thingamy-bob.

"Hmm," I said. "I want you to attach a cover note from me, Jill. Take this down. *Attached you will find the information you requested from Harvey. I'm sorry for the delay. I am now handling the matter personally, and you may rest assured that it won't happen again. Warmest personal regards, T. John Dick.* Did you get that? Oh, and make sure Rich gets a copy."

At 10 o'clock, Rich's P.A., Debbie, appeared at my door with a tall thin middle-aged man with thick spectacles and a brown and yellow tie.

"T. J., this is Peter Braithwaite, the candidate for VP of Engineering. Peter, this is T. John Dick, our Marketing Manager."

"Welcome, welcome," I said offering my hand. He shook it with a degree of firmness to which I gave only just a pass mark. I believe that you can tell a lot from a man's handshake. Peter's would certainly not have done for a marketeer, but for engineers one can accept lower standards in this regard, so I did not dismiss him out of hand, despite his nerdy spectacles and spotty complexion. I reminded myself again that he was, after all, applying for an engineering position.

"Take a seat. Would you like some coffee?"

"No thanks, I just had one in Bill's office."

I detected a foreign accent. "Are you from *Down Under*?"

"I beg your pardon?"

"You know. Austrian."

"No, I'm...."

"No, let me guess. English?"

"I'm from Wales originally."

"I knew it," I said. "My wife's aunt went to England once. Went all over the place. London, Cambridge, and that place where Shakespeare was born."

"Stratford."

"No, it wasn't that. Never mind. How long have you been over here?"

"Twenty-two years."

"And do you like it? Well, you must like it better than England. All that crappy weather."

"Yes, I love the weather down here in North Carolina."

"And all that Royal Family hanky-panky. I bet that really ticks you off, doesn't it? Fergie whooping it up all the time. Have you noticed they always go for Americans? Fed up with all those toothy inbred aristocrats, I suppose."

"I can't say I really pay it much attention. I'm an American citizen after all."

He didn't sound much like an American to me with that plummy accent.

"So tell me, Peter. What makes you think you've got what it takes to make it at Pumpex-SuperPumps?"

"Well, as you can see from my résumé, I'm currently at United Valve...."

I vaguely remembered receiving a résumé, but had no idea what I had done with it. "Ah yes. United Valve."

"....where I'm Director of Electrical Engineering. I feel that my experience there, plus my academic background would stand me in good stead at SuperPumps."

That stuck-up Limey accent was really getting on my nerves, confirming my initial handshake-related reservations. This guy was a no-hoper. I decided to finish up quickly, give him a quick tour of the department and deliver him back to Debbie.

"Well Peter, is there anything you'd like to ask me?"

"Well, Bill and Ronnie explained most...."

"Good, well I expect you'd like a quick tour of my department." I got up and motioned toward the door. We stepped out into the open plan area of the office. Randy's desk was first on the tour, but Randy wasn't there.

"Where's Randy today, Jill?"

"He had to go to the podiatrist."

"Couldn't it have waited until after work?"

"He said it was an emergency."

"Oh. Well, if you'd like to follow me Peter, I'll introduce you to Mike, one of the star performers of the Pumpex-SuperPumps team. He's very good with computers, a real prodigy. Do you have computers in England?"

Chapter 9

"Being a Model Corporate Citizen"

When I returned to my office after escorting Peter back to Debbie's desk, where Rich was waiting to take him to lunch, I remembered with a stab of annoyance that I had left my Mission Statement on the coffee table at home. I had been reading it through the previous night, when one of those Hair Club For Men infomercials had come on the television and I had stopped to watch it. Not that I am in any way balding; I have high temples and a distinguished brow. But I try to keep up with the latest developments in hair technology, in case, in years to come, I might need to take some action. I personally am devoid of vanity, but marketing is a dynamic, young man's arena and you need to be aware of the importance of how you present yourself to the world. I had laid down the Mission Statement to watch the infomercial and left it lying there. This was annoying, as I wanted to show it to Rich that afternoon.

I decided therefore to go home and retrieve the document at lunchtime. I picked up the phone and called Grace to tell her I would be coming home for lunch. She sounded genuinely surprised and delighted. With a spring in my step, I walked out to my car.

It was a beautiful spring day. As I drove toward home, I hummed along to my *Twenty Classical Favorites* cassette (a successful executive career does not have to stand in the way of a keen appreciation of the arts). As I approached the entry to Regal Pointe, I saw a familiar vehicle pull out of the gate and head in the opposite direction. It was Randy's old pick-up. His podiatrist had to be one of the top practitioners in the county to have an office in the prestigious Regal Pointe area.

Randy's truck was a good reflection of the kind of man he was. He was the same age as me, 42, but seemed faded and past his prime, having a hard time keeping up with the fast pace at Pumpex. He had been a salesman and was popular in his way with a certain kind of small-time customer. He had then moved into Marketing, but had never made it past Product Manager. I sometimes asked myself whether Pumpex needed a washed up loser like Randy. The Pumpex team is made up of winners and achievers. I would have to review his position in the company quite carefully. Randy had not even once been married, and I had to wonder if he wasn't perhaps gay.

When I got home, I was surprised to see Grace still in her dressing gown. Her hair looked like it hadn't been combed. She explained to me that she hadn't been feeling well that morning. She did look a little flushed. So I sent her back up to bed, while I made us both a sandwich. As we sat on the bed eating it, I told her about my coup in being put in charge of the two million safe work hours celebration.

"That's nice," she said, smiling, but somehow I got the impression her mind was elsewhere. Sometimes I almost get the feeling that Grace doesn't really want to feel part of the Dick team.

Back at the office, I gave Rich a call.

"Do you have a moment, Rich?" I asked in a voice that hinted that I had something important to discuss with him.

Rich's sigh spoke volumes. His was a heavy load. Hearing about my Mission Statement would be just the kind of boost that would lift his spirits.

"Yes, I suppose so, T. J. I have a two o'clock with Ronnie though, so we only have a few minutes."

I took my Mission Statement and walked briskly along to Rich's office.

Rich was on the phone. He gestured to me to take a seat. "Yes, Ray," he said into the phone, "the local TV station WCUP is going to be there. And Senator Phil White. He's up for re-election, needs all the local exposure he can get. He'll be making the presentation." Rich paused, while Ray spoke. Then he resumed: "Yes, I think it will be excellent publicity. Two million safe work hours; it shows we care for our employees. This will be very helpful after that big lay-off last week." (Our soft sales had necessitated a down-sizing of the manufacturing work force. Some, unable to see the economic big picture, had reacted emotionally, and in a small town like Falling Rock this soon became news. This was all the more galling, as Pumpex prided itself on being a model corporate citizen. I made a mental note to revise my Mission Statement to include *Pumpex-SuperPumps will be a model corporate citizen.*). Rich continued: "There's still some ill-feeling about our firing the old management lock, stock and barrel. This will show we're a company with heart. OK, bye Ray. Yes, we'll look forward to seeing you next week."

Rich put down the phone and sat down at his desk, giving me one of those convivial smiles I've never seen him give anyone else. Certainly not Ronnie. How he could put up with that crawler I'll never know.

"Now then T. J., what's up?"

"Well Rich, as you know, I have always been keenly aware of the broader picture, anxious to contribute to the global strategy at Pumpex. You'll remember my plan for increasing manufacturing efficiency...."

"Bill will never let me forget it."

"Yes, I'm sorry he had to react so personally to what was after all constructive criticism."

"He called it something else."

"Well, I suppose it did show him in an unfavorable light, but for the company's sake I had to tell it like it is."

"He said you never spoke to anyone actually involved with manufacturing. Most of them don't know who you are."

I found it hard to believe that anyone in the company didn't know who the Marketing Manager was, but I let this pass. "Of course, I didn't speak to any of them. I didn't want to impact the objectivity of my assessment. People have opinions, which can cloud the issues. I based my study on in-depth observation of working practices."

"You know we had complaints," said Rich.

"No, I didn't. I suppose some people might fear criticism. I personally never ...."

"No, it wasn't that. Several of the female operators on the PX-Line complained that there was a strange man watching them. *Lookin' at us real funny.*" Rich said this last phrase in his comical southern accent. (We have the kind of relationship where we often like to share a joke, and we both have an excellent sense of humor). "Human Resources had several calls about it."

I made a mental note to find out who had made these calls.

"Anyway," Rich continued, "that wasn't what you came to see me about."

"No, Rich. I'd like you to take a look at this." I put my Mission Statement on the table and turned it so that he could read it. "You and I both know that bringing a company like SuperPumps up to the Pumpex standard is going to need some radical new thinking. So, I prepared this Mission Statement to give direction to the company. Something everyone can get behind. Work towards a .... uh…"

"Common goal?" said Rich. It is amazing how much our minds are in sync. It's little wonder we form such an effective team. Rich must sometimes think of this when he's trying to get some sense out of Ronnie or Bill.

Rich read it through, nodding approvingly. Like me, he had an MBA and fully appreciated the vital role of the Mission Statement.

"I'm planning to revise it a little, I said. "Add a bit about being a model corporate citizen. Of course, if you have any comments or want to change anything, change the whole thing even…."

Rich looked at his watch. "No, it's OK I think. I really need to get ready for my meeting now." He started shuffling papers on his desk.

I got up to go. "You bet, boss." I said the word "boss" with a kind of jokey respect, the kind of informality that oils the machinery of our working and personal relationship (a big contrast to the Ostrich's greasy sucking up and Bill's ridiculous ranting).

"Oh, by the way," said Rich before I reached the door, "what did you think of Peter?"

"Hopeless," I said with a sad smile.

"Really? I found him impressive."

"Yes, well in some ways…."

"I've never seen such qualifications."

"No, nor have I." I could say this honestly, since the precise nature of Peter's qualifications was not at my fingertips.

"Oxford. Ph.D. at MIT. Very impressive. And glowing references."

Not knowing exactly what Peter's references said (or where I might have put them), I decided to steer the discussion to other areas. "I was put off by those big thick glasses."

"Yes, well I think we're going to hire him."

"I think probably on balance, it's a good decision." Flexibility and an open mind have always been among my greatest strengths.

"Ronnie and Bill both thought he was the right man," said Rich. He looked at his watch again. "I'd better get moving or I'll be late for my two o'clock."

Back in my office, I cursed those two crawlers Ronnie and Bill. They had probably got wind of Rich's liking for the Brit and fallen into line. I was glad I wasn't that kind of spineless yes-man. At least I had stated my opinion in a forthright manner. I consoled myself with the thought that Rich would be bound to respect the way I had made my point, and turned my attention to my Mission Statement. I decided to have a copy printed for everyone in the company, from the real contributors in Senior Management right down to the cleaners and assembly line workers. Everyone, even those with insignificant jobs, should get the message that Pumpex is above all else a team that values all its members. In addition, I would have copies posted on the notice boards throughout the plant. This would undoubtedly be the kind of thing Ray would be pleased to see, as a sign that we were serious about turning this company around and knew how to do it. I penciled in the addition about being a model corporate citizen and took it to Jill.

"Jill, I need you to type this up and make three hundred copies."

Jill looked at the Mission Statement, obviously impressed. I doubted whether she had ever seen anything like it before. Certainly the old SuperPumps management wouldn't have had it in them to come up with anything like this.

As I turned to go back to my office, I noticed that Randy was at his desk. "How's your foot?" I asked.

"What?" he said, looking at me blankly. It was easy to see why Randy had never made it to Senior Management.

"Your foot? How was your podiatrist's appointment?"

"Oh yes. Fine, thanks." A stupid grin spread over his big round face. "Not too painful?"

"Oh no. Not painful at all. Quite pleasant really."

"Yes, well be careful. We can't have you ending up in bed."

For some reason, Randy's stupid grin got even larger and stupider. I really couldn't think what he, of all people, could have to smile about.

Chapter 10

"A Single -Minded Sense of Purpose"

I have always been known as an ideas man. You can't rise to the top in a demanding field like marketing just by being superbly qualified with an MBA from one of the top schools in the country. Creativity is the magic ingredient that distinguishes top executive material from plodders, the greyhounds from the mutts, as I like to put it. So it was not long before I was brimming over with ideas for the Two Million Safe Work Hours Presentation. However, I have always been a team builder, so I decided that this would be an excellent opportunity to involve the troops in a major project. I therefore sent Jill around to gather everyone together in my office for an impromptu department meeting. When everyone was assembled, I kicked off the meeting:

"I expect you all realize that there's something very important happening next week."

"I didn't realize you knew," said Harvey.

"Knew what?" I said, trying not to let my irritation show.

"If we don't get those valves in here by Friday, the whole darned PZ line will have to close down." For some reason he looked at Mike as he said this. "This could cost us big time. Half the factory idle and…."

"Oh, for God's sake, Harvey!" I said severely. "This is *really* important." I was not going to be side-tracked. A single-minded sense of purpose is one of the strengths I bring to my work. It was one of the reasons I was a key member of Senior Management while Harvey was a Product Manager. "Next week we have a visit from Ray."

"Ray who?" asked Randy.

I gave him a withering look. "Ray Hacker."

Randy withered visibly. Like many who did not know him as well as I did, Randy obviously did not care for Ray. If he and my wife were ever to meet, I think they might find themselves in agreement on the matter of Ray.

I continued: "So of course I want everything to be spotless. I have a feeling Ray will want to see round the department, maybe even talk to some of you, ask how you're getting on, that sort of thing." I looked around and was surprised to see that only Mike showed any real excitement. I would certainly have to steer Ray in Mike's direction, let him see the caliber of the new men I was bringing on board. Rachel was staring fixedly at the framed copy of the advertisement featuring the runner-up in the Miss North Carolina Pageant, and seemed to be muttering something under her breath. Harvey's face appeared to be screwed up in an expression of disgust. When I caught his eye, he smiled apologetically and said:

"Sorry. Got some barbecue caught between my teeth. Can't seem to get it out with my tongue."

I gave him a look that made it quite clear he was skating on thin ice. Then I went on: "This happens to coincide with a presentation by Senator Phil White of a plaque to the company to celebrate two million safe work hours. Rich has asked me to handle the arrangements for the occasion. I thought it would be a good exercise to ask for your input. We need to make this a very special prestigious occasion." I looked at Rachel. Here was a chance to draw her out, start breaking the ice.

"Rachel, have you got any ideas?"

She looked at me in a way that suggested there was still some way to go before the ice was completely broken:

"You could start by getting someone other than that bloated phallocratic bigot to make the presentation."

I looked at her, astonished. It was true that Senator White, a heavily built man, was a noted conservative Republican with strong views on issues like immigration, women's rights and gun control. He had created some fairly heated controversy a few years back with his plan for the forcible sterilization of environmentalists. Nevertheless, Rachel's outburst was uncalled for. Firm action was required, and I decided there and then that I would definitely talk to her about it sometime.

"It seems to me T. J.," I might have known Mike would be the one to come forward with the first idea, "that we really need to put on a spectacular show. At Universal, we had an auditorium that was ideal for this kind of thing. It held four hundred people, had a stage, lighting everything."

I shared an understanding look with Mike. We had both known what it was like to work in a top rank professional organization. What a contrast with SuperPumps, where so much of the building seemed to be given over to manufacturing. It was hard to see how a truly creative executive could reach his full potential in such conditions. My own office was scarcely three times the size of an engineer's cubicle.

"I was thinking," he went on, "that we could use the factory floor. Build some sort of a stage, put in lighting for the cameras. We could rent some chairs so that the whole work force, plus press and dignitaries, could watch in comfort."

Mike's idea was brilliant, but it seemed to me that in his youthful exuberance he was overlooking one vital fact. "Won't the factory floor be in use? All those workbenches and machinery and things?"

"Well actually, no. Due to a screw-up by Production in failing to interpret my forecasts correctly, we're running out of valves for the PZ line. It looks like that part of the factory won't be in use for most of next week. We could put the people to work at clearing away the equipment to make room for the stage and the chairs. There's a guy I work out with at the gym who runs the local amateur theater group. He could get hold of the stage and the lights and anything else we need."

I looked at Mike warmly. If only I had more like him! I noticed approvingly that he was wearing a similar tie to my own.

"Sounds like an excellent idea, Mike. I was thinking very much along the same lines myself."

Chapter 11

"Fire Half of Them and See What Happens"

When I arrived the next morning, Mike was waiting outside my office.

"Morning Mike," I said. "Did you want to see me?"

"Yes, T. J. If you have a moment?"

"Of course, Mike. Come on in. Take a seat." I had a busy morning ahead of me, deciding exactly where the copies of my Mission Statement were to be posted, but I decided to make time for Mike.

"I saw Clifford at the gym last night," said Mike, sitting down in the chair opposite my desk. I noticed approvingly that his socks matched his suit. Dark blue and neatly pressed. The suit that is. Of course, his socks might also have been pressed for all I knew. Mike is fastidious in everything, a quality that helps make him the top performer in the department. I had noticed that Harvey's socks were frequently an imperfect match for his pants.

"Clifford?" I asked.

"The guy with the stage and the lights and everything. He said it's no problem. The amateur theater group has all we need. They have a collapsible stage that can be assembled without too much trouble. I've already been down to look at the PZ line area. There's a couple of beams we can hang the lights from. The sound system should be no problem. All we have to do is get a couple of hundred chairs. I'm sure we can rent them somewhere."

One of the keys to my success as a leader is my ability to delegate. I decided to let Mike quarterback this one. I of course would be the coach, ready with advice and direction. "Mike," I said, looking him in the eyes.

"I'm going to let you run with the ball. Do whatever it takes, but make it happen."

"You bet, boss," he said, and got up to leave.

"And Mike."

"Yes, T. J."

"You must come round for dinner some evening."

"Thanks T. J."

When he had gone, I turned my attention to the question of where my Mission Statement should be posted. I took my pen and notepad and wrote down: *Mission Statement Distribution Plan*. Under this I wrote:

1. Circulate copies in internal mail

2. Main Notice Board

3. Cafeteria

4. Marketing Notice Board

5. Human Resources Notice Board

After this, I couldn't remember where the other notice boards were. I decided to research the subject myself by making a tour of the facility. Grabbing my notepad, I strode out of my office and, after a brief pause to check with Jill that a copy of the Mission Statement had been circulated to everyone in accordance with item one of the *Distribution Plan*, I went on a tour of the plant that took up the rest of the morning.

By the time I returned to my office just before lunch, I had expanded my list by four notice boards. I gave the list to Jill with the instruction to make sure a copy was posted on each board by the end of the week, and then to create a *Notice Board* file in which to keep the list for future reference. Then I strolled along to Mike's office.

"How about some lunch, Mike?" I said. "I'd like to go over the plans for next week."

Over tortillas at Pepe's Mexican Cantina, I consulted with Mike about the details of the presentation.

"How do you see the program, Mike?" I asked.

My aim was to give him as much discretion as I could reasonably allow, while subtly guiding him in the direction that would assure the success of the project. In this way it would be both a learning and a motivational experience for him. I am always keen to develop and nurture the talents of my people. It's one of my greatest strengths as a manager.

"Well, I had an idea."

I gave him an encouraging look. "Yes."

"I think we should start with a speech from Ray. It's a great chance with the whole work force assembled. A few words of inspiration."

"Yes, Mike. Very good."

"Then the Senator will want to say a few words, with the press there and everything."

"More than a few words, I would think," I chuckled.

Mike chuckled too. He has a lively sense of humor.

"Then he'll present the plaque, and this is where my idea comes in."

I looked at him quizzically.

"Instead of having him present the plaque to Ray or Rich or you, we have somebody from the factory floor accept it."

"What? You mean some complete nobody?"

"Yes. By having somebody unimportant receive the plaque for the company, we show how everyone counts here at Pumpex-SuperPumps. Good for morale. And for the press."

"You're a clever young devil," I said with a smile. "I wondered if you'd hit on that idea."

"Yes, well I figured you would have something like this in mind. I thought that we could choose the lucky person by a drawing. Put everyone's name in a hat and pull out the winner who gets to shake hands with the Senator."

"A good idea, Mike. Get onto it."

I drove Mike back to the plant and dropped him off at Human Resources. We had decided that Jerry, the Director of Human Resources, should organize the draw. It would give him something to do aside from lounging around all day reading magazines, which, as far as I have ever been able to determine, is what Human Resources people do. I went back to my office and spent the next couple of hours arranging the overhead transparencies Jill had prepared for the New Product Development Procedure Meeting the following morning.

About 4 o'clock, I was disturbed by a visit from Bill. By this stage, I had separated the overheads into six piles and run out of room on my desk. I was about to place a pile of them on one of my visitor chairs, when Bill came in and sat on it. I gave him a look which clearly showed my annoyance at being obliged to put the overheads on another chair, which was further from my desk and totally unsuited to the task of efficiently sorting them out. He didn't seem to notice. In fact, he seemed rather preoccupied.

"T. J.," he began "I'm worried about what's happening out in the factory. Because Mike screwed up the forecast, we're just about out of valves for the PZ line. That means I'm going to have to lay some more people off next week, and the others will be messing around with that darned stage thing you're putting up. Morale's at an all time low. Quite frankly, it's not the first time Mike's screwed up. The only reason he doesn't screw up even more often is that he doesn't seem to do anything most of the time. Except play around with that computer of his."

I looked at Bill with the stoniest expression I could muster. It had taken Mike two years of post-graduate study at one of the finest schools in the country to learn how to play with his computer. But you couldn't expect someone like Bill to understand that.

"We can't let it happen again. Put Harvey back in charge of the PZ line."

This was preposterous. I had taken Harvey off the PZ line when Mike came aboard, judging that the line could benefit from a more professional approach.

"Out of the question, Bill," I said firmly. "Mike's the best man for the job. Now if you'll excuse me, I've got a whole heap of stuff to get ready for Ray's visit next week."

"That arrogant asshole!" said Bill.

I was shocked. He was talking about the President of the Pumpex Group of North America, a hard man but an effective leader.

"A nasty piece of work. If you ask me, the guy's a psycho. Crazy. And he's getting worse. When he came down here just after the take-over, you know what he said about my staff?"

I said nothing. I was concentrating on making my expression even stonier than before.

"*Fire half of them and see what happens!* That's what he said. Right there in front of them. That's not management. That's just being an asshole. No wonder those drawings appeared on the bathroom walls."

I was even more shocked. I had not seen any drawings of course. I had never been anywhere but the Executive Restroom. Still, it was quite intolerable that anything like this could be allowed to happen.

"I hope you found out who was responsible and fired them," I said.

"Hell, no! It could have been anyone. Could have been Rich for all I know. I'm sure he hates the son-of-a-bitch too. Only he's scared shitless like the rest of us. It's a damned culture of fear."

I was not prepared to listen to any more of this. "I think you'd better leave," I said tersely.

"I'm going," he sighed. "Don't worry, I'm going."

When he had gone, I called Harvey. "Harvey," I said. "I want you to go down to the bathroom in Production and make sure the walls are absolutely clean."

Chapter 12

"An Ability to Remain Calm in the Most Stressful of Situations"

The New Product Development Procedure Meeting was due to begin at 8:30 am. in Meeting Room A. When I arrived at 8:24 with an armful of overheads and hand-outs, I was surprised to find the room occupied by a large group from Production Control. I opened the door and went in.

"What the hell's going on?" I demanded in a voice that left no doubt that I was thoroughly displeased to see them there.

"We're having our monthly scheduling meeting." The speaker was Ed, Bill's Production Control Manager. His expression was smug. It beat me what somebody whose talents extended only as far as Production Control could possibly have to be smug about. It was very irksome the way some of these people used the fact that my official title was Marketing *Manager* as an excuse to speak to me as if I were on their level, despite my pivotal role in the organization and direct line of reporting to Rich. I had mentioned this to Rich, but with so much on his plate he had not got around to changing my title to Vice President.

"Don't you know there's an important Senior Staff meeting in here at 8:30?" I said in the no-nonsense tone I'm known for in situations like this.

"Not according to the book." Ed's look was more than smug. It was downright insolent.

"What are you talking about?"

"In the book. There's no mention of any Senior Staff meeting in the book. I came round yesterday evening and looked. There was no meeting written in for this morning, so I reserved the room. Go and have a look if you like."

It was becoming clear what had happened. In my hectic schedule of the last few days, I had omitted to reserve the meeting room. It occurred to me that Jill should really have done it for me. With all the things to think about in my position as one who has to constantly focus on the big picture, I couldn't be expected to attend to every little thing. I went out to her desk to give her a piece of my mind, but before I could do so I was hailed by Rich, coming toward me, accompanied by Ronnie, Ken and Bill. Bill wore a telling smirk, which left no doubt in my mind about exactly who was behind the last minute arranging of the Production Control Meeting.

"All set for the meeting then T. J.?"

Behind Rich, Bill was grinning stupidly. Well, he hadn't won yet.

"I've changed it to Meeting Room B."

"The Blue Meeting Room? Why?" asked Rich.

"Yes, why?" said Bill.

"The overhead projector is better in there. As you can see, I have rather a lot of slides."

"OK, T. J." said Rich. "It's your show."

"Yes, it's your show T. J." said Bill.

He was beginning to sound like a parrot. "Good company for the Ostrich," I thought to myself. "It's like working in an aviary."

We walked along the corridor to Meeting Room B. As we approached I began to hear voices through the open door:

"......taking into account the provision we made for obsolete inventory, we're going to come out about 40% below....."

I burst into the room. "What's going on in here?" I said, controlling my voice so that it barely shook. An ability to remain calm in the most stressful of situations is one of my greatest strengths.

Ronnie had followed me into the room. "Oh, I forgot. I asked my department to put together a review of our financial position in the light of the recent poor sales performance. Come to think of it, they did mention something about a meeting on the subject this morning. I told

71

them not to forget to put it in the book. I told them I was right behind T. J. on this matter. If we can't follow a simple procedure...."

"Oh shut up, you stupid great ostrich!" I said.

Ronnie tried to look shocked. "Really T. J. There's no need to get personal. After all we were only following...."

I didn't wait to hear the rest. With great dignity I strode from the room. As I walked down the corridor, I heard Ken say, "Does this mean the meeting's off?"

Fifteen minutes later, I was standing at Jill's desk explaining to her firmly that she would have to buck up her ideas and that future mix-ups like this one would not be tolerated, when Rich came by.

"Do you have a minute, T. J.?"

We went into my office.

"I was thinking," said Rich, "that it might be better to reschedule the meeting for next Monday. Ray will be here and it will be a chance to show him how we're getting to grips with the organizational deficiencies we inherited from the old SuperPumps management and putting in place a professional procedure for new product development. Peter will be here Monday too, so it will give him a chance to see what we're doing."

"Sounds good to me, Rich."

So those cretins' little joke had really backfired. Now Ray would get to see me present the New Product Development Procedure. There would be no doubt who was bringing a professional approach to the organization. Ray would remember T. John Dick as the brilliant and energetic Marketing Manager who was doing more than anyone to put Pumpex-SuperPumps on the right track. And all thanks to Ronnie and Bill!

"And T. J." said Rich as he left. "Don't forget to reserve the meeting room." He grinned broadly.

When he had gone, I shook my head, smiling at Rich's wacky sense of humor, and reflected on how the healthy informality of our working relationship helped to make us such a successful team.

Chapter 13

"The Pressures of Running a Complex Organization"

"Well, wish me luck, dear," I said to Grace as I walked down the path to the car.

"What?" she said. She seemed to be waving at someone. I followed her gaze to the building site across the road. Dwight, who had already started to work, stopped to take off his T-shirt and then waved back.

"Don't you think you should at least have a dressing gown on?" I said. "Standing out here in that short nightdress. People might get the wrong idea."

She didn't reply. She was busy bending down to pick up some litter that had blown into our yard. Dwight gave a loud whistle. I gave him one of my withering looks, which had an immediate effect. He smiled apologetically and said:

"Sorry, Mr. Dick."

As I drove to work, I went over the schedule for the next two days in my mind. Today was the New Product Development Procedure meeting, beginning at 10 o'clock. Before that Ray would probably want to tour the department. And tomorrow was the Two Million Safe Work Hours Presentation. It would be a full two days. Full of opportunities for Ray to observe T. John Dick in action.

I swung into the parking lot, strode into the building and arranged myself at my desk. I looked around me. Tidy but busy was the appropriate look. I was struck by the realization that for someone who gets through as much work in a day as I do, my office was remarkably tidy already. To look at it, you wouldn't realize that this was the powerhouse of Pumpex-SuperPumps. This was of course a tribute to my organizational skills.

Nevertheless, I took some files from the small filing cabinet in the corner and laid some of them in my in-tray and some in my out-tray. I took one of them and placed it open on my desk. Then I went out to make a quick inspection of the department before Ray arrived.

Mike's office was as impressively tidy as mine. Mike too has a gift for organization, which has no doubt been sharpened by everyday exposure to my own skills. I smiled approvingly and passed on to Harvey.

Harvey was on the phone when I reached his cubicle. This gave me a chance to make some observations. His desk appeared to be somewhat tidier than the last time I had seen it. Still, there were many deficiencies which were jarring to the organized mind. His in-tray was full to the point that papers were in danger of falling out onto the desk or the floor. I noticed several paper clips lying loose on the desk. When he put the phone down, I said:

"This won't do, Harvey. Ray will be round at any moment. I want your desk tidy."

"Oh. Well, I did tidy it."

"Did you? Well, what's this then?" I picked up one of the paper clips.

He stroked his chin. "It appears to be some sort of a device for fastening together several pieces of paper."

I found Harvey's flippant attitude not only an impediment to his work but a bad influence on the department. I had pointed this out at his performance review.

"We'll talk about this later," I said in a tone that made clear my extreme displeasure. "In the meantime, get this place tidied up before Ray comes round."

I moved on to Randy's desk. It got a pass mark for tidiness, the more so as there was no sign of Randy. I was about to ask Jill where he was, when I saw the door to the Department open and Rich entered, accompanied by the short but distinguished figure of Ray Hacker. I turned into my office to await their arrival there.

A moment later Rich and Ray arrived at my office door. I heard Rich say:

"And this is T. John Dick, our Marketing Manager. You might remember him. He was Marketing Services Manager at Corporate before we drafted him down here."

They both appeared in my office. Ray looked at me and said: "Nope. Don't remember him."

I laughed. Of course he remembered me. I had been in his office. I had spoken to him for over three minutes at the Pumpex Christmas party in Boston. I had sent him a memo about Pumpy the Possum. Ray certainly had a dry sense of humor. I smiled at him in a way that made it clear that T. John Dick was someone you could share a joke with.

"What's this then?" he said, picking up the file I had placed on my desk. I realized that I had not actually looked at it to see what it was.

"Oh just some stuff I'm working on," I said.

Ray took a paper from the file and read it aloud. *"Twelve Ways to a Better Short Game."* To my horror, I realized that what he had in his hand was a page from my file of golfing hints. I had been saving cuttings from *Golf Magazine*, to which I had subscribed since shortly after coming to work for Rich. *"If, like many of us, you're giving away too many shots around the green, maybe you should take a few tips from veteran king of the short game, Gary Player."* Ray paused. He had very thin lips, which now spread into a smile that bared his teeth. "Well, I'm glad to see you have your priorities right. I'd hate to think you were wasting company time trying to correct your slice."

Why did he have to go poking about on my desk? He hadn't even noticed the Mission Statement displayed prominently beside the framed advertisement featuring the runner-up in the Miss North Carolina Pageant. Uncertain of how to react, I decided to laugh. He looked at me in a way that made me feel this had been the wrong decision.

"OK," he said. "Let's have a look around."

"Um, before we do, I thought you might like to just glance at this," I said, pointing to the wall behind me.

"What?"

"I think you might…"

"It's that damned rat!"

"What? Oh no, that's Pumpy the Possum. I was referring to the Mission Statement that I've…."

"The rat! The damned rat!" Ray was turning a strange purplish color.

"I think perhaps we should tour the Department now," said Rich.

"Damned rat!"

"Why don't you lead the way, T. J?"

75

"Yes, of course Rich. Please, this way. I think you'll be impressed with what you see. I run a pretty tight ship."

I ushered them out the door and led the way to Mike's office.

"This is Mike Rothstein, Product manager for the PZ line." I said. Mike stood up and delivered a firm handshake.

"Really?" said Ray. "Perhaps Mike can tell us why PZ sales are down twenty percent this month?"

"Well, I'm afraid it was inevitable, given the mess I found when I got here a couple of months ago," Mike replied. "I'm confident that the steps I've taken to correct the situation...."

"Tidy office, I notice." said Ray. "What's next?"

Next stop was Harvey's cubicle. Ray looked at Harvey. From his expression, he didn't seem to like what he saw. "And what do you do?" he asked.

"I'm Product Manager for the PX line," said Harvey. He didn't get up or shake Ray's hand.

"Oh," said Ray with obvious distaste. I feared he must have noticed the paper clips still lying loose on Harvey's desk. "What's next?"

We walked the two steps to Rachel's cubicle.

"Rachel is our Marketing Communications Manager," said Rich. "Handles all our promotional material and product literature. A very creative young lady."

"So I see," said Ray. He was staring at something behind Rachel's desk. I followed his gaze. There on the wall was a large poster. It depicted a powerfully built man, grinning vacantly and flexing the muscles of one arm, while in the other he held a large bronze plaque engraved with the text of my Mission Statement. The man was naked. Ray turned to me. He put his face so close to mine that I could, in less stressful circumstances, have counted the pock marks on his cheeks. Ray was not a big man, nor was he what you would call handsome in the conventional sense. The Ostrich had once speculated that his small stature and teenage acne had turned him into what he called a "vicious little yellow-fanged snake."

Now he looked at me with an expression that confirmed that the tour was not going well.

Rich said, "Maybe we'd better go on the tour of Manufacturing now, if we're going to have finished in time for the 10 o'clock meeting."

"Yes, I think we'd better," said Ray.

Back in my office, I wished that I had a spare shirt. I had been perspiring quite heavily. I was about to get up and check the air-conditioning, when the phone rang. It was Ronnie.

"How did you get on?"

"What do you mean?" I asked.

"How did you get on with the Snake's tour?"

It occurred to me that someone referred to as the Ostrich even by his own staff had no business applying derogatory nicknames to the President of the Pumpex Group of North America. Before I could think of an appropriate way to voice this thought, the Ostrich continued.

"Rich had dinner with him last night. Said he was in a foul mood. Worst he'd ever seen him. Practically foaming at the mouth. I was hoping he really put you through it this morning. Might cheer him up before he gets to my office."

"Well actually, everything went pretty smoothly, all things considered," I said. I was not going to give him the satisfaction of knowing that the tour had gone less well than I had hoped. And after all, Ray had commented favorably on the tidiness of Mike's office.

"Oh. Well, good for you then, old buddy. Not so good for me probably. He'll want to make someone sweat before he's finished."

I put down the phone and went to check the air conditioning. The thermostat appeared to be defective. It was reading right on seventy.

At my desk, I took stock of the situation. It was not as bad as it might at first have seemed. Ray's prickly attitude during the tour of my department could probably be attributed mostly to his bad mood, which Rich had noticed the previous evening. The pressures of running a complex organization like the Pumpex Group of North America were bound to get to him from time to time. I could sympathize with this. There are times when the burden of masterminding the marketing strategy of Pumpex-SuperPumps while at the same time running a department which included difficult personalities such as Harvey and Rachel seemed almost too heavy for one person. Perhaps Ray would be in a more amenable frame of mind by the time the New Product Review Procedure meeting began. I looked at my watch. It was almost 10 o'clock. I grabbed my files and overheads and went quickly to Meeting Room A.

Ronnie and Ken were already there. So was Peter Braithwaite, who came over to me and shook hands with that lack of firmness I had noticed at the start of our interview the previous week. I said, "Welcome aboard" with as much enthusiasm as I could muster. Nobody could ever say that T. John Dick was not a team player. Whatever reservations I might have had about Peter's qualifications for a top position at Pumpex-SuperPumps, I was willing to give him a chance and to keep a completely open mind about his prospects, although frankly I thought he was a no-hoper.

Ronnie came over to where I was adjusting the overhead projector, which didn't seem to be working. He moved that long arm kind of thing with the mirror at the top of it, so that the light was pointing at the screen. The Ostrich is always interfering in things. It can be very annoying when you are trying to work.

"The snake appears to be slithering behind schedule," he said. "He never made it to my department. Must be giving poor old Bill a really hard time."

A few minutes later Rich and Bill turned up with Ray Hacker. By the look on Bill's face, the Ostrich had been right. His cheeks were flushed and I wasn't sure, but he seemed to make some sort of obscene gesture behind Ray's back. Either that, or he had just noticed some dirt under the nail of his middle finger. Anyway, we were all assembled. The meeting could begin. It occurred to me that if our competitors could see the depth of talent assembled in this room, it would surely cause them to quake in their boots. Ray, Rich and I would certainly be a frightening prospect.

Rich said a few words of introduction. He presented Peter to Ray, who didn't appear to be very impressed. Then he said a few words about the vital importance of putting together a viable New Product Development Procedure which would allow us to bring the right new products to the market on time and at a controlled cost. Then he turned the meeting over to me.

I began by also stressing the vital importance of putting together a viable New Product Development Procedure which would allow us to bring the right new products to the market on time and at a controlled cost. During this time I noticed that Ray had turned his back slightly to me and was talking to Rich. I decided to move briskly to the real business of the meeting. Ray was a busy man who obviously liked to come straight to the point.

"By now you will all have had a chance to read my proposed New Product Development Procedure." I looked around, but nobody caught my eye. Ken and Ronnie were busy shuffling their notes. Only Peter gave any indication that he had heard me. I continued. "I think that we should start by going through the procedure step by step. As we go through it you'll notice that its greatest strength is its simplicity. The process begins with a New Product Proposal Form, which is submitted to Marketing."

I put an overhead of the form on the projector. For some reason it seemed to be projecting things upside down. Probably something Ronnie had done while he was fiddling with it. Quick thinking under pressure is one of my greatest strengths, however, and I barely broke stride in the face of this obstacle which might have fazed less accomplished presenters. Quick as a flash, I rotated the slide on the projector and was pleased to see that it was now the right way round.

"As you can see, the form is simplicity itself."

"Can't see a damned thing actually." Ray had turned round to face the screen.

"I think you need to adjust the focus, T. J." said Rich.

I turned one of the little knobs on the projector. The long arm thing with the mirror at the end fell down, hitting my finger quite hard. I stifled a cry of pain and quickly and efficiently moved the long arm thing up again.

"I'm afraid your ideas are going completely over our heads," said the Ostrich, pointing at the ceiling, where my overhead of the New Product Proposal Form was now visible. On the credit side, it now appeared to be in focus. Wearing a broad grin, which I considered quite inappropriate for an important meeting about something as vital as the New Product Development Procedure in the presence of the President of the Pumpex Group of North America, the Ostrich came over and adjusted the projector so that it was pointing at the screen. As he returned to his seat, I located the correct knob and did the fine adjustment to the focus.

"Is he ever going to get on with it?" said Ray, turning to Rich.

"Anybody with an idea for a new product can fill out this form and hand it to Marketing," I continued.

"Where are you going to get the ideas from?" said Ray. "It seems to me you're a bit short on them. Otherwise you wouldn't be millions of dollars behind budget."

"Well, of course most of the ideas will come from Marketing. We're constantly brainstorming, coming up with innovative new ideas. However, we encourage...."

"Such as?" said Ray.

I looked at him, trying to figure out what he meant. "Uh...well..." I played for time.

"What new ideas have you come up with recently?"

"Umm...well..." I was aware that my presentation was not starting as well as I had hoped. I have always been sensitive to the moods of my audience.

"Oh, never mind. Get on with it then." Ray turned once again and started talking to Rich.

"I review this form and pass it on to one of the Product Managers." My mouth felt very dry and I was aware of an uncharacteristic tremor in my voice.

"If I might interrupt you for a moment, T. J...." The voice was not immediately familiar. Then I recognized those plummy English tones. "At United Valve, I introduced a New Product Development Procedure which was very successful. I've read yours and, although I think it's very good, it does seem to have some deficiencies. I took the liberty of bringing in a copy of the procedure I developed. I think it would make more sense to adopt a procedure that is tried and tested." He began handing out folders containing stacks of papers. The Ostrich picked up my procedure in one hand and Peter's in the other as if he were a set of weighing scales. He let the hand with my procedure drop sharply. "I like this one best," he said, looking at Peter's unimpressively thin folder. I sensed that the meeting might be beginning to slip away from me.

"If we could stick to the subject of the meeting," I said, "my Procedure has...."

"Which procedure are we supposed to be looking at?" asked Ray, who had turned back round in his seat and was flicking through Peter's folder.

"The other one," I said.

"Well, why the hell did you give me this one then?"

"I didn't."

"Well how did it get there?"

"Umm...well...Peter...."

"You guys are pathetic," said Ray, his face coloring. "Can't organize a damn thing. A complete bunch of cretins!" He began to crumple up his copy of my New Product Proposal Form in his hand.

There was an awkward moment of silence. I tried to think of an appropriate way to relaunch the meeting in its intended direction, but nothing came to me. I wondered once again if the air conditioning was working properly. It seemed very hot in the room. My head was swimming and I really didn't feel very well all of a sudden. Then a voice came from the far end of the room.

"You should feel right at home then Ray." We all turned to stare at Bill, who had fixed the President of the Pumpex Group of North America with a look in his eyes I had never seen before. If this had been someone more impressive than Bill, I would have called it a steely glint.

"What did you say?" asked Ray in a voice which, after the meeting, the Ostrich described as a hiss.

"You should feel right at home amongst a bunch of cretins, you jumped up, arrogant, greasy little shit."

Ray's lips moved but nothing came out.

"You are undoubtedly the rudest son of a bitch I've ever met, as well as one of the ugliest. You think we have to take this shit from you just because your momma never whapped your bony butt and taught you manners? Well you can take your damned arrogance and stuff it up your ass!" With that, he got up and left the room. At last Ray found his voice.

"You're fired." he squeaked.

I looked at the Ostrich, who seemed to be suppressing a giggle.

"Has Bill gone mad?" I asked.

The Ostrich leaned toward me across the table and whispered, "No, not gone mad. Just gone. He starts as President of Scientific Pumps next week."

Chapter 14

"The Spirit of the Jungle"

All was quiet where I sat at the wrought iron table that gave our deck something of the French rustic look. Building work had stopped for the day. I was staring at the future residence of Steve Taylor of Taylor Chrysler Plymouth Dodge, but this evening I was unable to appreciate its unusual beauty. My mind was on the events of the day. It had certainly not been the kind of success that I had hoped for and that all my hard work deserved. On the other hand, Bill's outburst had deflected some of the attention away from my difficulties in the meeting. In fact, after his departure things had gone considerably better. There had been no further interruptions from Ray, or indeed from anybody else, and after about five minutes Rich had said:

"You know, I think we've seen enough of your procedure. Since nobody seems to have any comments, I vote we accept it."

I was a little disappointed at the time. I still had over forty overheads left to show. However, the main thing was that my procedure had been accepted. As I gathered my overheads together, I couldn't help directing a smile of triumph at Peter, who was dejectedly collecting up his folders. There are times when, just for a moment, I have a heightened awareness of the spirit of the jungle that pervades the executive's life. Today Peter was the gazelle and I was the lion.

The door to the deck opened and Grace came out, rather unsteadily it seemed to me, carrying two margaritas. She handed one to me and sat down with a thump in the chair opposite mine at the table. "Whoops! Nearly spilled it," she giggled. She took a generous sip of her margarita, looked at me and giggled again. "Did he really say that, T. J? Oh, I'd have given anything to be there! Just to have seen the bastard's face!

Well, well, good old Bill!" She started to laugh and then let out a violent hiccup and put her free hand to her mouth, while the margarita wobbled perilously in the other. "A toast!" She raised her glass. "To Bill! May he have every success at wherever it was you said he was going."

Nobody could ever accuse me of not having a sense of humor. However Grace's irreverent attitude to the shocking events of the day overstepped the limit. I gave her one of my sternest looks.

"Oh for God's sake, T. J., you're just jealous," she said.

"Oh. And why should I be jealous, pray?" My voice was heavy with irony.

"Because Bill's going to be President of something. When are you ever going to be President of anything?"

"It's only a small company. Well, not as big as Pumpex anyway."

"At the rate you lot are going, it soon will be," she laughed, getting to her feet, not without difficulty. "Another margarita?"

"No thank you." I was coming to the conclusion that I would never make Grace into a real team player.

When she had gone, I turned my thoughts to tomorrow and the Two Million Safe Work Hours Presentation. Resilience is one of my greatest strengths. As I watched the sun go down over the construction site, I felt my old confidence return. Tomorrow, Ray and the rest of them would see what T. John Dick could do.

Chapter 15

"The Show Must Go On"

The next morning, I entered the plant not through the executive offices as usual, but through the factory entrance with the ordinary workers. Everywhere there were signs that this was a very special day. Above the entrance was a banner with the words *2,000,000 Safe Work Hours—Together We Can*, a clever echo of my Mission Statement. Parked directly outside was a colorful van with *WCUP ACTION NEWS* emblazoned on the side. A man with a camera balanced on his shoulder was smoking a cigarette just outside the door (Pumpex-SuperPumps is a non-smoking facility).

Once inside the plant, I found my way to the PZ line production area. Mike was already there, holding a ladder and talking to somebody at the top of it. When he saw me coming, he waved to me and shouted, "Hi, boss! Clifford's just gone up to check the lights and then we're all set to go." I looked at the rows of seats arranged neatly in a semi-circle around the stage, which had been erected where the final assembly and packaging work stations were normally located. The stage was draped with a cloth in the purple Pumpex company color. It was all really most impressive. On the stage was a microphone stand and a few chairs for the dignitaries—the Senator, Ray, Rich, the Mayor of Falling Rock and, of course, me.

"Good, Mike. Very good. I see you've laid everything out just as we discussed."

"Yes. It really wasn't that big a deal. We drafted in a few of the operators from the line, and it was done in no time."

I noticed three women standing against the wall. I waved to them and shouted. "Thanks for the help, ladies." One of them made a gesture, which I decided I would definitely have to report to Bill, before I remembered that Bill was no longer around. I would have to think of someone else to report it to. Another of them said:

"Hey, Charlene, ain't that the guy who was standin' there lookin' at us all creepy all that time last month."

I turned back to Mike. "Well it looks like you've got everything under control. I'd better get on up to Meeting Room B to meet the Senator. They're probably waiting for me."

As I walked back through the factory toward the executive offices, I went over the day's agenda in my head. After a brief reception in Meeting Room B (an informal affair with coffee and doughnuts, which I had arranged to have brought in), I would take the Senator, Ray and the Senior Staff down to the PZ line area for a brief rehearsal. Then the workers and office staff would be assembled and the presentation would start. First I would say some words of welcome. Then Rich would introduce the Senator. The Senator would make the presentation to the winner of our drawing, who would accept it with a few words on behalf of Pumpex-SuperPumps. Then Ray would give a short inspiring address to close on a high note. As I arrived at the Meeting Room, I allowed myself a mental pat on the back for another splendid piece of organization.

In the Meeting Room, the reception was in full swing. As I helped myself to coffee, I caught sight of the Senator talking to Ray, Rich and Ronnie. Ronnie! The Ostrich! It was typical of him to somehow insinuate himself into the Senator's conversation. I walked across the room to join them.

The Senator was a powerfully built man, with a perfectly bald head and a gray, sharply tailored suit. His tie was red, slightly darker than mine, I noticed. His voice matched his large frame, booming out across the room. I reflected whimsically that perhaps we wouldn't need the microphone for the Senator's speech. At that moment he appeared to be commiserating with Ray about the appalling number of scroungers claiming workmen's compensation and driving up costs to industry.

"And then half of them start claiming disability benefits!" he boomed. "In the next Congress, we intend to do something about it. Make it tougher for them to scrounge off the Government because of some piffling little so-called injury."

Ray was nodding his head in vigorous agreement. "About time something was done."

"In a caring way, of course. We are a party with heart."

"Of course, Senator."

Ray had shifted his position, forcing Ronnie to stand behind the Senator, so that he no longer formed part of the group. The Ostrich caught my eye and grinned at me in that stupid way of his. He was moving his arm in a circular motion, as if he were winding the Senator up. It was just like him. I sometimes wonder if the Ostrich has any respect for anything.

"Soon fix the freeloaders," the Senator continued. I had found a gap between Ray and Rich and now stood facing the Senator.

"Who are you?" said the Senator.

I reached out my hand, which the Senator shook with vigor. "T. John Dick, Marketing Manager."

"Yes well, I hope you'll remember which party represents the interests of industry when it comes time to vote."

"Oh yes. You'll have my vote, all right. Oh yes."

"It's time to put a stop to all the abuses. Welfare. Out of control immigration. Damned fairies in Hollywood and in our schools. This country needs a return to the family values that made it great. Vote for America! Vote Phil White."

I was on the point of applauding, but caught myself just in time. Phil White certainly was an inspiring speaker who had caught the mood of an angry nation. It was easy to see how he had made such a name for himself in Washington. He shifted slightly and I caught sight of the Ostrich behind him. He was holding his belly and looked as if he was about to throw up. I wondered if he had eaten too many doughnuts. Thankfully, he moved away and helped himself to more coffee.

"Well, gentlemen," I said, "if you don't mind, I think we should be getting down there. I want to do a quick run-through, so that everyone knows what's happening."

"Right. Lead the way then," boomed the Senator. I could see that my brisk efficiency had not failed to impress him.

I led the way down the corridor to the factory floor. Everyone seemed to be in a good mood. Even Ray seemed to have forgotten the unpleasantness of the previous day. We passed the PX line, which was still working. Harvey was standing there, talking to one of the line supervisors. I had had to speak to him before about spending too much time on the factory floor, but I was feeling generous, so I smiled at him as I led my column of VIPs toward the PZ area.

"T. J." he called out. "I need to speak to you about...."

"Not now, Harvey." I wasn't feeling so generous that I would neglect my distinguished party to talk to one of my Product Managers.

"It's important. It's about your drawing to decide who gets to accept the award. The guy who won it....."

"I said not now Harvey. Can't you see I'm tied up here with the Senator? Shouldn't you be helping Mike?" I noted once again how little of the Pumpex team spirit had rubbed off on Harvey.

As we entered the PZ area, I sensed the powerful effect the sight of the stage and the neatly arranged rows of seats had on the dignitaries. This was reinforced when Rich whispered in my ear, "For God's sake, T. J! How much did we spend on this lot?"

I had no idea how much we had spent. "Oh, you'd be surprised how little," I said.

Mike came toward us accompanied by a dapper little man of about fifty in a pale blue silk shirt and white pants. His graying hair was swept back dramatically off his brow and he wore a floral patterned silk cravat.

"This is Mike," I said. "My right hand man. He's done a lot to help me put all this together."

Mike delivered a firm handshake to the Senator, who grunted benignly. "Glad to meet you. Always pleased to meet the young blood of industry. Nation's future."

"Ahem!" The little man in the silk shirt cleared his throat.

"Oh yes," said Mike. "This is Clifford D'Arcy from the local amateur dramatic group. He's the one we have to thank for the stage and the lights."

Clifford bounced forward and reached out his hand to the Senator, who shook it without enthusiasm. Clifford's handshake appeared to have none of the firmness of Mike's. It was not the kind of handshake to impress someone like Senator White.

"How simply *too much* to meet you Senator. I have to say I never cared much for your politics, but I simply *adore* watching you on C-Span. Making your little speeches in the Senate. How forceful! How dramatic! Tell me, Senator, have you ever thought of a career in the theater if you don't get back in next time."

The Senator appeared to be unwell. He was turning bright red and breathing heavily.

Clifford had tilted his head to one side and was holding his hand against his cheek. "I can definitely see you as a thespian," he enthused.

The Senator turned to me: "Is this some kind of a joke, Dick?"

"Why don't we go on up to the stage?" suggested Rich.

As we moved up to the stage, I whispered my displeasure to Mike. "Just what kind of a gym do you meet someone like that in?"

"Sorry, T. J. I'd forgotten about the Senator's forceful views on the subject of the Cliffords of this world."

It was all very well for Mike to apologize; I sensed that the whole carefree mood of a few minutes earlier had evaporated. The Senator was pissed, so Ray was pissed, so Rich was pissed. I decided to get right into the rehearsal, pick up the mood again.

"Senator, you sit here. Rich there, Ray there. First of all, I say a few words of welcome. Then Rich introduces the Senator. Senator, you present the award to one of our workers. His name's on this card. He'll say a word or two of thanks. Then Ray winds everything up. OK?"

I looked at my watch. Five to ten. Clifford climbed up onto the stage.

"Places, everyone. Almost time for curtain-up."

This was absurd, of course. There was no curtain. Still, there was no time to point this out. The workers were streaming in and taking their seats. The local press were already seated in the front row, notebooks and video cameras at the ready. I made a sign to Mike at the back of the building. The lights went off. In the darkness, I heard Clifford scramble off the stage, then the Senator's booming voice, "Damn' faggot!"

I took my seat and waited for the stage lights to come on. Nothing happened. I waited another thirty seconds. Still nothing. There was a growing murmur from the audience. Chairs scraped on the concrete floor. Then it occurred to me that maybe I was supposed to walk to the microphone before the lights came on. It would be a dramatic opening to have the lights come up with me already poised at the mike. I got up from my chair and fumbled toward the center of the stage. I found the mike stand and grasped it, peering out toward the audience. Still no lights.

This technical hitch might have floored a man with a less potent mix of initiative and coolness under pressure. I decided the only thing to do was to follow the old showbiz adage: *the show must go on.* Unfortunately I couldn't see to read the speech that I had prepared. I would have to wing it.

"Ahem!" I cleared my throat and tapped the microphone three times. The murmur in the audience stopped. "Most of you will recognize me...."
I began.

"Cain't even see you, boy!" someone shouted. There was laughter. Just then the lights came on. There was a wave of thunderous applause. I had to wait for it to die down.

"....but for the benefit of some members of the press who don't, my name is T. John Dick, Marketing Manager of Pumpex-SuperPumps." I fumbled in my pocket and found my speech. I opened the paper and read: "I'd like to welcome everybody to one of the brightest occasions in the brief history of Pumpex-SuperPumps." Just then the lights went out again.

"Don't seem like a very bright occasion to me!" somebody howled. This idiotic remark produced a riot of impolite laughter.

"So...um. Yes....well, welcome," I improvised coolly. "Yes, indeed. Welcome. Welcome indeed....everyone." The lights came on again to an even more thunderous round of applause. People were stamping their feet on the floor. Through the noise, I heard Rich's voice. He had left his chair and was standing next to me at the mike.

"For God's sake, T. J., go and find out what's happening to those lights! I'll take over now."

Rich had clearly overlooked the fact that he was standing next to the mike. His voice boomed out over the sound system. A few voices in the audience shouted in unison: "For God's sake, T. J., go and find out what's happening to those lights!" This provoked some ill-mannered laughter from the unruly elements.

I jumped down from the stage and strode to the back of the building, where Mike was coming down from a ladder.

"What the hell's going on, Mike?" I shouted.

"It's Clifford."

"What about him?"

"He's gone."

"What? Why?"

"I don't know. He stormed off in a real temper. Shouted something about not hanging around any longer just to get insulted. Then he said he was going to vote Democrat for sure next time. He said some very unpleasant things about the Senator. The thing is, I don't know how to operate the lights. There's a bunch of switches down here, but they could mean anything. So I climbed up there and tried to operate them by hand. I guess I screwed up a couple of times."

I looked up at the beam to which the two spotlights were attached. "OK, Mike. I'll take over now." I climbed up the steps of the ladder, clambered on to the beam and settled myself into a position between the lights, where I could reach either one. Below me, Rich was well into his speech of welcome.

".....and I'd especially like to welcome the Pumpex-SuperPumps workforce, the people who have shown that good work can be done safely...."

I noticed that the right spotlight was not directed precisely at Rich. I leaned over and nudged it slightly. Unfortunately I must have nudged it slightly harder than I had intended, because it swung over to spotlight Ray, who at that moment appeared to be engaged in picking his nose. Once again there was a howl of laughter from the unruly element, accompanied by wild applause. I quickly swung the light back to focus on Rich.

"....thus proving beyond a doubt that together we can." I was gratified by Rich's quotation of my Mission Statement. "Without any further ado, I'd like to introduce the senior Senator for our State, Senator Phil White."

There was some applause, although, I noticed, less than that of a moment before when the light had settled on Ray with his finger in his nose. The Senator rose from his chair. I swung the light over to where he stood and moved it to follow him over to the mike. I was getting the hang of this now. I have always had a gift for anything technical. The Senator stared intently at the audience. A hush fell on the building. He had the look about him of a man with a vision.

"When I first went to Washington as Senator for North Carolina, I was proud to represent a State that stood for everything good and wholesome in America," he began. "Now we find ourselves assailed on all sides by demons that would eat away at the very fabric of our society." His voice rose in passionate intensity. "Affirmative action. Unbridled illegal immigration. What's happened to the America we knew? Well, I believe that it's in places like this that we find it still. That's why it's such a great pleasure to come here today to present this plaque to a company that still stands for all that's best about America. At a time when it's sometimes hard to find anything made in America, it does the patriotic heart good to see that at Pumpex Americans are once again showing the world what we can do. And so it gives me great pleasure to present this beautiful plaque for two million safe work hours to…" —he looked at the little card I had given him—"…Mr. Jorge Ramos."

Applauded by his colleagues a slight young man in a tee shirt and blue jeans jogged up on to the stage and over to where the Senator stood. He beamed through his bushy black mustache as he took the plaque from the Senator, grabbed his hand and shook it enthusiastically. Then he turned his face to the microphone and said:

"Es con mucho gusto que accepto este premio para dos milliones de horas de trabajo sin sinistra, por la parte de Pumpex-SuperPumps. Gracias." (I am able to relate this pretty much word for word thanks to Rich, who has twice vacationed in Puerto Vallarta.) I don't know if the Senator understood, but it was clear that he was far from pleased. He had turned a kind of purple color, which almost glowed in the spotlight I had trained on his face. As Ramos left the stage to deafening cheers, still beaming and waving the plaque aloft like a trophy, the Senator turned and stomped back to his seat, muttering something under his breath. By his expression at the time, I thought it was just as well that he was out of range of the microphone.

Ray rose to his feet and walked to the mike. The laughter and applause died down immediately. He tapped his feet and stood there, glowering at the assembled workers and press. "We have one man in particular to thank for this morning, and I can assure everyone that when I next see Mr. Dick, I will have a few very special words to say to him."

This came as quite a surprise to me because, quite frankly, I was a bit disappointed with the way things had gone. Although of course I could not be blamed for any of the mishaps, I had been prepared to take my share of the criticism. A pat on the back was totally unexpected, and especially from Ray, whose expression even now seemed almost to contradict his words of praise. Sometimes, I think, I'm too self-critical, always striving for perfection, unable to see that my efforts are successful in the eyes of others. It is, I think, my greatest weakness.

Ray paused, glowered at the audience again. "Never," he said, "never have I been witness to such a horrible shambles. If this is indicative of the kind of organization at SuperPumps, I think we might as well fire the lot of you." After such a positive beginning, Ray's speech was certainly turning out to be less upbeat than I had expected. He had now begun to move about the stage, shouting, so that he had no need of the mike. I was having quite a job keeping the spotlights on him as he paced back and forward.

"However, it's not practical to fire the lot of you. Not yet anyway."

He had arrived back at the center of the stage and, as he leaned forward over the mike stand, his features were contorted with rage. In the spotlight that I had had to swing rapidly into position, his face looked even more purple than the Senator's had a few moments earlier. The Ostrich told me later that, in the harsh glare of the light, it had "a positively demonic aspect."

The reason that I have to refer you to the Ostrich's description is that I had very little time to look at Ray's face myself. That last swing of the spotlight had thrown me off balance and, to stop myself falling, I grabbed one of the cables attaching the lights to the beam from which they were suspended. Clifford must have made a very poor job of fixing the cable, because it came loose from the beam, and I felt myself falling. From below, I heard Ray's voice:

"So I might as well start with someone. Dick, wherever you are, you're....."

Ray never finished his sentence. At that moment, I fell from my position on the beam and plummeted into the audience. Fortunately my fall was broken by Big Shawna of the PZ line, who was occupying several chairs directly below the lights. She was of course startled and screamed in panic, but her presence undoubtedly saved me. A less corpulent employee might well not have been adequate to prevent a fatal accident.

Ray was less fortunate. The loosening of the cable from the beam caused both spotlights, which had been attached to it, to fall. One of them toppled forward in an arc directly onto the center of the stage, which was of course occupied at that moment by Ray. It struck him on the head with a noise that was heard throughout the building, even over Big Shawna's screams. He fell to the floor of the stage and lay there in silence.

The other spotlight also fell onto the stage, though fortunately not on top of anyone. It bounced twice and rolled over to where the Senator was sitting. He jumped to his feet, but I guess years of large lunches with Washington lobbyists had taken their toll. He was not quick enough to avoid the light, and it struck him hard on the leg, before falling off the stage and smashing on the concrete floor. The Senator let out a howl of pain and began dancing up and down on his uninjured leg, holding the other one and shouting, "Communists! Terrorists! Arabs! Environmentalists! We're being attacked!"

The Senator's shouts were now the only sound in the building. Big Shawna had stopped screaming and was looking at me in astonishment. For a moment nothing happened. Everyone was too shocked to move. I had recovered my composure—a cool head in a crisis is, as I have said before, one of my greatest strengths—but I was unable to move without causing an excruciating pain in my leg. At last, the Ostrich got up and ran onto the stage. He knelt down beside Ray, who was lying face down, and turned him over. The fallen spotlight lay on the stage, its beam directed at the two figures, so that their giant shadows were projected on the wall. For a moment, both shadows were immobile, as Ronnie looked at Ray. Then he bent down and put his ear to his mouth. Still nobody else moved. The Senator had by now fallen off the stage, knocking himself unconscious. There was absolute silence as Ronnie lifted Ray's wrist and held it between thumb and forefinger. Then he bent over Ray's face again, pinched his nose, held his head back and started to blow into his mouth.

Gradually, people were recovering from the shock. Rich came to help Ronnie and others rushed onto the stage to see what was happening. Big Shawna seemed unaware of, or unconcerned by, what was going on. She held me tightly in her powerful arms and shouted across the hall: "Hey Latisha! Look what I got!"

It was at that moment that smoke first became visible. A burning smell was coming from the stage and in seconds the purple cloth draped around it was in flames. (The Fire Department later issued a citation for the use of a non-flame-resistant material at a public event. Their report blamed the fire on either the smashed floodlight or sparks from the electric cables attached to it.) Pandemonium broke out. Few people knew what to do. (A further citation was subsequently issued to Pumpex for failure to carry out any fire drills since the take-over, an omission that the local press seized on in an attempt to cast doubt on the company's claim to care deeply about the well-being of the workforce).

My memory of the events that followed is decidedly hazy. The pain in my leg was intense. I remember looking up into Big Shawna's face as she bustled through the crowd, repeating, "Don't you worry suh! I ain't gonna let nuthin' happen to you!" After that, everything is a blur.

EDITOR'S NOTE

There is a gap of several weeks in T. John Dick's account, immediately following the fire at the Pumpex-SuperPumps facility. During this time, Dick was recovering in hospital from a broken leg, back injuries and the effects of concussion. I would not wish to be the cause of unnecessary anxiety to his friends and admirers, so let me eliminate any painful suspense by assuring you that he made a full recovery. However, not surprisingly, given the extent of his injuries, there is a break in the story following his account of the events leading up to the fire. On the subject of the disaster itself he is silent. Feeling that some knowledge of the aftermath of the fire would be helpful in understanding subsequent events, I have pieced together some newspaper accounts of the time.

The editor is indebted to Ms. Paige Turner of the Falling Rock Public Library for her assistance in compiling these newspaper accounts.

*From the **Falling Rock Chronicle** of Wednesday, April 26, 2000*

One Dead, One Missing in SuperPumps Inferno
Senator Injured in Blaze

The Pumpex-SuperPumps manufacturing facility on Jim Bakker Boulevard was badly damaged yesterday in a blaze that took firefighters from Falling Rock and towns as far away as Statesville over five hours to bring under control.

The dead man was Mr. Ray Hacker, the President of the Pumpex Group of North America. Eyewitnesses told of having seen him slump to the ground after being hit by a falling spotlight during a celebration to mark two million accident-free work hours at the plant.

Still missing is Mr. Randy Philips, a Product Manager, who could not be accounted for at a roll call taken after the building was evacuated. Rescue workers continued to search the building, but at the time of going to press no sign had been found of Mr. Philips.

All others were evacuated safely, the only injuries being to Senator Phil White, who was visiting the plant to present an award for the two million safe work hours, and Mr. T. John Dick, the company's Marketing Manager. The Senator sustained serious injuries to his knee and severe concussion when he fell from a makeshift stage that had been erected for the occasion. Mr. Dick is being treated for a broken leg, shock, concussion and injuries to his back, received when he fell from a beam above one of the plant's assembly areas in circumstances which are at present unclear.

*From the **Falling Rock Daily Record** of Thursday, April 27, 2000*

SuperPumps Hero says "No Big Deal"

Shawna McBride doesn't look like a hero. The 38 year old from Falling Rock works as a gimlet joister at the Pumpex-SuperPumps facility, where co-workers describe her as "just one of the girls." But when the SuperPumps factory was consumed by fire on Tuesday, Shawna showed that the most ordinary of people are capable of the most extraordinary heroism. She carried Mr. T. John Dick, the company's Marketing Manager, who had sustained a broken leg, from the blazing building and delivered him to medical crews in the parking lot outside. Shawna was typically modest in describing her rescue of the stricken executive:

"I was just sitting there minding my own business when this white boy falls into my lap. From nowhere. Well I don't meet many men these days, so when this one landed on me out of the blue, I wasn't about to let him go again. To tell you straight, I didn't really know who he was. I'd seen him hanging about the factory about a month ago, looking at the girls all funny, sort of strange. Some of them complained about it, but I never minded. Next time I seen him he was standing on the stage mumbling something while the lights was goin' on and off. Then he disappears and a few minutes later he falls out of the sky and the building's on fire. It was no big deal."

From the obituary column of the **Boston Daily Herald** *of Thursday April 27, 2000*

Raymond Hacker, 1946-2000

Raymond Hacker, who died in a bizarre fire at the Pumpex manufacturing facility in Falling Rock, North Carolina was noted for an abrasive management style that endeared him to few of those who knew him. During his time as President of the Pumpex Group of North America, he presided over massive downsizing of the group's workforce, as reported in this paper. His oft-stated philosophy was "Fire half of them and see what happens." What happened was a dramatic slide in the company's fortunes under his leadership.

Born in Philadelphia, Hacker attended private school and Northern University, where he graduated in Business Administration. His real break seems to have come in 1978, when he married Thelma, only daughter of Pumpex founder and owner Ralph Crump. His sensitivity on the subject of the role his marriage had played in his meteoric rise within Pumpex was legendary. Few reporters dared question him on the subject, after he broke my nose in the course of an interview during my stint as a business correspondent in 1992. There have been few obituaries I have looked forward to more eagerly than this one.

*From the **Falling Rock Chronicle** of Thursday, April 27, 2000*

Missing SuperPumps Man Found Safe
Saved by bad back!

Randy Philips, a Product Manager at the Pumpex-SuperPumps factory partially destroyed by fire on Tuesday, turned up alive and well at his North Falling Rock home yesterday wondering what all the fuss was about! Philips, 42, was absent from the building when the blaze hit, attending an appointment with his chiropractor.

*From the **Falling Rock Chronicle** of Friday, April 28, 2000*

Dick Questioned in SuperPumps Blaze

Police yesterday questioned Mr. T. John Dick in connection with Tuesday's fire at the Pumpex-SuperPumps facility. Dick, who is recovering in Cook Memorial Hospital from injuries sustained in the fire, was not charged. Sergeant Mike Flatt of the Falling Rock Police Department told reporters: "Unless they make it a crime to be a horse's ass, there's nothing we can charge him with."

*From the **Falling Rock Daily Record** of Friday, April 28, 2000*

Day of Mourning at SuperPumps

Workers at the SuperPumps factory will today officially mourn the death of Group President Ray Hacker in Tuesday's dramatic fire. There will be a moment of silence this morning and the flag will fly at half staff until lunchtime. The scheduled family night and mini-golf tournament at the Optimists' Park will go ahead as planned.

*From the **Boston Daily Herald** of Saturday, April 29, 2000*

Pumpex Widow Philosophical Over Husband's Death
Agence France-Presse

Thelma Hacker, wife of slain executive Ray Hacker, appeared to be taking the tragic death of her husband in her stride. When reached at a party given for about forty close friends at her villa in Antibes, she commented. "They should give that Dick guy a medal." (T. John Dick, Marketing Manager at the plant where Hacker was killed in a fire on Tuesday, was initially suspected but subsequently cleared of involvement in the blaze.)

Mrs. Hacker has no plans to return to the US for the funeral, which takes place on Monday.

*From the **Boston Daily Herald** of Tuesday, May 2, 2000*

Pumpex Stocks Soar

Despite the recent fire at their North Carolina facility, Pumpex stocks rose sharply. Analysts attribute the surge to revised profit forecasts released yesterday, which project a much brighter picture for the remainder of the year than was previously predicted.

*From the **Raleigh Echo** of Thursday, November 30, 2000*

Ex-Senator Draws Disability

Phil White, defeated in the recent Senate elections is down on his luck. The right-wing firebrand, who once referred to this paper as a liberal rag he wouldn't even hang in his bathroom, is now struggling to repay massive debts accumulated in his campaign. According to reliable sources, White, who injured his right knee in a recent fire, is now drawing disability allowance.

Chapter 16

"The Stuff that Senior Staff are Made of"

My first day back at Pumpex-SuperPumps was exhilarating. The ten days in hospital followed by three weeks at home had been a time of great frustration for me. Inactivity is not a natural state for a Dick. We are a dynamic up-an'-at-'em breed and I had been bursting to get back in the saddle even on crutches with a leg still in plaster. I have always taken physical discomfort in my stride. It is one of my greatest strengths.

Everyone was delighted to see me back, of course. Mike offered to help me climb the stairs to the Department, but I insisted on doing it on my own. "Thank you Mike, but I can manage," I said with a smile that masked my pain. I felt it was important for Mike to see the kind of grit and determination that is the stamp of a leader; the boy might need it some day himself.

In my office, I was pleased to find that nothing had been touched or moved. One of the keys to my efficiency as a manager is my attention to organization. I can instantly get Jill to find any file or document in my office. Of course, someone in my position can't be absent for more than a month without his in-tray filling up with documents requiring his attention, and I noticed that this was indeed the case. But before I got down to that, I set off on a tour of the department. It was important for my people to sense the presence of their leader again. I dreaded to think in what directions my ship had drifted without its captain.

My worst fears were confirmed when I stopped at Jill's desk and reviewed the Meeting Room Reservation Book. There were no entries at all for the period of my absence. I walked the few steps to Meeting

Room A, where, as I suspected, there was a meeting in progress. This was the first indication that things had to a significant degree fallen apart without my firm hand at the helm. I would have to mention it to Rich, of course, but for the moment I was in too good a mood to worry, and, I must admit, viewed what would normally be a disturbing episode as a gratifying confirmation of just how essential my management skills were to the smooth running of Pumpex-SuperPumps.

Randy was not at his desk.

"Where's Randy today?" I asked Jill, in a friendly voice that conveyed that I did not hold her personally responsible for the meeting room situation. It was the responsibility of the meeting organizer to fill out the form and give it to Jill, as I had made abundantly clear in eight memos on the subject. Without the form, Jill was powerless to act.

"He had a dental appointment."

"Again?"

"Actually, it's his first absence in quite a while. Almost three weeks."

I moved on to Harvey's desk. He was not there either. I picked up his phone and called Jill.

"Hi, Jill. T. J. here."

"Oh hi, T. J., you're at Harvey's desk."

"I know. Where is he?"

"He had to go see Clayton Sipe at Pumps-R-Us. He'll be back tomorrow."

"Oh. Another crisis, I suppose."

"Well, no. I think he said something about clinching a big deal for PX-3s."

I was not pleased. Not only would it have been more appropriate for Harvey to have been present to brief his Department Manager than to have gone on a jaunt to his buddies in South Carolina, but I was seriously concerned that he should have taken on something as important as this, without waiting for me to return. The trouble with Harvey was that he was a loose cannon, going off in all directions, where a more experienced executive would be more likely to achieve results. "Well," I thought to myself, "cannons have a way of getting fired, if they're not careful." I made a mental note to share this joke with Rich. It would certainly appeal to his lively sense of humor.

101

"Well, when he calls in, tell him I want to talk to him." I put the phone down and headed to Mike's office. Mike was busy at his computer but, when he saw me coming, he quickly switched it off in order to be able to give me his full attention. He got up and moved a chair to a position where I could sink into it and lean my crutches against the wall.

"It's great to have you back, boss. How's the leg?"

"Oh, not so bad." Of course I was still in considerable pain, but I remembered how important it was to let Mike see the stuff that the Pumpex Senior Staff are made of.

"I bet it itches though."

It was a pity that Mike mentioned that. Through the rigorous self-discipline that is one of my greatest strengths, I had succeeded in banishing thoughts of the itch under my plaster cast, and had not thought about it since breakfast, when I had got Grace to scratch it with a meat skewer from our fondue set.

"I had a cast once. Broke my leg skiing. It's the itch I remember most. Euh!" He shuddered.

I felt the skin on my leg begin to tingle. "Yes, well. Tell me what's been going on while I've been away. Have you been managing?"

"We've been getting by, T. J. I've done my best to...."

"Right. Well I'd better get back to my office. A lot to do." The itch in my leg was killing me! I got up on to my crutches and made my way to my office as quickly as possible. Once there, I sank into my chair, opened my drawer and reached for my ruler. It wasn't there. Someone had taken my ruler. I called Jill.

"Jill, my ruler appears to have disappeared. Have you any idea who took it?"

"No, sorry. I don't. I've got one, if you'd like to borrow it."

That was hardly the point. Still, I was desperate. "Yes please, Jill. Quick as you can."

After what seemed like an age, Jill appeared at my door with a ruler.

"Sorry, Mr. Dick. It took me a little while to find it." Here was another indication that things had grown very slack in the department in my absence. She stood at the door for an unnecessarily long time. "It's good to have you back, and I hope...."

"Yes, yes, thank you Jill. That'll be all for now."

When at last she had gone, I stuck the ruler down inside my plaster cast and wiggled it about vigorously.

"Lost something, T. J?" It was the Ostrich. Typical of him to turn up just in time to catch me at a disadvantage.

"No. No, I'm just....uh...." It annoys me that I can never think of the appropriate cutting response to Ronnie's idiotic comments until after he's gone. Instead of saying "Well I wouldn't mind losing you, you stupid ostrich!", which would have been suitably stinging, I said: "Nothing really."

"Itching to get back to work, huh?" he said with that moronic smile he always has when he thinks he's said something funny. "Anyway, I've got to run to a meeting. I'll stop by later on for a chat."

This time I was ready. "I'll look forward to it," I said in a voice dripping with irony. The Ostrich just smiled. I'm afraid my irony is too subtle for the likes of him.

When he had gone, I called Jill into my office.

"Jill, I'd like you to send an internal memo to everyone in the department. Take this down:

Subject: Writing/Drawing Utensils.

It has come to my attention that the above-mentioned utensils are being borrowed and not returned. This can seriously impact the smooth running of the department. If a new utensil is required, the procedure is to address a request to Jill, who will fetch the required item from the Departmental Stationery Cupboard (DSC). If you have any questions or do not fully understand the procedure, please contact me. Thank you for your cooperation.

With this out of the way, it was time to turn my attention to my in-tray. There was a memo from Rich explaining that the PZ line would be out of operation for at least two months while repairs were carried out to the building. There were several sets of sales figures covering the period of my absence. They showed a slight improvement, which I attributed to seasonal factors. Finally I came to a memo on Pumpex Group of North America letterhead. I picked it up and read:

To All Pumpex Group Staff
Subject: Appointment of Group President

The Board is actively seeking a replacement for Ray Hacker as President of the Pumpex Group of North America. As you can imagine, Ray's shoes are hard to fill and the search for the right man may take some time. In the interim, the Board has asked Mr. Hans Kartoffel, recently retired President of Pumpex Europe to step into the breach as acting President of the Group. Please join with the board in wishing Hans every success in his assignment.

I put down the memo in disbelief. With home-grown talent of the caliber of Rich and myself within the organization, why would they want to give an important assignment like this to some ancient Kraut, who probably couldn't even speak English properly? I was still sitting there with the memo in my hand when the Ostrich stuck his head around the door.

"Ah, T. J. I was hoping you'd still be there." He came in and took a seat.

"I'm very busy, as you can imagine." I looked at him pointedly.

"Yes, yes, of course. So how are you feeling? You look right as rain. Except for your leg, of course."

I sighed. It looked like he had settled in for a chat.

"I've just come from a review of our financial position. Did you know things have never looked better. You really dug us out of a hole when you decided to burn the place down. Bit rough on old Ray, I suppose, but it's hard to find anyone who's too sorry. I heard his wife sent you flowers in hospital. Is that true?"

I nodded. Thelma Hacker had sent me a bouquet and a very nice get well card.

"Bit rough on me too. I was the one who had to give him mouth to mouth, after all. You know, his breath was foul. Well not his breath exactly, since he wasn't breathing, but the general area of his mouth. Really horrible. You know what I think?"

"No."

"I think it was his soul. The smell. It was the rotten son-of-a-bitch's soul. The stench of evil."

I gave him one of my looks, but I was confused and not really sure which look I gave him. There is sometimes no appropriate look to give the Ostrich.

"And you know what else?"

"No."

"I'm sure he tried to bite me. Even though he was probably dead or unconscious, he tried to bite my lip. Right there." He pointed to his upper lip.

"What did you want to see me about?" I asked, trying to restore a little sanity to the situation.

"What? Oh nothing really. I just wanted to tell you about how the Great Fire of Pumpex turned out so well. You know all that excess inventory we had? The stuff you hadn't a clue how to shift?"

I looked at him incredulously. "You know perfectly well that once the advertisement campaign featuring the runner-up in the Miss North Carolina Pageant holding a PX-2 compressor has had a chance to bite, we'll move that inventory damned quickly." I do not usually use language like that, but the Ostrich's suggestion that I didn't have an effective plan for increasing sales was too much.

"Yes. Of course. Well we won't have to now. It all went up in flames. So instead of writing it off, we collect the insurance. Brilliant. Were you ever in the Mob, T. J?"

"Don't be absurd."

"Sorry. By the way, that excess inventory. It was all PZs. How were you going to boost sales of the PZ by pictures of semi-naked floozies holding PXs?"

Bean counters like the Ostrich understand nothing of the fine art of marketing. Almost immediately I replied. "The PX ad was calculated to raise awareness of the whole company, thus boosting...."

It was too late. He was gone.

Chapter 17

"Pain is no Barrier to a Determined Senior Executive"

A fter the Ostrich had departed, I looked at my watch and saw that there was still some time to go before lunch. I decided to go for a walk round the plant to see how the repairs were going and to boost morale amongst the workers by letting them see that I was back at the helm. It took me some time to get to the factory floor on my crutches, but pain is no barrier to a determined senior executive, and I persevered.

The damage to the PZ line area was considerable, and repairs did not seem to be progressing with any great urgency. A few men in hard hats were standing around talking beside various pieces of machinery, but there was very little sign of activity. The contrast with the hectic world of the Marketing Department was striking. By coincidence, Rich was there also, checking on the status of the work.

"Hi, T. J. Welcome back." The welcome was clearly heartfelt. Rich would certainly have missed my support in these trying times.

"Good to be back, Rich." I was conscious of the fact that I must have cut something of a heroic figure, standing there on my crutches in the midst of this scene of destruction. This upset my natural modesty, but there was very little that I could do about it.

"Quite a job you did here!" said Rich. I was getting tired of the suggestions that I was in some way responsible for the previous month's fire, which was clearly the fault of the idiot Clifford's sloppy work and young Mike's inexperience. However, I recognized Rich's wacky sense of humor at work and took no offense.

"The repairs don't seem to be progressing too quickly," I said.

"To tell you the truth T. J., that suits us just fine."

I looked at him with intelligent curiosity.

"You know as well as I do that we can't even give away a PZ at the moment," said Rich.

I knew no such thing of course. I had high hopes of the exposure we were getting from our advertisement featuring the runner-up in the Miss North Carolina Pageant. However, I let it pass. My intelligent curiosity wanted to hear what he had to say.

"Well, it turns out our insurance covers us not only for the inventory you sent up in flames but also for lost production. Every day that we lose, we get compensated for. It's wonderful. I come down here every day to watch the PZ line make money for the first time since the take-over. Our stock price is way up, you know."

We watched the inactivity in silence for a moment. Then Rich continued.

"Ronnie recommended we hire this construction company. They built the extension to his house. The slowest work he'd ever seen, apparently. Took twice as long as scheduled."

At that moment a man in a hard hat came over to us. He wore cleaner dungarees than the others.

"Mornin', Mr. Pickens," he said to Rich.

"Morning, Stan. This is T. John Dick, our VP of Marketing."

"It's a real pleasure to meet you," said the man called Stan. "I'd just like to say thanks for what you did here. To tell you the truth, business has been real slack recently. This job is helping us out of a bit of a hole." He beamed at me in a way that suggested that he regarded me as his benefactor. "If there's any work you need doing, Mr. Dick. Renovations, extensions, anything at all. You just let me know. As a token of our appreciation."

I started to say: "Actually, I was in no way responsible....." Suddenly, something struck me. I turned to Rich. "*VP* of Marketing?"

"Yes, T. J.," he smiled. "It's the least we can do for the man who has single-handedly turned the company around."

I am not a vain man. I have never attached much importance to titles. It has been enough for me to know that I do an outstanding job. Nevertheless, as a token of appreciation for all my hard work and consistent contribution to the company's success, the promotion was welcome. I admit that I was very pleased.

Rich looked at his watch. "How about lunch?"

On the way back through the factory, we went by the PX line, which was still working. As we passed the gimlet-joisting work station, I caught sight of a very large African-American woman waving at me. I frowned. It can be very dangerous to use a gimlet-joister without paying due attention.

"Hey, baby!" she shouted. "Come to Momma!"

There was ribald laughter from the other women, which I considered most inappropriate. This lack of respect for Senior Staff was no doubt a legacy from Bill's days. I had heard that he would sometimes actually sit down on the line and chat with the girls. This was undoubtedly a cheap way to gain popularity, but there is far more to leadership than popularity, and I have always been conscious of the need to maintain a proper distance. Not that I am not popular, of course. It's just that I know how to command respect in a way that Bill never did.

"I thought Big Shawna was on the PZ line," I said to Rich.

"She was. Only with PZ production at a halt, we had to lay them all off. We could hardly do that with Big Shawna though, could we? Can you see the headlines? *Pumpex Fires Fire Hero.* Imagine the fun they would have with that. All the puns they could make with the word *fire*."

Over lunch at Bolick's Barbecue, Rich filled me in on some up-coming projects.

"The Annual Sales Meeting is next week. As you know, we're getting the whole sales force together at Wakiah Island. It's Ken's show, of course, but the sales force will expect to hear something from Marketing and see the new products that are coming up. You don't have much time to prepare."

"We'll be ready, Rich."

"Good. Hans Kartoffel will be there. He's making a tour of all the companies in the Group to get acquainted. He gets in here Monday. Then we all go down to Wakiah Island."

I had dropped a lump of barbecued pork on my tie and was rubbing it with my napkin.

"Are you listening, T. J.?"

"Of course. Hans Kartoffel. Yes." It is one of my strengths as an executive that I can deal with many tasks at the same time. My attention to my tie in no way interfered with my ability to concentrate on what Rich was saying. I believe they call this multi-tasking.

"I expect he'll want to do the usual tour. Better make sure your department's in good shape. You're just making it worse."

"What?"

"Your tie. You're making it worse. You need to dab your napkin in some water. Here."

Rich put his glass of water beside my plate (my own glass was empty). I wet my napkin and continued to dab at my tie as he continued.

"On Monday night he wants to go out for dinner with the Senior Staff. Bit of a problem there. We can't go back to Chez François since you and Ken were thrown out for brawling, and there's nowhere else decent in town. Being from Europe, Hans probably likes a good dinner. It's how they do business over there."

I nodded. I had never been to Europe, but I knew Rich had spent a couple of days in Amsterdam once, so he should know all about this kind of thing.

"The important thing," he continued, "is to let him see we're sophisticated people he can relate to."

The spot on my tie was proving extremely stubborn. I had already sloshed half of Rich's water on it, much of which had unfortunately run onto my shirt and the front of my pants.

"Just because we live in a hick town in North Carolina doesn't mean we left our cosmopolitan sophistication behind in Boston," Rich went on, handing me his napkin.

I think one of the waitresses must have jostled me, because at that moment the arm which I was using to mop up the water from my shirt slipped and struck the ketchup bottle, which someone had left unnecessarily close to the edge of the table. Neither Rich nor I had taken any ketchup, so it was definitely the fault of some careless waitress. The bottle toppled off the table and fell onto my lap. The same negligent person who had incorrectly positioned the bottle on the table had omitted to check that the top was securely fastened. As a result of this inattention to detail, the top came off and most of the contents emptied onto my pants before I could retrieve the bottle.

Rich was looking at me in astonishment. Clearly he too was shocked by the standard of service that could allow such a thing to happen to a senior executive. Recovering my composure quickly, I hailed the nearest waitress, a tall thin girl with alarmingly blond hair. When she came over, I pointed at my lap and said "Take a look at what's under my napkin!"

Before I had a chance to lift my napkin, the stupid girl slapped me in the face and said: "You dirty son-of-a-bitch!" She stormed off before I even had time to say that if she was in the habit of leaving half-open ketchup bottles dangerously close to the edge of the table, she had no right to make such a scene when customers got dirty.

Moments later, she was back, accompanied by the manager. He glared at me.

"You're right, Darlene. He looks pretty sick to me."

This was too much. Not only had the idiotic girl, by her negligence, caused a serious accident with consequent damage to a senior executive's suit; she had also obviously delivered a garbled message to the manager, who was under the impression that I had been sick. Furthermore, I didn't appreciate the way he was looking at me.

"Look," I said with justified but controlled anger, "this has nothing to do with being sick. I was on the point of suggesting to your waitress where she should put her bottle of ketchup. But now that you're here I want to know what you're going to do about it."

"I'll show you what I'm going to do about it," he shouted. He reached over and grabbed my crutches, which were leaning against the table. "Here, Darlene. You take these. I'll take this." He grabbed me by the collar and pulled me to my feet, causing considerable pain to my leg. He was a very powerfully built man. Nevertheless, I am confident that without my injury, I would have been more than a match for him. As it was, I was powerless to prevent him dragging me to the door and throwing me out into the parking lot. I was, of course, outraged.

"Is this any way to respond to constructive criticism from customers?" I said sharply. "If you knew the first thing about marketing...."

I never finished my sentence. At that moment he threw one of my crutches at me. It hit me on the head, and for a moment I was dazed.

When I fully recovered my senses, Rich was helping me into his car. As we drove to the Emergency Room, he said, "Well, I guess that's another restaurant we can't go back to."

I looked at him and for a moment I thought he was grinning. I must have been mistaken. My vision was still blurred.

Chapter 18

"What Makes the VP of Marketing Tick"

"Is there a dentist's office somewhere near Regal Pointe?" I asked Grace. We were standing on our deck, enjoying the calm of the construction workers' afternoon break.

"I don't know. Why? Did that guy loosen a tooth as well as bash your brains out?"

I rubbed my head beneath the bandages the nurse at the emergency room had wrapped around my head. A week they said I had to wear them! "No. I just wondered. As Rich was driving me home, we passed Randy—he's one of my Product Managers—going the other way, just before we turned into the development. He was at the dentist this morning."

"Oh. Isn't there that place down on 29th Avenue Drive North-East?" Falling Rock's road numbering system was feeling the strain of the town's growth. Three new roads had been built between 29th Avenue and 30th Avenue—29th Avenue Drive, 29th Avenue Lane and 29th Avenue Drive Lane.

"I don't remember seeing one there."

"Oh, well maybe it was on 29th Avenue Lane. Somewhere down there. Would you like a drink? Take your mind off the pain."

"Yes, maybe a glass of Chardonnay would be appropriate under the circumstances."

As she passed through the door into the house, I couldn't help noticing that she was looking especially good today. It was almost as if she had been expecting me, although how she could have managed to change into that revealing black nightdress in the few minutes between my call from Rich's car and my arrival at the house was beyond me. In any event, I appreciated her efforts to make me feel better. I just hoped she understood that my head injury would not allow me to respond romantically to her touching efforts at seduction. When she returned, I said:

"You know, I think we should extend this deck."

She handed me my glass. "That would be wonderful. I've always said we should extend it to the end of the house."

"Yes, well I don't think it would be such a big job really. Then we wouldn't have to lean so far over to see the lake."

"What made you decide on this now? You always said it would be too expensive. Did that bump on the head soften you up?"

"No. I just thought it would be a nice thing to do. Of course, if you don't want to....."

"I want to, T. J. I'm just surprised, that's all. I reckon that bump on the head did do something." She came over and kissed me on the cheek. Now it was my turn to be surprised. Grace is not a very physical woman, and such uninhibited gestures are rare. I was only sorry that the pounding in my head prevented me from responding with my customary passion. The cool self-control that makes me such a successful executive at Pumpex is not the only side of T. John Dick!

We stood for a moment at the edge of the deck, watching the construction workers at the building site next door as they sat around drinking sodas and smoking cigarettes. A couple of them waved at us. One of them shouted:

"Hey Grace! Who's your Indian buddy?"

I didn't waste my time trying to figure out the meaning of such an idiotic question. My head was extremely hot under all the bandages. I walked back to the table, which stood in the shade of the house, and sat down in one of the chairs.

"You know it's the National Sales Meeting next week?"

"Yes." She stood with her back to me, looking out on the building site, where the men were beginning to return to work.

"I'll be away for three days. It's a nuisance, I know, but there's no getting out of it."

"I expect I'll find some way to keep myself occupied," she said bravely, continuing to look at the building site. She didn't turn round. I sensed it was easier for her to be brave without looking me in the face. For a moment I felt a pang of guilt. I was actually looking forward to the Sales Meeting.

By the time she turned to face me, she had managed to compose herself and there was a smile on her face. What a truly remarkable woman she was! I decided this was the time to give her my good news.

"Hans Kartoffel is going to be here on Monday. The new acting Group President."

"That's a strange name."

"Yes, he's from Germany. And he wants to go out to dinner with the Senior Staff on Monday."

"Well just be careful with him. Don't kill him or anything."

"Grace you know perfectly well that I was in no way......"

"Just kidding, T. J., just kidding."

"Yes, well I don't think such a tragic accident is anything to joke about."

"No, I suppose you're right. Everybody's doing it though. I heard another one today. 'What were Ray Hacker's last words?— I feel a bit light-headed.' She started to giggle. "I even heard one about you. 'How did T. J. introduce Ray Hacker?— Today, the spotlight falls on the President of Pumpex.'" She was laughing so hard now she had to hold on to the rail of the deck.

I gave her one of my sternest looks. Nobody could ever accuse me of not having a sense of humor, but these jokes were certainly in poor taste.

"Where did you hear those jokes?" I couldn't think who of our Pumpex friends would repeat such tasteless so-called humor. Certainly not Rich or his wife.

"I can't remember. Just someone I bumped into." She stopped laughing suddenly. My stern look had obviously had its effect, and I decided to let the matter drop.

"So where will you go for dinner?" she said after a moment. "Not Chez François, I suppose."

"No. It's a bit of a problem really. There's nowhere in Falling Rock that's likely to measure up to the kind of place he's used to. Europeans like to dine in style. I don't think the Imperial Dragon Chinese Pagoda or Harry's Rib Shack is really what we need."

"Why not invite them all over here? We could get those caterers from Charlotte. You know, the ones Ralph had for his party. They were classy. Good food too."

I thought about her suggestion for a moment. It had merit. It would be an opportunity for Hans to see the Dicks as a team. Get to know what makes the VP of Marketing tick. The informality of the occasion would lead to a lowering of the barriers, a chance to forge the personal bonds that are so important in an organization like Pumpex. There was only one problem.

"Where would we put everyone?" I asked.

"On the deck, of course. You said you wanted to get an extension built. Well, here's an incentive to get moving. We've got a week."

It wasn't long, but I remembered the warmth of Stan's gratitude. It just might be possible. As I went in to call him, Grace said:

"You don't get to meet many European men round here."

Chapter 19

"Talent, Dedication and an Ability to Get Results"

There are times when a top executive owes it to the company to clear his desk and his mind, and sit back to do some strategic thinking. I have always been keenly aware of how many people—shareholders, colleagues, subordinates and customers—depend on the breadth of my vision and the sharpness of my business insight.

On Tuesday morning, I closed my door and sat back to do some thinking. Of course it wasn't but a minute later that the disturbances began, and no surprise that it was the Ostrich who barged in without knocking and settled himself into the chair on the other side of my desk. It was also no surprise that he was wearing that idiotic grin of his.

"Hi there, Gandhi!" he said. "How's it going? I thought an open door was one of your management strengths."

"I'm trying to do some thinking," I said stonily. I did not want to encourage him to stay. Bean counters have no idea how much we marketing people have to get through in a day.

"Some thinking, huh? No wonder your head's all bandaged up."

I intensified the stoniness of my expression, but it had no effect. I think the Ostrich's lack of subtlety immunizes him against my looks, which are normally so effective. (A mastery of non-verbal communication is one of my greatest strengths.) He continued, still wearing that idiotic grin.

"We were all wondering, you know. Why you were wearing the bandages. Ken figured you wanted something to go with the plaster on your leg. Accessories make such a statement, he maintains. Peter thought you'd got tired of hobbling along on your crutches and had taken to walking on your head. Quite an imaginative guy, Peter. I suppose engineers need to be to invent things. You know, like reasons why projects are a year behind schedule. Anyway, I said you must have joined some kind of an Indian religious movement. Turns out we're all wrong. You're just taking some very wise precautions before cranking up your brain."

It was time to clear this up once and for all, before silly rumors and gossip got started. Although I shun such things myself, I am aware of their prevalence in the office environment.

"Well, if you must know, I had an accident in the parking lot of Bolick's Barbecue. I fell and hit my head on one of my crutches, that's all."

"You didn't have the ribs, did you? With a plateful of those in your belly, anyone's equilibrium could be impaired. Your center of gravity shifts down to the area of your waistline. If you're not expecting it, a sudden gust of wind can blow you right over."

I very much doubted the Ostrich's theory, which clearly demonstrated his kind of shoddy reasoning. A lower center of gravity would surely have the effect of *more* stability, not *less*. However, I didn't have time to argue. He was eating into my strategic thinking time.

"Is there anything in particular you wanted to talk to me about?" I asked.

"No. Just happened to be passing. Wondered about your head, that's all."

"In that case, if you don't mind, I need to get on with my strategic thinking."

"Oh yes, sorry. Wouldn't want to interfere with the strategic thinking. The big picture. Next time I'm passing and wonder about your head, I'll wait and come back when your door's open."

After he had gone, of course, the ideal comment came to me. I should have said something along the lines of, "I suppose it's difficult for you to see the big picture with your head stuck in the sand." It is a great regret of mine that, although I am known for my razor sharp wit, few people are aware of just how sharp it is because the perfect comment comes to me after the ideal moment has gone.

I sat back in my chair again. I had much to think about, but the Ostrich's interruption had irritated me. Vice Presidents of Finance are seldom fully occupied. I have noticed that there are always copies of the Wall Street Journal lying around their offices. You won't find the Wall Street Journal in my office! The hectic world of marketing allows no time for reading newspapers. And you won't find me wandering about disturbing other people's work with pointless conversation.

Just then, I noticed Rich walking past. I decided to go and get a cup of coffee to help me think.

"Hi, T. J. How's the head?" asked Rich at the coffee machine. He was obviously concerned. We are more than just colleagues. His question was spoken in the tone of voice you would use to a friend.

"Not too bad, Rich. Hurts a bit but I'll survive. I just dashed out to get some coffee. Doing a bit of strategic thinking."

"Ah yes, strategic thinking. I just bumped into Ronnie. He said he thought that was why your head was bandaged." He laughed.

This so-called joke of Ronnie's was a sore provocation. I decided to unleash my own wit.

"Yes, well his head's stuck in the ground and he can't see very well."

Rich looked at me. "Are you sure you're OK, T. J?"

I was aware that my delivery hadn't done justice to my joke. Perhaps it was too subtle to begin with, even for someone with a lively sense of humor like Rich. I changed the subject.

"I had an idea about dinner next Monday," I said.

"Oh yes?" said Rich, sipping his coffee. His interest was obviously aroused.

"Yes. I was thinking about what you were saying about not being able to go to Chez François and there not being any other decent restaurants in Falling Rock. Well, why not have everyone round to my house? We know of a superb caterer. It would be more informal but still provide the sophisticated atmosphere Hans is used to." Rich had seen my Swedish furniture and impressionist prints.

"Hmm. I don't know. It's an idea. I would have everyone over to mine, except we have the decorators in. Where would you put everyone at your place?"

"On the deck."

"As I remember it, T. J., your deck is pretty small."

I had, of course, anticipated this question. "By next week it'll be a lot bigger. Stan's people are starting work tomorrow."

"You crafty old devil. So you found a way for Stan to show his gratitude."

"He might have to pull a couple of men off the work here," I said.

"Great. OK, T. J., let's do it. Let me know if you need any help. I'm sure Liz wouldn't mind popping up and giving Grace a hand."

This was an unexpected bonus. Grace would be delighted at the chance to get to know Rich's wife better. I had tried to encourage her to see more of Liz, but she seemed reluctant to do so, and I had not been able to help her overcome her shyness. I was so pleased with Rich's reception of my suggestion that I completely forgot to mention the continued flouting of the Meeting Room procedure, which I had intended to bring up.

Back in my office, I turned my attention to another important matter. My promotion to Vice President of Marketing would require a reorganization of the department. I had noticed for some time that my span of command was too wide. I could not be expected to concentrate on vital strategic decision-making if I had to devote so much time to the guidance and management of my staff. It was essential that I move quickly to appoint a Marketing Manager to relieve me of some of this burden. There was, of course, only one possibility. As I was thinking this, I happened to glance up and see Harvey through the window in my door.

"Harvey," I shouted. He didn't stop. Of course my door was closed and it was possible he didn't hear me, although I think a more professional executive would have. I went to the door, opened it and called after him. He turned round and came back. To my surprise, he was smiling.

"Hi, T. J. Good news, isn't it?"

"What?" I asked.

"About the PX-3 deal with Pumps-R-Us. It ought to keep the production lines busy for a while. Good price too."

"Yes, well that's what I wanted to talk to you about. Have you any idea how stupid it was going charging off down there yesterday?"

He looked at me with his mouth gaping stupidly.

"You could have blown the deal," I continued. "You should have waited until I got back. This kind of thing is important. It should be left to Senior Staff."

"But Clayton asked specifically that I go down there."

"Maybe he did. But you should have waited until I could go with you. Negotiations like these are best handled by a senior executive with experience and training, who knows how to handle the big accounts. You could easily have screwed it up. It could have been very costly."

"But, T. J., he told me if you ever came within a hundred yards of the place he'd set his dogs on you."

I didn't like Harvey's tone. I gave him one of my sternest looks. So this was what Harvey called "trying to respect me more."

"Have you seen his dogs? They're mean."

Clayton Sipe's dogs, of course, were completely beside the point. I was not going to get led off down that alley after a red herring. I looked at him even more sternly.

"Well, things are going to change around here, Harvey. I can promise you that." I turned, went back into my office and picked up the phone.

"Mike. Have you got a moment to pop along to my office?"

When Mike arrived, I gestured to him to sit down on one of the chairs round the little conference table in the corner of my office.

"How long have you been here now, Mike?"

"Oh God, you're not going to fire me?"

"No, of course not. What made you think that?"

"Just that every other time....I mean...nothing. What were you saying T. J?"

I must have disturbed Mike in the middle of a very intense program or calculation or something on his computer. It was not like him to babble.

"I've been very impressed with you in that time Mike. Very impressed with your professionalism and ...um...leadership."

"Thank you, T. J."

"That's why I'm promoting you to Marketing Manager."

"Thank you." Mike grinned broadly. I felt a pang of nostalgia at the memory of my own first major promotion. There was much of me in Mike. He would go far.

"It won't be easy," I went on. "Keeping control of Harvey and Randy and Rachel, but I think I'm a pretty good judge of a man's character. I'm sure you'll be up to the job."

"Thank you, T. J."

I picked up the phone. "Jill, will you get everyone together and bring them along here for a brief departmental meeting?"

While we waited for everyone to arrive, I discussed the implications of his promotion with Mike.

"Of course you'll have to recruit someone to replace yourself. Oh, and of course there will be some more money in it for you. We can't expect you take on this kind of responsibility just for the fun of it, can we?"

There was a knock at the door and Jill, Harvey and Rachel came in. I motioned for the girls to sit down. There wasn't another chair, so Harvey sat on my desk. I like to keep my staff meetings informal, but there is a limit. I gave him a disapproving look. He got up and stood by the door.

"I have some good news," I began. "As you all know, I was recently promoted to VP of Marketing. This will be a big boost to the department. I'll be able to represent us with even more authority at Senior Staff level. It also means that my old position as Marketing Manager becomes vacant. As you know, at Pumpex we like to promote from within, to reward talent, dedication and an ability to get results. That's why I've decided that Mike is the man for the job." I smiled at Mike.

There was a moment of silence, broken by Harvey.

"What?" he said almost under his breath. He seemed to mutter something else.

"What was that, Harvey?" I said.

"Nothing. I mean..... I need to take a wizz." He opened the door and went out. I looked at Rachel and Jill.

"Congratulations, Mike," said Jill. I thought she could have sounded a bit more enthusiastic. Rachel said nothing, but looked at me with strange intense eyes. I sometimes got the impression she was trying to figure out exactly what made T. John Dick tick. I sensed that I held a certain fascination for her that went beyond admiration of my leadership qualities. "Just what kind of a man is this T. John Dick?" her eyes seemed to say.

I looked for Randy's reaction. It was only then I realized he wasn't there. I looked at Jill.

"Doctor's," she said.

"As I was saying," I continued, "Mike has shown that he's a motivated self-starter, who knows how to use a computer better than anyone else in the department. What he has achieved you all can achieve if you apply the same level of skill and dedication."

"Oh, for God's sake!" said Rachel. I sensed that the appointment had not gone down too well with her. She probably saw some kind of evidence of sexism in the promotion of Mike rather than her, despite the obvious difference in talent and qualifications. There is just no pleasing some people.

When they had all left, except for Mike, I got up and shook his hand.

"Congratulations, Mike. Tomorrow we'll talk about your first big project, the National Sales Meeting."

Chapter 20

"My Sensitive Understanding of Grace's Unique Personality"

"What, that stuck-up bitch! No way! You must be joking. Not in a million years!"

For a moment, I was afraid that Grace would spill her margarita on the head of the workman below. She turned round violently and stood with her back leaning against the rail of the deck.

"I don't need her coming round here sticking her nose in. I'm perfectly capable of organizing a damned dinner party, for God's sake!"

There was no need for this kind of language. I gave her a very disapproving look.

"Goodnight, Mr. Dick. Goodnight, Grace. See you tomorrow." The voice came from below.

"Goodnight, Sam," Grace called after the departing workman.

I looked at the ground below the deck. There was a heap of earth and some tools, not much to show for a whole day on the job.

"He doesn't exactly seem to have been hard at it," I sighed.

"Oh, I wouldn't say that," Grace said, and her eyes glazed over in a way that suggested to me that she would have done better not to fix herself that last margarita. Her face now wore a slightly silly smile, which was at least preferable to the surly expression of a moment earlier.

"All I'm saying," I resumed, "is that Rich said he was sure she would be pleased to lend a hand."

The surly expression returned. "And because she's the boss's wife, I'm supposed to let her walk in here and tell me what to do! I don't like her, T. J. She's just a condescending, stuck-up ...."

"Grace!"

"I could tell you a few things about Mrs. Perfect down there in her big house next to the lake."

"I really don't see...."

"She's no better than the rest of us, I can tell you."

I didn't say anything. I thought it better to let the subject drop for the moment. We could return to it when Grace was in a more rational mood. This outburst was probably related to the time of the month or something. One of the secrets behind the success of our marriage is my sensitivity to things like that. I changed the subject.

"I hope they manage to get more done tomorrow. There's only four days till the party, and two of those are the weekend. Stan said they would have it finished by Monday, whatever it takes. He's just going to have to put more men on the job. One guy on his own will never get it up."

Grace seemed to choke on her margarita. Then she burst out laughing. She was still giggling as she swayed back into the house. One of the great strengths of our marriage is my sensitive understanding of Grace's unique personality. Still, there are times when I'm darned if I can figure out what she's thinking.

Alone on the deck, I picked up the binoculars and put them to my eyes. As I swept along the lakeside, I happened to stroll over to the edge of the deck and crouch slightly down into the corner, so that my eyes inevitably alighted on Rich's house. As I watched, the door opened and a man emerged. He made his way rapidly up the driveway to a truck parked near to the gate. As he got in, he waved in the direction of the back door of the house. I was sure I recognized him from somewhere. At that point, I chanced to move the binoculars slightly and caught sight of Liz standing in the doorway. She was wearing only a bathrobe, so of course after a few seconds I swung my binoculars away. Nobody could accuse T. John Dick of being a peeping tom. I watched the truck as it moved up the road toward me. I had seen that truck somewhere before too. As it got closer, I suddenly remembered. I saw that truck every day, parked at the building site opposite our house. And the man I had seen was the workman, Dwight.

I put the binoculars down, puzzled. Rich had mentioned having the decorators in, but I didn't remember him saying anything about any construction work he was having done on his house.

Chapter 21

"Management Secrets"

"I'll want you to take the lead in the new product presentations, Mike." We were discussing the National Sales Meeting. Wednesday afternoon was to be given over to presentations by the Marketing Department.

"Of course, T. J."

"We'll start with a presentation by me, of course. I thought I would spend some time on the Mission Statement. I expect that will provoke some pretty lively discussion."

"Bound to."

"Then I'll talk a bit about the big picture. Marketing strategy. The impact of the New Product Development Procedure."

"Sounds good."

"Then I'll hand it over to you. You can go over the new products that are coming out. What new products are coming out, by the way?"

"Um. Well, there's the whatsit. The PX-3. And.....well, that's all I think."

"Good. Well, talk about the PX-3 then. Of course, you might have to talk to Harvey to get some of the technical stuff. How it works. What it is. That kind of thing."

"Yes. That might be a good idea."

"Don't let him give you too much of that stuff though. The trouble with Harvey is that he'll never be a real marketeer. He knows too much about the product. You can't be too interested in that kind of thing and have the breadth of vision you need to excel as a marketing professional. That's Harvey though. You'll never change him."

I shook my head sadly as I walked with Mike to the door. He shook his too. I felt that we were going to work well together as a team.

I had just sat down again at my desk, when I saw Rich walk past. I grabbed my coffee cup.

"How's the deck coming along, T. J?" asked Rich.

"A bit more slowly than I had hoped. Still, Stan assures me that it will be finished on time." I took a sip of my coffee. "By the way, you never told me you were having some building work done yourself."

"What?"

"Yes, I happened to notice Dwight coming out of your house yesterday evening. One of the construction workers from the building site. Is it official, or is he just doing a bit on the side? What's it going to be? An extension? Your house is pretty big already. You'd better be careful you don't upset the neighbors by making their houses all look tiny," I chuckled.

"I'm not having any work done." Rich looked puzzled.

"Oh." I thought for a moment. "Well, I expect he was just fixing the shower then. Are you alright?"

Rich had gone quite pale.

"It's nothing to worry about. It probably just goes very hot for a moment, that's all. Dwight knows how to fix it. You won't have any more trouble." I didn't seem to have put his mind at ease. He still seemed unnecessarily worried about his shower. I wished I hadn't mentioned it.

"What?" he said. "Oh, yes. Of course. Excuse me, T. J. I ...uh...have a...," he looked at his watch "...a 10 o'clock. With...uh....Ronnie." He headed off in the direction of his office. I wondered for a moment if he was feeling ill, but then put it down to worry about the Sales Meeting and Hans' visit. Worry is one of the unwelcome companions of leadership, as I was only too well aware with my own heavy responsibilities. I decided to go and check the Meeting Room Reservation Book.

There were still no entries in the Meeting Room Reservation Book. I checked both meeting rooms and was pleased to find that neither of them was in use. Thus the meeting room status could be said to correspond to the Meeting Room Reservation Book.

I was reviewing my overheads from the New Product Development Procedure Meeting, deciding which ones would be appropriate for my presentation at the National Sales Meeting, when Mike appeared in my doorway.

"Ah, Mike," I said. "Come in, come in."

"If you're in the middle of something, T. J....."

"No, no. Come on in. Pull up a chair."

When he was seated in the chair opposite my desk, Mike pulled out a calculator from amongst the papers he was carrying.

"Have you seen one of these, T. J?"

"A calculator? Of course I have" I laughed.

Mike laughed too. Despite the stresses of an executive's responsibilities, office life can actually be fun, if two people share a lively sense of humor.

"No, of course I don't just mean *a* calculator. I mean *this* calculator," Mike said through his laughter.

I looked at it. "No, I don't think so. What's so special about it?"

"It's a Texas Instruments BA-20 Profit Manager. It lets you calculate margins just by pressing a single button. Give me a cost price."

"For what?" I asked.

"It doesn't matter. Just make something up."

"Ten dollars."

"OK," Mike said, entering ten dollars on his calculator. "Now give me a selling price."

"Twenty dollars."

Mike entered $20 and pressed another button. He turned the calculator round to show me.

"You see?" said Mike. "It automatically calculates the margin for you. We all had them at Universal. I don't know how I would manage without one."

I looked at the calculator.

"Twelve point six two five percent. That doesn't seem quite right to me."

Mike took the calculator back.

"Oh. I must have pressed the wrong button. I should have done it this way."

As he spoke, he entered the calculation again. He frowned.

"No, it wasn't that. Hold on a moment."

He pressed some more buttons and frowned again.

"Anyway, the point is it allows you to do these calculations far quicker than with ordinary calculators, where you have to divide the thingy price by the other one. It's a great aid to efficiency."

"Yes," I said, giving him an encouraging look. I wanted to see where he was leading. He went on:

"So I want to make sure each of the Product Managers has one. I've noticed that Harvey, for instance, uses an ordinary calculator. If we're going to turn this department into a center of excellence, we're going to have to make some radical changes in the way things are done around here. This could be an important step in the right direction."

I nodded agreement. I liked what I heard. In fact, in Mike's incisive analysis of the problem and eagerness to get to grips with it, I recognized, with a little nostalgia, something of the young T. John Dick.

"Go ahead and order them, Mike. I'll sign the requisition."

"Thanks, T. J." He got up to leave.

"No, sit down a moment, Mike," I said with a warm smile. "That is, if you have a minute."

"Of course."

He sat down again in the chair in front of my desk. I got up and closed the door.

"You know, Mike, I think you've got great potential."

"Thanks, T. J."

"That's why I promoted you to Marketing Manager, and not someone like Harvey."

We both smiled at the thought of Harvey as Marketing Manager. I continued:

"That's also why I'm going to share with you some of what I like to call my 'Management Secrets.' The things that make me an outstanding executive of VP caliber. Now this is some pretty hot stuff, you understand, and I wouldn't want it to fall into the wrong hands, so you've got to promise it won't go any further."

"Of course, T. J."

"Could you imagine what might happen if someone like Ronnie got hold of this stuff? He might try to use it against me. I'd lose some of my edge over him, and that would be bad for our department and the company."

"God forbid, T. J. My lips are sealed."

"Good." I leaned forward in my chair and clasped my hands on the desk in front of me. "Now, Mike, what do you think it is that separates a great manager from a mediocre one?"

"Hmm. Let me think. Well, it must be..... no not that, it's ....um.....could it be intelligence? No .....uh.....decisiveness maybe?"

"No, no, nothing like that. The secret of great management, Mike, my boy, is not decisiveness or intelligence, or any of that stuff. I couldn't have risen to where I am today just because of outstanding intelligence, skill and dedication. These helped, of course, but the real key is meetings."

"Meetings?"

"Yes, meetings. How you handle the whole meetings thing will determine whether you have a future as a top manager. I mean, think about it. To you and me it's obvious that I run my department like a well-oiled machine. We see cutting edge management techniques in action every day. But how much of this does Rich really see? He sees the results, of course, like the advertisement with the runner-up in the Miss North Carolina Pageant holding a PX-2."

"Pretty impressive results, T. J."

"I know. But Rich only too rarely has a chance to actually see my managerial skills in action. The only time he really gets a close-up look at what T. John Dick is made of is in meetings."

"Yes, I see. Of course."

"So it's vital that you get the hang of meetings. Now, there's a couple of tips I've picked up over the years. You might want to make a few notes, Mike."

"Ready!" He had already picked up his pad, and his pen was hovering eagerly above it.

"Well, the first thing, of course, is to attend as many meetings as possible. Even if it's a subject that doesn't directly concern me, I find that my breadth of vision and strategic thinking are always invaluable."

"I see."

"Yes. The exception, of course, is a meeting that Rich isn't attending. There's not much point in going to one of those."

"No."

"If I find myself at one of those, I just look at my watch, gather up my papers and walk briskly from the room."

"I see."

"The next thing to remember is always to be on time for meetings. You know why?"

"Well, ..um...it's polite?"

"No. You see, Mike, being on time automatically gives you a moral advantage over anyone who arrives even a minute late. Whatever you have to say will appear more important and credible because *you* were on time and *he* was late. I don't know why this is. It just is."

"Gosh! That's amazing, T. J."

"Yes, so if you feel you need to disagree with someone, pick someone who arrived late."

"Gosh! Yes, of course." Mike was scribbling furiously in his pad.

"I hope I'm not going too fast for you, Mike."

No, no. I'm fine."

"Now, if you are the one who has actually called the meeting, the most important thing to remember is the doughnuts."

"Doughnuts," Mike repeated slowly, writing in his pad and underlining it with a flourish. "Doughnuts?"

"A meeting with doughnuts is always seen as an important meeting. I owe a lot of my success to doughnuts. Never forget that, Mike."

"I won't. Doughnuts. Of course."

"Yes, a couple of boxes of doughnuts at an 8 o'clock meeting is one of the best investments you can make. As a man who has doughnuts at his meetings, you will enjoy unrivaled prestige."

I leaned back further in my chair and thought for a moment. Mike looked at me eagerly, pen poised.

"Presentations are another thing that can be very important, of course. Now here, the secret is, wherever possible to avoid making them. A top executive is able to display his incisive mind and breadth of vision better by his comments during someone else's presentation than by actually making one himself."

"I would have thought that a presentation would be a good chance to show your vision and incisiveness," said Mike.

"Only rarely, Mike. Usually they just provide an opportunity for heads of other departments to pick your ideas apart and make you look like an idiot. It's much better to get one of your people to make the presentation for you. That way you show you're a top manager who knows how to delegate and is anxious to let his people run with the ball."

"I see. So you should never make a presentation?"

"Not unless it's to a large audience."

Mike looked blank.

"You're safer with a large audience. If someone asks you a difficult question, you can just say to the audience 'What do *you* think?', let them argue for a moment, then look at your watch and say you have to move on, so that everyone has a chance to ask a question."

"Wow!"

"Yes, it's much easier to look good in front of a large audience. Particularly if you have what I call 'presence.'"

"Presence?"

"Yes, it's hard to define exactly, but a top executive has it. Poise, confidence, class. I always give an outstanding performance in front of a large audience. That's why we're making presentations at the National Sales Meeting."

Mike scribbled in his pad for a few seconds. Then he looked up, scratched his nose thoughtfully with his pen and asked:

"So, it's all about meetings. There's nothing else?"

Mike's pen seemed to have developed a leak. There was blue ink all over his nose. I handed him my pen.

"You seem to have a bit of a leaky pen there, Mike. Try this one."

"Thanks." He wiped his nose with his handkerchief.

"Well, no. It's not *all* about meetings. There's a few other things too. I think probably one of the most important things is not to try to do too much. It won't be appreciated by those above you and will increase your risk of arriving late to meetings. A manager who packs his day with things to do is guilty of bad planning. A good manager avoids doing things as much as possible."

"Hmmm. Yes, I see."

"After all, we have people to do things. That's why we're managers. Best just to let them get on with it most of the time while we're in important meetings exercising our strategic vision and focusing on the big picture. Why have a dog and bark yourself?"

"Good one, T. J."

"Thank you. And another thing. If you observe my management style"—here I couldn't suppress a certain justified pride—"you will notice that, although I always have my finger on the pulse of the department, I try not to obscure the clarity of my strategic vision by an excessively detailed knowledge of what my people actually do."

"No."

"If I did, it would just clutter my mind and get in the way of my ability to see the big picture. I mean, look at my desk. Tidy, streamlined. The desk of an executive with vision. Then look at Harvey's desk."

Mike laughed.

"I think you can see my point," I said with a wise smile. "Some of us have what it takes to be Senior Management, and some of us don't. That's why I picked you for the Marketing Manager's position and not Harvey. It's all in the desks. If you want to know who's got it and who hasn't, take a look at their desks."

Mike nodded intelligently. I got up from my desk and sat down closer to him at the little conference table.

"Of course, it can be pretty stressful, Mike. Leadership can be a heavy burden and you have to learn how to manage the stress. I find performance reviews help a lot."

"Performance reviews?"

"Yes, schedule them as often as possible. It never hurts to give your morale a bit of a boost by reminding yourself of how much better you are than your staff. Analyzing the shortcomings of your people can be a great stress reliever. As well as a great help to them, of course."

"Of course. Yes."

I looked at my watch. It was getting close to lunch time.

"Well, I've enjoyed our little chat, Mike."

"So have I," said Mike, getting to his feet. "It's been a great help. I think I've learned a lot. Thank you."

"Any time, Mike. If you ever need any more advice, you know where I am."

Mike opened the door and almost bumped into the Ostrich, who was standing with his hand raised ready to knock.

"Oops, sorry, Mike. Almost punched you on the nose there by mistake." He took a step back and stared at Mike with a particularly idiotic expression on his face. " Looks like T. J. already did! Is this some sort of a new management style, T. J? You call your staff into your office and punch them on the nose?"

"What are you talking about?"

"Well look at the boy's nose! That's a hell of a bruise. Or are you going to tell me he walked into the door? Incidentally, I thought your door was always open."

"Oh, for heaven's sake! It's ink."

"Well quite frankly, T. J., I don't think sticking a pen up his nose is a whole lot better than punching him. You won't be happy until your whole department's as bandaged up as you are. You have to be stopped. I'm going to have to report this to Human Resources."

"Oh, for heaven's sake!" I said again. But it was too late. He had already gone.

Chapter 22

"A Marriage Based on Mutual Respect"

"I had hoped we'd be a lot further on than this," I said, directing at Stan a look that made my displeasure unmistakably clear. Well, unmistakable to anyone but Stan. He didn't seem to notice it at all, but replied in that irritatingly jaunty way that was beginning to, well, irritate me:

"Don't worry, Mr. Dick. We'll have it ready for you by Monday."

I looked at the four poles sticking out of the ground that were all there was to show for three days work. Two of Stan's men were unloading planks of wood from a truck. It was Friday afternoon and I was beginning to lose confidence in Stan's assurances. To make matters worse, it was hot and my head was sweating under the bandages, my leg itched in its plaster cast and I had spent a large part of the morning explaining my side of the pen incident to Jerry in Human Resources. This had been particularly annoying as it turned out that the Ostrich had not reported the matter at all, so that Jerry seemed to have some difficulty understanding why I was making a complaint against myself, especially if it wasn't true. I tried to explain my natural concern that no scurrilous rumors should be allowed to start. That was why I was so anxious to explain the whole incident to him. Even the most senior position in Human Resources does not demand a sharp mind, and it had taken me almost an hour to make him understand the situation. It was no wonder that I was not in the best of moods, and now I found that there had been almost no progress on the deck. It was time to make my extreme displeasure plain to Stan.

"I'm extremely displeased, Stan."

He looked genuinely taken aback.

"I sure am sorry to hear that, Mr. Dick. After all you did for me! I had no idea you were unhappy. I called yesterday and spoke to Mrs. Dick. She seemed real happy with my men's performance."

Nobody could ever accuse me of being sexist, but there are some things that you really can't expect women to know about.

"I really don't see how my wife could be in a position to judge your men's performance, Stan. You should have spoken to me."

"Well, the important thing is not to worry. My men will work through the weekend and have everything ready in plenty of time. You'll see."

I am slow to anger. The responsibilities of a top-flight executive require an ability to keep a cool head under pressure. Now, however, something snapped. There was a lot riding on Monday evening's reception and buffet dinner, and this idiot just didn't seem to be able to grasp its importance. My irritation at his bland assurances turned to fury. I swiveled sharply and swung my foot at a pail of water that was standing next to one of the poles. Unfortunately, what I had assumed to be water turned out to be cement that someone had carelessly allowed to set and placed within range of my foot. My exclusive English leather shoe provided little protection against such an impact. As my toes crumpled in pain, I made to grab my foot, letting my crutches fall and tumbling backwards into one of the workmen, who was passing with a plank of wood. Stupidly, he tried to catch me, dropping the plank, which struck me on the head.

Grace's remarks as she drove me to the Emergency Room fell far short of the kind of support that a husband has a right to expect from his wife at a time like this. I think perhaps she thought that I couldn't hear her or was too dazed to comprehend. From the way she was talking, you would almost think that I was in some way to blame for the accident.

"I could sue them, you know," I said.

"Oh, you've come round have you?"

"I've been conscious for some time now," I said pointedly. "And I don't think that 'dumb asshole' is an appropriate way for a wife to refer to her husband in a marriage based on mutual respect."

"Sue who?"

"Whom. Stan and his company. Leaving pails of cement around a building site. It's negligence."

"I don't think you'd have a leg to stand on. Oh, that's funny!" she laughed. "Leg to stand on!" She knocked on my plaster cast with her knuckles.

"Look out!" I yelled. She was so busy giggling that she allowed the car to veer over the center line. She had to swerve quickly to avoid an oncoming truck.

"And you, asshole!" she shouted as the truck passed, horn blaring. I wondered how many margaritas she had had. She turned to look at me again. "Think about it, T. J. All they have to do is call the doctors from the hospital to testify that in the last few weeks you've been treated for concussion, back injuries, a broken leg and concussion again. Today makes three concussions. Nobody's going to award you damages. They might lock you away for your own safety, but they won't believe anyone has to be negligent for you to inflict injuries on yourself. They'll probably think you do it on purpose. I read about it somewhere. Monchausen's syndrome, or something. Are you sure you don't have a syndrome?"

"Maybe I do, getting in the car with you! How much have you had to drink?" I said.

"Perhaps you'd like to drive then?"

We finished the drive in a silence broken only by the occasional hiccup. I reflected on how difficult it had become lately to sense in Grace any of the spirit that made the Dicks such a formidable team. At last, we arrived at the emergency room. An orderly came to meet us with a wheelchair. When he saw me, he smiled.

"Oh, it's you Mr. Dick. How're you doin'?" This was of course a stupid question. If I was doing well, I would hardly be arriving at the emergency room. I gave him a look that made it clear that I was in no mood for cheek from hospital orderlies.

Sorry, Mr. Dick'" he said. "Hey Keesha, Mr. Dick's back!"

A particularly fat nurse, whom I vaguely recognized from previous visits, came waddling out to the car. A large black face appeared, framed by the door.

"Hey, Mr. Dick! How're you doin'? I swear if you come down here any mo' often, we'll have to invite you to our Christmas Party this year!" The large black face laughed. I considered her behavior totally inappropriate to the arrival of a quite seriously injured executive, who should be treated promptly and with respect. I was about to tell her so, when there was a loud noise from the other side of the car, where Grace had been standing a moment before but was now nowhere to be seen. It sounded like something hitting the pavement.

"Better bring another wheelchair, Keesha. This one's fallen on her ass."

Chapter 23

"The Only Rule in My Book is a Hands-On Approach"

Monday was going to be a busy day. There was Hans' visit to the plant and then the buffet reception in the evening. I arrived early to make sure the department was ready for inspection. The last thing I needed was a visit from the Ostrich.

"You make it very difficult, you know, T. J." he said, settling uninvited into the chair opposite my desk.

"In what way? I make what difficult?" The Ostrich had a very obscure way of talking that would never have let him make it in the world of marketing, where clear and effective communication is vital. That, no doubt, was one of the reasons why he was stuck in the drab world of accounting.

"Well, I never know how to begin a conversation with you. How's your head? Or how's your leg? Or your back? And now your foot!"

I had hoped to keep the story of my foot injury quiet. There was no serious damage done. No bandages or outward sign of injury, except for a limp that was not noticeable since I was still on crutches.

"I heard you took a swing at a pail of cement. Impaled yourself, you might say." He laughed. One of the many annoying habits of the Ostrich is that he always laughs at his own jokes, no matter how feeble.

"Well, if you must know, everything's just fine. The bandages and the plaster come off tomorrow, before I head down to Wakiah Island for the National Sales Meeting."

"I'm pleased to hear it. Jerry in Human Resources passed through a letter to me that he got from our health insurance people. They're threatening to put the premiums up."

"What?"

"Yes. All your visits to the hospital are adding up."

"That's ridiculous! How could one person out of three hundred making a couple of hospital visits cause...."

"T. J.," he interrupted. "Don't get steamed up under that turban of yours. It was just a joke."

I sometimes wonder where the Ostrich got the idea that he had a sense of humor. Nobody could ever accuse me of not being able to appreciate a good joke. Just ask Rich. But Ronnie's so called jokes were just stupid. I started to shuffle papers around on my desk to show that I was busy. Of course, he failed to take the hint.

"Are you ready for Hans' visit, T. J.?"

"I think the department will pass inspection with flying colors, as usual."

"Not with that, you won't." He nodded toward the wall behind my desk.

"What?"

"That poster of the floozie with the big boobs. I've heard Hans is really straight-laced. He won't like that kind of thing."

"There's nothing wrong with the poster. It's an integral part of the PX-2 promotional campaign."

"If you say so, T. J. What do you know about Hans?"

"Not a lot. Only that he managed some little Pumpex operation in Europe for years."

"Not so little. He built it up to where it's as big as the US operation. And much more profitable. He's a bit of a star in the organization. Not universally popular at Corporate, of course. Nobody likes to be shown up."

"Well, he'll find that at Pumpex-SuperPumps we run a pretty tight ship."

"I hope so. Rumor has it that Rich is in line for a move back up to Corporate. That means that they'll be looking for someone to step into his shoes. Hans is bound to have a major say in who it is. Why do you think he's making a trip down here so soon?"

I stopped shuffling my papers and looked at Ronnie. His expression showed no sign that this was another of his idiotic jokes.

"It'll be a pretty hard choice, of course. There's me, who just counts ever-decreasing numbers, Ken, who provokes major customers to physical assault, Peter, who's still trying to remember the way to the bathroom, and, of course, you who burns down half the factory and slaughters the Group President. Hard to pick among us. Maybe they'll go outside the company. Anyway, got to run now. Make sure my own department's spick and span."

I waited until he had left before taking the framed poster of the runner-up in the Miss North Carolina Pageant holding a PX-2 compressor unit down from the wall. I had it in my hands, when the Ostrich stuck his head round the door.

"I was just joking, T. J. The guy's from Germany, for God's sake! They have some pretty naughty stuff over there. A friend of mine went to Hamburg once. He told me some things that would make your hair curl."

It was typical of Ronnie to assume that I had fallen for his pathetic attempt at a joke.

"I was just cleaning it," I informed him, replacing the poster on the wall.

"Of course," he said. "Good luck with Hans."

"Thanks," I said, sitting down at my desk.

When he had gone, I got up again and took the poster down. Better not to take any chances.

Before making my inspection of the department, I took a few moments to take stock of the situation. This was exciting news! If Hans was indeed going to use his visit to size up a possible successor to Rich, then I had quite a lot in my favor. Rich had a keen appreciation of my contribution to the company; he was bound to suggest me as his replacement. On top of that, the buffet reception at my house that night would provide the ideal opportunity to make a deep impression on Hans. A good showing at the National Sales Meeting at Wakiah Island ought to just about seal it. My rivals for the position were, frankly, a pretty sorry bunch. Peter was too new. Ken's experience in Sales had too narrow a focus—a successful President would need the breadth of vision gained in a field like marketing. Ronnie was perhaps the greatest threat, not because of any outstanding qualities on his part of course, but because people in Finance just had a habit of getting themselves promoted to presidents of companies. I had never understood why this should be so, when Marketing provided a so much richer soil in which to grow the talents required of top management.

Fortunately, the Ostrich would find himself outflanked. He would not be hosting a buffet reception and, although he would be at Wakiah Island (all the Senior Staff attended the National Sales Meeting), he would not be making any presentations or taking a leading role as I would. It was with a mixture of excitement and confidence that I left my office and began my inspection of the department.

I first went to Mike's office. I thought that it would be good experience for him to do the inspection with me and perhaps pick up a few tips. I had given the matter some thought, and almost decided to delegate these inspections to Mike. It seemed to me that they could be handled by a competent Marketing Manager, with the VP of Marketing playing only a supervisory role.

"How's the department looking, Mike?" I asked. "Hans will be coming round sometime this morning, you know."

"Yes. I had a quick blitz first thing this a.m.. The usual problems. Harvey's desk was a mess. I had a word with him. Told him to shape up."

"Good. I thought that we might just have a final look round together. But first there's something important I need to talk to you about." I closed the door of his office so that we wouldn't be disturbed.

"You can't fire me. You just promoted me!"

"What? Who said anything about firing anyone?"

"It's just when you closed the door. They always close.....sorry."

I sat down in the chair opposite Mike at his desk. The color, which had drained from his face, was returning.

"Are you feeling OK?" I asked.

"Yes. Yes, I'm fine."

"Oh. Well, what I want to talk to you about is confidential. Keep it to yourself."

"You can rely on me, T. J."

"I have heard from my inside sources that Rich may soon be called back up there." I pointed up toward Boston on the map that hung on the wall behind Mike's desk.

"God! I didn't even know he was ill."

"What are you talking about, Mike?"

"Mind you, he has looked a bit pale recently."

"There's nothing wrong with Rich."

"But you said...."

"I said he might be called back up to Boston. To Corporate."

"Oh! I thought you meant......"

"If he's called back up there, they'll need someone to take his place down here. Obviously the ideal replacement would be one of the Senior Staff. Someone who knows what makes the operation down here tick."

"Obviously, T. J. And I'm not saying this to flatter you or anything, but you're the obvious choice."

I said nothing, but gave him a look that encouraged him to go on. It was important to get an objective view.

"It's vital that Pumpex-SuperPumps gets a more marketing-oriented perspective, if we're going to survive in the increasingly competitive pump market."

I nodded agreement. He had certainly hit the nail on the head.

"You've been able to achieve miracles in your current position; the Mission Statement for example. But it's nothing compared to what an outstanding marketing man could do at the top. This company needs you to be President."

Mike's was certainly a shrewd analysis.

"I agree. For the company's sake, it's vital that I get the job."

Mike nodded his head.

"Of course," I went on, "if I do get the job, that will free up the VP of Marketing position. I'm sure I would have no difficulty finding the right man to fill it." I looked at him and smiled. He smiled back.

"I'm sure that we can make sure that the right man is picked for President," he said. "For the good of the company."

"Yes, Mike. That's what matters. The good of the company. Now, let's go and have a look round the department before Hans arrives."

To my astonishment, Harvey's desk was even more of a mess than usual. Not only was there the usual jumble of papers, but a large lump of metal with a pipe attached to it was lying there, right in the middle of the desk. I was flabbergasted. Mike was the first to speak:

"Harvey, I'm flabbergasted!" he exclaimed. "Here we are right before an important visit, and you have that thing on your desk! Didn't I say to tidy things up?"

"This 'thing' is a 5 inch flange joist for the PX-2. There's a problem with the groove bore. Manufacturing are waiting for me to tell them if it's acceptable, before they start up production. It won't take a moment to check it."

"Do it later, Harvey," said Mike. "Hans could be here any moment. What kind of impression do you think this will make?" He pointed to the metal object with obvious distaste. I didn't intervene. Instead I limited myself to directing one of my most withering looks at Harvey. Mike was shaping up well in his new position, but it would be a long time before he would be capable of the kind of looks that are such a strong weapon in my managerial armory.

"But the whole production line is waiting," Harvey protested.

"I said do it later. Get rid of it."

Harvey gave a deep sigh, shook his head and picked up the object.

"Mein Gott, is not that a 12 centimeter flangenjoist that you in your hand are holding?"

I turned and saw Rich, accompanied by a short, almost ball-shaped man with gray hair and round spectacles perched on his nose. So this was Hans. I was not terribly impressed. His suit was a little too stylish in a flashy kind of way, the sort of thing you could probably get away with in Europe I supposed, but not the classic cut we expect to see on American executives. And his tie! It was dark blue. Hardly calculated to make an impression. I thought to myself how soft the competition must be in Europe if someone like Hans could make it to the top wearing dark blue ties.

In spite of my poor first impression of the man, I was, of course, aware of the need for me to make a good impression on him. The future of the company depended on it. I stretched out my hand toward him.

"Hans Kartoffel, I presume. T. John Dick, VP of Marketing."

My voice and my eyes held just the right mixture of confidence and respect and I produced one of my warmest smiles, but to my amazement he walked right past my outstretched hand to Harvey's desk.

"I have not seen such a flangenjoist since many years. Do you mind if I look at it?"

"No, go ahead," said Harvey and handed him the object.

Hans beamed as he held it. "We used to use these in our compressors in Europe. We had to phase them out because of problems with the angels."

There was a pause in the conversation, while Rich and I exchanged glances, looking for clues.

"The angels?" said Rich.

"Yes, the angels were too small and this has led to a grinding of the balls with the feather."

"Hmm, yes," I said to break the silence that followed this observation. "Feather. Yes."

"I think you mean angles," said Harvey to Hans. Then turning to the rest of us, "Hans is talking about how the angle of the flange can be too narrow, leading the ball bearings to grind against the spring." He turned to Hans and said: "It's *spring* in English. The German word *Feder* is a spring, not a feather in this case."

In my opinion, a Product Manager has no business knowing German. Nobody with an in-depth knowledge of marketing has time to waste on things like knowing German. Or on angles of flanges, come to that.

"Yes, spring, that's it, of course," said Hans, still cradling the object. "You know, it's good to see Marketing taking a hands-on-it approach. I like that."

"Excuse me a second," I said. I hurried the few steps to where Jill was sitting at her desk. "Jill," I whispered, "get me one of those."

"One of what, Mr. Dick?"

"Those things. Like what Hans is holding now. A flange thing."

"A joist?"

"Yes, that's it. Run down to Production and get me one. Put it on my desk. Quick as you can."

"I'll need you to sign a requisition and....."

"Never mind the procedures, Jill. This is urgent. Just get me one." I have never had much patience with those who are so hung up on procedure that they let it get in the way of action. "Go on! Hurry!"

Jill rushed off in the direction of Production, and I rejoined the group. Mike had one of the new calculators in his hand.

"So, of course, I've made sure that everyone in the department has one. I'm confident that it will increase our efficiency still further."

Mike's comments in praise of the Texas Instruments Profit Manager seemed to be making little impression on Hans, who was still gazing at the object in his hand. He turned back to Harvey.

"Are you not also grinding your balls with this part? Surely must it be a problem."

"Actually," said Harvey, "we do have some of those problems. We minimize them by adding an extra grommet here, next to the flange extension." He pointed to a part of the object.

"Hmm. Ja, that is an excellent idea."

"Let's say, for example, that you have a cost price of twenty-seven dollars and you sell the product for thirty-nine dollars." You had to admire Mike's tenacity. He was not giving up. "You just enter the figures here and....."

"Thirty-one percent. A margin of thirty-one percent. Ja, ja, very interesting."

To a keen instinct like mine, it was clear that Hans was in fact anything but interested in Mike's calculator. Of course, Mike could not have known that Hans would turn out to be a walking computer, but he was not helping matters now by standing there with his mouth open, looking like a codfish. The boy's inexperience was showing. It was time for me to take a hand.

"Yes," I said, "that grommet thing was certainly the key. If we hadn't come up with that, we would have had to ....well, come up with something else. I'm certainly glad we came up with the grommet. I should emphasize that I was only the leader here—it was a team effort, the whole grommet thing. A fine example of how my department works together for the good of the company." I beamed generously at Harvey and Mike. A willingness to share credit for a job well done has always been one of my strengths as a manager. I think this was certainly clear to Hans. He put down the object and asked:

"Shall we be going further, please?"

"Yes, we shall," I said.

The rest of the tour went quickly and smoothly. Rachel and Randy had tidied their desks to an impressive standard that reflected great credit on the motivational skills of their new Marketing Manager. A few minutes later, we arrived at my own office. Through the open door I could see that Jill had succeeded in procuring for me an object similar to the one on Harvey's desk. As we entered, I picked it up casually from my desk, combining the gesture skillfully with a remark about the importance of a hands-on approach to marketing.

"To some people marketing is like an ivory tower, far removed from the nitty-gritty of the products. Not here at Pumpex-SuperPumps. No, a hands-on approach is what we like to see. Yes, indeed. You'll often find me closeted in my office with a ...." I suddenly realized that I couldn't remember what the thing in my hand was called. I hesitated for a fraction of a second. Mike must have sensed my problem, because as I looked over Hans' shoulder, I could see his mouth moving silently. I read his lips.

"....joint. Yes, closeted in my office engrossed in a joint."

Hans was giving me a very peculiar look. Mike, for some reason was holding his head in his hands. Hans turned to Rich.

"Is this man serious? Do you not have rules?"

"The only rule, Hans," I said, giving him a forthright straight-talking look, "the only rule in my book is a hands-on approach. If anyone in my department needs to get their hands on a joint for any reason, they should be able to go down to Production and ask for one."

Hans' eyes were nearly popping out of his head. I was clearly making a big impression. Again he turned to Rich.

"Never have I met such a manager!" he exclaimed.

I smiled modestly.

"Joist!" hissed Mike, who had moved round so that he was now standing behind me. I realized instantly that, thanks to a lack of clarity on Mike's part, I had been using an inaccurate term to describe the object in my hands. This could, of course, have led to an embarrassing situation for someone less cool headed and quick in his reactions than myself.

"Of course," I said, "some people call it a joist. That's the European term, I believe. Some people here use it too. Just like some people prefer the metric system. Me, I like the good old US terms. Oh yes. Not that I'm not international in my outlook, of course. No, I've got a feeling for the global economy all right." I had elegantly turned the situation to my advantage, not only neatly explaining my use of a non-standard term for the object in my hands, but even creating a chance to emphasize my global perspective, which could be a vital consideration in determining who would be Rich's replacement. As I may have mentioned, coolness under pressure has always been one of my greatest strengths.

"Your tie!" said Hans.

"Ah yes. Silk, actually." It was strange that he should mention my tie now, I thought, although I was not surprised that he had noticed it. I am a great believer in the ability of my ties to project the dynamism of my personality and today I had chosen to wear what was probably my most dynamic tie of all, fire-engine red.

"The flange extension is dripping oil onto your tie. You are holding it upside down without the oil nozzle cap on the oil nozzle. Have you never held one of these? Do you not know this will happen? Now your red tie is turning brown, Herr Dick. At least it does not hurt my eyes now. Ha! Ha!"

"Ha! Ha!" I said, and shook some more oil onto my tie, skillfully seizing the opportunity to show Hans that T. John Dick was a man with a lively sense of humor.

Chapter 24

"The Merger of Two Great Companies"

The sun was shining brightly when I left work, with just the hint of thunderclouds building up on the horizon. I had left a little early to give myself time to check on the preparations for the reception and buffet. Grace had assured me that everything was going according to plan, but I thought that it was asking a lot of her to see to the arrangements without my organizational expertise to fall back on. One of the things that makes our marriage such a success is that we each bring different qualities to it, which results in a kind of synergy, rather like the merger of two great companies. In addition to sensitivity and dynamism, I bring my organizational talents, honed to perfection in the hectic corporate world in which I have risen to prominence. This is undoubtedly a great boon to Grace. For her part, she brings a faithful devotion to me, which is a comfort among the stresses of a top-flight executive's life.

I had spent the afternoon reading a book that I had picked up at lunchtime. It was called "This is Germany—A Guide to the Land and its People" by Rudi Wekening. I smiled as I thought of how I would be able to talk knowledgeably to Hans at the buffet reception, thus strengthening my position still further against the Ostrich, who would certainly not have thought to prepare himself so thoroughly. It was just the kind of detailed preparation that lay behind my success as a senior executive.

I had asked Randy to give me a ride home, since my plastered leg still prevented me from driving. On the way I reflected on the morning's events. There had been some rough moments brought on by young Mike's inexperience, but on the whole it had been most satisfactory. I was sure that I had succeeded in making an impression on Hans and almost certainly improved my position even more in the race against poor old Ronnie for the top spot at Pumpex-SuperPumps. And ahead of me lay the chance to consolidate that position still further by a good performance at the reception and buffet. I permitted myself a confident smile, as we turned into Regal Pointe. A few minutes later, I snapped out of my reverie as we drew up outside my house.

"Thanks, Randy," I said. Then something occurred to me. I had never invited Randy to my house. Not out of any kind of snobbery, of course. Nobody could ever accuse me of being a snob. But the quality of life at Regal Pointe depended on a certain exclusivity, and out of consideration to your neighbors you could hardly have people like Randy in their pick-up trucks cluttering up the subdivision.

"How did you know which house was mine?" I asked.

"What? Oh, I saw the photographs. You know, the ones you brought in just after you bought it. Recognized it from the photos."

"Ah, yes. And I suppose you know your way around here, what with your dentist and podiatrist."

"Yes, that's right."

"Well, see you tomorrow at the airport."

"Oh, I'm not flying down."

"Yes, of course." I remembered that as part of an effort to control costs, only the executive staff were flying down. The Product Managers and Rachel would drive the six or seven hours to the coast. In the Marketing Department, we are not afraid to make sacrifices for the good of the company.

"Well, have a good trip anyway."

"But, I'm staying here remember. Somebody has to hold the fort, you said."

"Yes, of course." I had forgotten. Randy was not going to the National Sales Meeting. We couldn't leave the Marketing Department completely unmanned, and quite frankly Randy would not really be missed at Wakiah. "Well, I'm sure there will be plenty to keep you busy while I'm away."

As Randy drove off, I made my way up the path on my crutches. Thank God this would be the last day I would be forced to use them! Instead of entering through the front door as usual, I went round to the back of the house to inspect the deck. True to his word, Stan had had his men working on it through the week-end, but it had still not been completed when Grace had driven me to work that morning.

I was relieved to see that the deck appeared to have been finished. A couple of men were clearing up their tools and loading them onto the back of a truck. Stan saw me and approached, beaming.

"All finished, Mr. Dick. Just like I promised. What a beauty, huh?"

"An impressive job, Stan. Most impressive."

The extension certainly looked good. It rested on two tall poles that went from the ground at the level of the basement up to the floor of the deck, level with the first floor of the house. I walked over to one of the poles and pushed it with my hand. The whole structure swayed gently. I looked at Stan with some alarm.

"It moved."

"Oh, you don't want to worry about that, Mr. Dick. That's just it settling. Besides, it's best for it to move a little. Makes it more resistant to the wind, you know."

I am no expert on building, but I am also no fool. I remembered the fable about the oak tree uprooted by the storm, while the reed swayed in the wind and survived. Stan's explanation made sense. I nodded thoughtfully. He could see that he was dealing with a smart customer.

"Well, thanks very much Stan."

"Oh, it was nothing," he said. "After the work you put our way with your fire, it was the least we could do."

It irritated me that Stan referred to the tragic blaze at Pumpex-SuperPumps as *my* fire, as if I had been in some way responsible, but I had neither the time nor the inclination to correct him. I left him and his men to finish clearing up and went inside.

Inside, everywhere was a hive of activity. Two young men in tuxedos were laying out plates and silverware on a long table that ran the length of the dining room wall next to the door to the deck. In the kitchen, a young black woman was bustling about with surprising agility for someone of her ample proportions, putting the finishing touches to platters of smoked salmon, shrimp, lobster, some sort of spicy chicken and various other delights. Her efficiency was all the more remarkable, since she had to maneuver around Grace, who, margarita in hand, was issuing superfluous directions, accompanied by sudden gestures, which threatened to tip over the platters.

"Oh hi, T. J." she said. "Come and have a drink. I've had a little one already. To steady my nerves, you know."

"No thanks" I replied frostily. I felt that Grace's nerves were by now probably too steady by a long way.

"Oh well, please yourself. What about you, Tundra?"

"Tondra, ma'am. No thanks. I'm on duty."

"Well it might as well be Tundra. You're about as much fun as a vast frozen wasteland. About the same size too."

"Whatever you say ma'am," said Tondra, with a trace of insolence that did not escape me. I made a mental note to mention it to her employers. At the price we were paying, we had a right to expect a better standard of behavior.

Just then the door flew open and one of the immaculately groomed young men in tuxedos burst into the kitchen.

"Ready with the smoked salmon are we then, Tondra? Yes? Lovely. Off we go then."

He disappeared even more quickly than he had appeared, carrying a silver platter in each hand. A fraction of a second later the door flew open again and the other young man swept into the room.

"Chicken, Tondra. Quick as you can, dear. Thaaaank-you." He beamed ingratiatingly at Grace and me, before vanishing through the door to the dining room. I followed him out.

I had to admit everything looked splendid. The long buffet table was draped in a crisp white cloth, the silverware, plates and food neatly and attractively arranged on it. Tasteful displays of flowers were dotted about the room. Even the young men themselves in their smartly pressed tuxedos added to the overall impression of elegance. Everything seemed to be just about ready, and there was still half an hour before the guests were due to arrive.

"Well done, Grace," I said. "Most impressive."

There was no reply. I turned and saw that she had settled down in one of the armchairs for a nap. I strolled over to the window and looked out onto the deck. The extension had doubled its area, so that there would now be plenty of room for everyone to mingle under the stars after helping themselves to the buffet. The freshly varnished wood glowed in the setting sun. Work had stopped for the day on the various building sites. A perfect setting. Hans was certain to be impressed. Easy sophistication was the impression of T. John Dick that he would take away with him. Just the kind of man to mingle with the captains of industry as head of a company like Pumpex-SuperPumps. I went into the bedroom to shower and change.

When I returned, wearing a more casual jacket and slacks with a dark blue tie that I had bought that afternoon, Grace had awoken from her nap and was deep in conversation with one of the young men.

"I really don't know why she put up with him for so long, Grace. I really don't."

"Oh, I know, Lance. It's not just all that Camilla Parker-Whatsername stuff. But those ears. Can you imagine living with those all those years?"

"Oh you're wicked, Grace, wicked! You know I was just a boy, but I cried when they got married. Such a gorgeous ceremony. And her dress!"

"Who are you talking about?" I asked.

"Oh hi, T. J. Lance and I were just discussing how a lovely girl like poor Princess Diana put up with such a cretinous husband for so long. I consider myself quite an expert on that kind of thing, actually." For some reason this made her laugh so much that she lost her balance and fell onto the young man named Lance, who caught her in his arms. I had no idea what led her to consider herself such an expert on the British Royal Family's marital problems. I did however see perfectly well what was going on here. I am no fool. I know when someone is making a pass at my wife, and my sophisticated outlook does not extend to tolerating such things. There is a primal T. John Dick that you cross at your peril.

"Get your hands off my wife!" I said, a steely glint in my eye.

"Ooh! That's the first time anybody's ever said *that* to me!" said Lance. "Did you hear that, Jerome?"

The other young man joined us from the far side of the room, where he was putting the finishing touches to the floral arrangements on the buffet table.

"I heard it, Lance. You're very lucky, Mrs. Dick, to have such a strong man to defend your honor."

For some reason this made them all laugh. I put a stop to that with one of my sternest looks, one that was almost menacing.

"Lance, you heartbreaker! We'd better retreat before you do any more damage," said the one called Jerome. The two young men retired to the kitchen, leaving me alone with Grace.

"For God's sake, Grace! What are you thinking of, letting that guy flirt with you like that?"

"Flirt with me? I think he's more likely to flirt with *you*, T. J."

From the kitchen came shrieks of laughter. This was too much. I strode across the room and flung open the door to the kitchen. I did not need to say a word. My look said it all. The laughter stopped. I closed the door and went back out to the dining room. The laughter, when it resumed, was much quieter.

Grace was refilling her glass when I returned. I was about to ask her what exactly she meant by her last remark, when the doorbell rang.

Chapter 25

"...A Most Extraordinary Man"

R ich and Liz were the first to arrive. Jerome took their coats and ushered them into the dining room.

"Rich! Liz!" I said. "Welcome. Come on out on the deck. Have a drink."

"Thanks, T. J." said Rich. "I'll have a Scotch. On the rocks."

Lance appeared immediately with a Scotch on the rocks.

"What about you, Liz?"

"I'll have a Slow Comfortable Screw."

"Liz!" I exclaimed.

"It's OK, T. J." said Grace, "It's a cocktail. Rather a common one, actually."

"Yes," said Liz. "I understand that the construction workers round here are very fond of the occasional one. Aren't they, Grace?"

This seemed unlikely to me. I had never seen any of the workers drinking anything but sodas or perhaps a beer at the end of the day. They didn't really strike me as a cocktail crowd. Before I had a chance to mention this to Liz, the doorbell rang again and we were joined by Ken and his wife, Nancy, together with Peter and Jennifer, who I noticed, like all English women, closely resembled a horse. They were immediately followed by Mike and by Jerry from Human Resources with his wife, Gina. Lance and Jerome bustled between the dining room and the deck, fetching drinks.

"I see you got the deck finished on time," said Rich.

"Yes, it was close but I laid it on the line to Stan and he pulled out all the stops to get it done. It's just a matter of knowing how to handle these people."

"I'm sure Grace was a great help handling the workers," said Liz. "Ouch!"

"Oh sorry, Liz," said Grace. "Was that your toe? Clumsy of me, and with these heels on too!"

"That's OK," said Liz, "with feet that size I guess accidents are bound to happen." She looked around the deck. "I hope it's big enough to accommodate everyone. If we didn't have the decorators in, I would have suggested we have everyone over to our house. We have a very big deck, and it's so nice down by the water. We wouldn't have had to squeeze everybody in."

For some reason I couldn't understand, Liz's remarks seemed to irritate Grace, who muttered something about Liz always being ready to accommodate everyone in her 'frigging big house down by the lake.' This in turn seemed to rile Liz, who glared at Grace. There appeared to be some tension between the two ladies.

"Either this whiskey is extremely powerful," said Ken, looking down, "or the deck is moving."

"Settling, Ken." I said, grateful for the interruption. "Just settling."

"Oh, I see. Yes. Settling."

"If you ask me, it's quite *un*settling," said Peter. This, I supposed, was what passed for humor in England. Nobody laughed. What really was unsettling, I thought to myself, was his wife's face.

"Hi, everyone! Having fun?"

It was the Ostrich. To my horror, I noticed that he was accompanied by Hans.

"Sorry we're a bit late," he continued. "Hans and I took a little longer than we had thought going over the figures this afternoon. Then, I'm afraid we stopped for a drink on the way here."

This was an outrage. The Ostrich had practically kidnapped Hans and dragged him off to some bar, causing him to miss the start of my buffet reception! No doubt he had used the opportunity to indulge in some shameless brown-nosing that I was going to have to work hard to make up. I also noticed that Hans had removed his tie.

"Hans," I beamed. "What would you like to drink?"

"Ah, Herr Dick! You also are here."

"This is my house, Hans."

"Ach, ja. I will be having a Scotch please with ice on the rocks."

"Yes, I thought it would be nice just to have everyone around to my house. Nice and informal. Give you the chance to get to know everyone. See the kind of guys we are."

Jerome brought Hans his Scotch.

"Which part of Germany are you from Hans?" I asked.

"My family are many generations of Hamburgers." He took a large swig of Scotch.

"Hamburgers. Yes."

"From Hamburg, Herr Dick. In the north of Germany. I have Hamburger blood in my veins."

"Ah yes. Hamburg." I cursed my bad luck. The book I had bought began in the south of Germany, and I had only managed to get about three quarters of the way through it. I had not yet got as far as Hamburg. However, as usual, I was equal to the situation.

"It must be very different from Munich, with its many churches and its lovely setting in the foothills of the Alps."

Hans looked at me blankly. No doubt he was astonished by my knowledge of his native land.

"Or Nuremberg," I went on," with its famous Christmas Market."

"Why are you talking to me of Munich and Nuremberg? Have you visited these towns?"

"No. But I have always felt drawn to Germany. I have an interest in many countries. Part of my international outlook. Especially Germany."

"This Scotch must be very strong. It is as if the ground beneath my feet would be moving."

"Oh, that's just settling. The deck is new, you see."

"If you say so, Herr Dick. It is fortunate that we Hamburgers are men of the sea. Otherwise, I would perhaps be sick."

I laughed politely. An understanding of what is amusing to people of other countries would certainly be an asset in the next President of Pumpex-SuperPumps.

"Is it true, Herr Dick, that you are the one who toasted my predecessor?"

The abrupt change in the direction of the conversation surprised me. I was irritated that the absurd rumor that I had been in some way responsible for the fire had made it as far as Europe. My instincts told me that this would not help my chances of landing the President's job.

"Certainly not. It was an accident, caused by the carelessness of...."

"I heard that you threw a large lamp at him. Is this true?"

"No, it fell on him. It was a tragic loss. Ray will be sadly missed."

"That son of a dog! Herr Dick, please do not be ridiculous. You did us all a favor."

I smiled modestly. It seemed the best thing to do. I thought it was time to change the subject.

"Have you been to the castle of Neuschwanstein and been entranced by the fairy-tale atmosphere of this 19th century folly, perched high on a sheer rock?"

Before he could answer, Ronnie said. "I think it's starting to rain. Probably just a shower. Perhaps we should all go inside and get stuck into that delicious looking buffet."

"Good idea, you old Straussvogel!" said Hans, slapping Ronnie on the back.

As they passed, Ronnie whispered to me: "It's German for ostrich."

I was not pleased. At this stage it seemed almost as if Hans were being completely taken in by Ronnie's disgusting attempts to suck up to him. My own powerful personality had had little chance to impress itself on Hans, thanks to the Ostrich's monopolizing of him. It was imperative that I broke this stranglehold, for the good of Pumpex-SuperPumps. I stood there for a minute or two in the rain, trying to get my thoughts together. The rain became heavier. Everyone had followed Hans and the Ostrich in to the buffet. I decided I had better make my way inside as quickly as possible and find some way of separating Hans from the Ostrich.

In the course of my career it has become evident to me that I am not what you might call a fortunate man. I have watched as people with far less talent than myself have somehow progressed up the corporate ladder by pure luck. How else, for example, could you explain someone like the Ostrich making it to Vice President of Finance. My success as an executive has been achieved by skill, vision and hard work, often in the face of bad luck that would break a weaker man. So what happened now should have come as no surprise to me. As I tried to turn to go inside, I found to my dismay that my left leg in its plaster cast would not move. It appeared to be stuck to the deck. I pulled as hard as I could, but still I couldn't lift it. I bent forward as far as my crutches would allow to see what had happened. Around my foot I noticed a dark discoloration of the deck's new varnish. It had obviously not dried properly and the rain, which was now falling very heavily, had caused it to become sticky. The mixture of water, varnish and plaster must have created a kind of glue, and now my foot was stuck firmly to the deck. I am not one to curse, but I admit that I muttered some pretty strong words on the subject of Stan and his workmen. Their incompetence had put me in a very embarrassing position. It would certainly not create the kind of impression I wanted, if Hans were to see me stuck to my own deck. I am not the kind of man who is in the habit of looking ridiculous, and certainly not when the top job at Pumpex-SuperPumps is at stake. At that moment, the French window opened and Ronnie stuck his head out into the rain.

"What are you doing out there, T. J? You're getting soaked."

As so many times before, my quick thinking saved me.

"Just checking the roof, Ronnie." I looked up at the roof above where he was standing.

"Checking the roof?"

"Yes. We've been having some trouble with it recently."

"So you have to check it now, in the pouring rain."

"It's the best time. The gutters, you see."

"Ah yes, the gutters."

Ronnie said something else. By the look on his face, it was probably one of his stupid wisecracks, but at that moment there was a loud clap of thunder, which drowned out his words. Then I heard a different voice.

"Herr Dick, why are you standing under the rain?"

"It's OK, Hans," said Ronnie. "He's just checking the roof."

"Yes," I said with a smile. "It's the gutters. Just checking them." I kept my eyes fixed on the roof, turning my head slowly to follow the course of the gutter.

"Are you not afraid of catching a cold?" Hans had to shout now to make himself heard above the rain which was falling in deafening torrents on the deck and the roof.

"We Dicks are a hardy breed," I bellowed back. "Toughness is one of my greatest strengths as an executive." I was not sure whether he heard me above the rain. I could not make out his expression through the water that was dripping from my hair and running down my nose. By the time I had removed my glasses and wiped my face, the French window had closed and Ronnie and Hans had turned to look toward the inside of the dining room. I was not sure what had drawn their attention away from me, but I seized the chance to resume my efforts to extricate my foot from the deck. I pulled as hard as I could and felt something give. I was pulling again with all my strength, when from inside the house I heard the sound of raised voices.

I looked up from my efforts and saw in the bright light of the dining room what appeared to be two people fighting. Then suddenly, there was a loud crash and a splintering of glass, and Grace came flying out onto the deck, landing on her bottom beside me. She sat up, wiping her mouth and muttering, "Bitch!"

I don't know if it was the impact of Grace hitting the deck, but there was a tearing sound and my foot was suddenly free. Taken by surprise, I fell backwards and landed next to Grace. At that moment, I caught sight of Liz striding through the gap where, until a moment earlier, the French window had been. Her hair was disheveled as if someone had pulled it.

"Slut!" she hissed loudly, and then immediately disappeared from view.

I stared in astonishment. The woman had completely vanished. It was as if she had been "beamed up" to the Starship Enterprise. For a moment there was nothing but the sound of the rain. Then Grace let out a gale of laughter. I looked round and saw that she was pointing in the direction of my foot. She seemed to be trying to speak, but was laughing so hard that she could only move her lips helplessly. Following her gaze, I noticed that a large piece of the deck fully two feet square was stuck to my foot. Rich and Ronnie had emerged from the house and were staring into a hole that had appeared in the deck. Then from below us came a cry:

"What are you staring at, you morons? Get me out of here! I think I've broken my damned leg!"

Above the rain, I heard Grace scream through her laughter: "T. J., I have no idea what you just did, but it was magnificent!" She leaned over and kissed me.

I looked over to where Rich and Ronnie were standing. By now they had been joined by most of the others. Jerome was supporting Lance, who appeared to have fainted. Rich turned toward me, and for a brief moment the rain in my eyes made it look as if he was smiling rather oddly. Then suddenly, the whole deck swayed violently. One of the ladies, or it might have been Jerome, let out a scream as, with a loud crack, the deck lurched away from the house. For a moment it swayed back and forth, and then it slowly collapsed, spilling us all onto the ground below. I found myself in a large puddle, with Grace still beside me, giggling uncontrollably.

From above us, came the sound of deep booming laughter.

"Herr Dick, you certainly are a most extraordinary man!"

I smiled modestly, but I don't think he saw it through the rain.

Chapter 26

"An Ability to Recognize and Develop the Potential of all my People, Regardless of their Sex or Gender"

The ambulance ride to the emergency room took place in a tense silence, broken only by the occasional moan or curse from Liz. Grace was still dazed from her injury, sustained not when the deck collapsed (thankfully, nobody had been injured in the fall), but when, still laughing uncontrollably, she had walked into one of the metal poles that had proved so incapable of supporting the deck.

I had not actually been injured, but it seemed that the only way of detaching the section of the deck that was stuck to my foot would be by removing the plaster. As we drove, I reflected gloomily on the evening's events. There could be no doubt about it. I had lost ground to the Ostrich in the race for the Presidency of Pumpex-SuperPumps. Although a rational, unbiased observer in full possession of the facts would certainly have concluded that I was in no way responsible for the series of mishaps brought on by Stan's incompetence and sheer bad luck, Ronnie was hardly rational or unbiased, and he was no doubt even now using the incidents as food for his idiotic humor. He would take any opportunity, however unfair and unjustified by the real facts behind the events, to make me look ridiculous. I was still brooding on the unhappy turn the evening had taken as we arrived at the hospital.

"Why, Mr. Dick!" said an irritatingly familiar voice, as the ambulance doors opened, "I do declare. We're goin' to have to fix you up with a season ticket fo' this place." The woman's impertinence did nothing to improve my humor. I fixed her with one of my sternest looks as I rose to my feet. My stern expression had the desired effect for a moment, but it was only temporary. She stared stupidly at the piece of deck attached to my foot and held her hand up to her mouth to suppress another torrent of idiotic laughter.

"What is it this time, Mr. Dick? Termites?"

"Termites!" laughed Grace beside me. "That's funny! Ouch!" She held her hands up to her head and groaned quietly."

I had come to expect this kind of stupid behavior from this fat idiot of a nurse, but I was entitled to expect more respect from my wife. I gave her a very stern look indeed, but she wasn't looking.

I am in no way a sexist. An ability to recognize and develop the potential of all my people, regardless of their sex or gender, is one of my greatest strengths as a manager of the new millennium. However, I have noticed over the course of my years as a top level executive that most women do not seem to want to have their potential developed, but would rather behave in a silly and irrational way. In marriage, of course, you are faced with this kind of behavior every day. I am just thankful that Grace is my wife and not one of my people at Pumpex-SuperPumps, where I would be forced to come down very hard on her. As it is, her attitude often causes me severe problems in the smooth running of our marriage.

I was thinking these thoughts as Grace and I sat in wheelchairs and Liz was carried past us into the hospital, still groaning loudly. As she passed us, Grace reached over and took my hand, squeezed it, giggled, hiccuped once and then passed out.

As I sat waiting for the doctor, I reflected again on the evening's events. It had certainly been a bad night for Pumpex-SuperPumps. If Ronnie was able to cash in on my misfortune and maintain his lead in the race for the top job, the company could end up being run by a bean-counter. Instead of my strategic vision and marketing focus, Pumpex-SuperPumps would be in the hands of an accountant, lacking both the qualifications and the personal leadership qualities vital to its survival. As these thoughts passed through my mind, a strange thing happened. Instead of feeling depressed or deflated, I felt a new determination well-ing up inside me. The fighting spirit of the Dicks surged through my veins. There was still time to make up the ground I had lost. I owed it to everyone at Pumpex-SuperPumps to chart the company's course into the new century as a dynamic marketing-driven organization.

"Darn it!" I said to myself. "I won't let that Ostrich beat me!"

"Seems this one's had a blow to the head too," said a voice behind me. "He's muttering something about fighting ostriches."

Chapter 27

"I Set my Face Firmly Toward the Future"

By the time I was sitting on the plane on my way to Wakiah Island the next day, I was once again in top form, ready for the fray and confident of success. It takes a lot to get us Dicks down. We are a family of fighters. I thought of my father, Captain Dick of the 81st, who had overcome an accidental shooting in the buttocks by his own men in Korea to emerge with a distinguished record from that conflict. His courage served as an example to his whole family. My brother, J. T., who had followed our father into the military had had need of the same kind of courage when unfairly blamed for the loss of a tank in a swamp during training maneuvers, due to a fault in the steering. Now it was my turn to draw on the famous fighting spirit of the Dicks. I put behind me the events of the previous evening, the collapse of the deck, the trip to the hospital and the exasperating two hours spent convincing three doctors that I was not suffering from delusions of being chased by birds. At least my leg was finally free of its plaster, and I could stretch luxuriously in the comfort of the first class cabin. I set my face firmly toward the future and the possibilities offered by the National Sales Meeting. I took out the agenda from my briefcase.

National Sales Meeting
Tuesday June 6
Arrive at Seabreeze Inn and Conference Center.
6.30 p.m —Dinner.

Wednesday June 7

8:00–9:00 a.m —Introduction. Rich Pickens, President.

9:00–10:00 a.m.—Review of the year. Ken Petersen, VP Sales.

10:00–10:15 a.m.—Break.

10:15 a.m.–12:00 noon—*Aims and Objectives—Growing Together in the New Millennium.* Ken Petersen, VP Sales.

12:00–1:00 p.m.—Lunch.

1:00–2:00 p.m.—Marketing Overview. T. John Dick, VP Marketing.

2:00–3:30 p.m.—New Products. Mike Rothstein, Marketing Manager.

3:30 p.m.—Golf.

7:00 p.m.—Dinner.

Thursday June 8

8:00 a.m.–12:00 noon—Team Building Exercise. Pratt and Poziemski, Organizational Motivation Consultants.

12:00 noon–1:00 p.m.—Lunch.

1:00–2:00 p.m.—*What makes a Top Salesman?* Ken Petersen, VP Sales.

2:00–3:30 p.m.—Regional Sales Teams Presentations.

3:30–3:45 p.m.—Break.

3:45–5:00 p.m.—*The Winning Instinct.* Tab Masterson, Coach of the 1984 South Carolina Water Polo Championship-winning Charleston Pelicans.

6:30 p.m.—Awards Dinner.

Friday June 9

8.00–10.00 a.m.—Closing Remarks. Hans Kartoffel, President, Pumpex Group of North America.

10.00 a.m.—Depart.

I took my pen and underlined *Marketing Overview.* That would be my first chance to show what I was made of. Then I underlined the word *Golf.* I smiled to myself, as I did so. I was in the same foursome as Hans, along with Rich and Ken. The Ostrich was stuck with three of the Midwest Sales Team. While I chatted to Hans about the future of Pumpex-SuperPumps in the global economy and demonstrated my dynamism and international perspective, the Ostrich would be immersed in details of pump distribution practices in Cleveland. I chuckled aloud.

"Are you all right?" The elderly lady in the next seat was looking at me with a concerned expression.

"Yes, I'm fine, thank you."

"Only you were making a very strange noise."

"That, Ma'am, was a chuckle."

"Oh!"

I underlined *team-building exercise*. This would be another chance to show my leadership qualities.

"Only it sounded very strange."

I gave her a look that anyone not completely senile would have taken as a signal that I was busy and not in the mood for idle chit-chat.

"I thought you were maybe having a fit."

"I assure you I am not in the habit of having...."

"My brother's fits always started like that. A peculiar gurgling noise like a waste disposal."

"If you don't mind, I'm trying to work."

"Oh. Sorry."

"Yes, well...."

"It scared me, that's all."

It took me several minutes to focus on my strategy for the Sales Meeting again. No top executive likes to hear his chuckles compared to a waste disposal, even by a doddery old fool. However, the ability to focus is one of my greatest strengths. I had soon put the foolish interruption behind me and when we landed in Charleston, I was once again pumped and ready for action.

It is a Pumpex Group policy that no more than four of the top executives can fly on the same plane. In this way, an accident cannot leave the company leaderless. For this reason, I had been booked on an earlier flight than the others. You don't like to consider these things of course, but it was a comforting thought that if the plane carrying Hans, Rich, Ken and Ronnie were to crash, I would be there to take command.

A few minutes later, I was sitting in the back of a limo for the half hour ride from the airport to the Seabreeze Inn and Conference Center. It was 2 p.m. I would have time to relax and compose myself before dinner. This would certainly give me an advantage over the Ostrich, who would barely have time to check in and change. The sun was shining as we drove along the coast. Life was good. I let out a contented sigh.

"'Zat you, or has my fan belt gone again?" asked the driver, without turning round.

"Just drive, will you?" I said, giving him one of my most withering looks, which was, unfortunately, wasted on the back of his head.

Chapter 28

"I am There to Listen and Advise"

The ability to maintain a healthy balance between the demands of my hectic life as a top level executive and my role as a caring husband has always been one of my greatest strengths. When traveling, I always make a point of calling home frequently, no matter how busy my schedule is. It is important for Grace to feel that I am there to listen and advise on any matter she thinks important, however trivial it might actually be. As soon as I had checked in to the Seabreeze Inn and Conference Center, I made my way to my room, sat down on the king size bed and called her.

"Hello."

"Hi, honey, its me."

"What? Oh, it's you, T. J."

"Who were you expecting? Prince Charles?"

Humor is one of the tools I use to maintain the spark in our marriage, in much the same way that a well timed quip often proves invaluable in maintaining the morale of the Marketing Department at such a high level.

"Huh?"

"Or your secret lover?" I chuckled.

"Of course not. How's the hotel? Have you burnt it down yet? Or has it just collapsed?"

For some reason, Grace seemed to find these silly remarks funny. I could hear her giggling into the phone. I sometimes think it is a pity that she doesn't share my sharp sense of humor, which always keeps Rich amused in our exchanges of repartee over the coffee cups. I doubt very much whether Rich would find such childish comments at all funny. I decided to ignore them.

"Actually, it's a very nice hotel. Right by the ocean."

"Pity I'm not there with you. We could go for a romantic stroll along the beach."

Sometimes I think that Grace has no idea what kind of a high pressure world it is for top executives at meetings like these.

"I hardly think we'd have time for anything like that."

"Oh?"

"No. I'm going to be very busy."

"Ah yes, of course. Tough at the top. Busy doing what?"

"What?"

"What are you actually going to be doing? Today, for instance."

"Well. Um. In a couple of hours Rich and Hans will be here."

"Yes, but what are you actually going to *do*?"

If I didn't know better, I might think that Grace asks these kinds of questions just to irritate me. However, I believe that a happy marriage like ours is based on communication and sharing, no matter how annoying it may be.

"I expect we'll have a meeting or something."

"Ah."

"Then there's dinner."

"Yes." There was a moment's silence. "Is that it?"

There is a limit to communication and sharing. " I've got to go now."

"Yes, of course. Only two hours till your meeting."

"Bye, honey."

"Bye, Sweetie. Have a nice time."

I put down the phone, took off my shoes and lay down on the bed to think. I went over my strategy one more time. There were three main opportunities for me to convince Hans of my suitability for the position of President at Pumpex-SuperPumps. My presentation the next day was, of course, vital. I smiled to myself at the thought that after three hours of listening to Ken drone on about salesmanship, the audience should be in a receptive frame of mind for a fresh and exciting presentation. The golf match was another opportunity. Again I smiled, this time at the irony that, despite all the Ostrich's crawling and week-end golf outings with Rich, it was me that would get to play in the game that really mattered. There would be many opportunities to show Hans what I was made of. Rich had once remarked to me over a cup of coffee that golf was like a metaphor for life. How a man coped with the challenges of the game could give you a pretty good idea of how he would stand up under the pressures of the business world. Hans could not fail to be impressed with the way I would conduct myself on the links, and draw the obvious conclusions for the future of Pumpex-SuperPumps. Poor old Ostrich! Hacking away with some Midwestern nobodies, while I impressed Hans with my lively interest in global business practices. Finally, there was the team-building exercise on Thursday. I had a pretty good idea what form this would take. On my recommendation, Ken had got Jerry from Human Resources to hire the famous motivational consultants Pratt and Poziemski to run us through our paces. I had attended one of their team-building exercises about three years earlier up at Pumpex Corporate Headquarters. I pretty much knew what to expect, and this would be to my advantage. The exercise would involve dividing up into teams and solving a problem like how best to build a bridge over an imaginary river or something. The team dynamics would develop during the discussion, planning and execution. A natural leader would of course emerge. This would certainly give Hans another chance to take note of my leadership potential.

There was still an hour and a half before anyone of consequence would arrive at the hotel. I had nodded to a few of our salesmen in the lobby as I was checking in, but there was little to be gained by spending the afternoon with them. I opened my briefcase and took out the book I had started to read on the plane: *Doing Business in Europe*. I was sure that the Ostrich would not have thought of doing this kind of research. Hans would certainly be in no doubt as to who had the international outlook that Pumpex-SuperPumps would need in the global marketplace and who was just a short-sighted bean counter with no idea of what happens in the wider world of business. I am a fast reader. By the time Rich and Hans arrived, I would have finished the book. A few off the cuff remarks over pre-dinner cocktails in the bar ought to give Hans a pretty good idea of my global perspective.

Chapter 29

"The Stresses of Executive Life will Take their Toll"

Sooner or later the stresses of executive life will take their toll. A man simply can't continue at the kind of pace my responsibilities require without something giving. It was unfortunate that it had to happen now, at such a critical moment for Pumpex-SuperPumps, when the future direction of the company was at stake. Still, I could hardly be blamed. It had been a hard week. The stress of organizing the buffet-reception, the late night run to the hospital, the early morning flight—all had taken their toll. In addition, the effect of sea air is well documented, particularly in conjunction with the soothing sound of waves on the beach. They even sell tapes of the darned waves.

I was certainly not, as the Ostrich put it, "lying face down on the bed snoring like a chain saw, surrounded by empty whiskey bottles." I had opened two miniature bottles of Jack Daniel's from the mini-bar, and not even finished the second one—hardly surrounded by empty bottles. But what really shows the Ostrich up as a liar is the fact that I don't snore and never have done. I pointed this out over coffee and ice cream in the restaurant and exposed his wild exaggeration for what it was.

It was certainly unfortunate that I missed dinner. I had several remarks concerning European business practices ready to slip into my conversations with Hans. All was not lost, however. I would just have to work them in rather more intensively when we all retired to the bar.

"Ah, Herr Dick," said Hans as I sat down beside him in the corner of the bar, unobtrusively easing one of the West Coast salesmen out of the way. "Good that you are here. Dinner was dull without you." I shot a glance at Ronnie, who was sitting opposite me, on the other side of the little table. He was smiling that silly facetious smile of his, but he could not have failed to take in Hans' compliment to me. I turned to Hans:

"I suppose, Hans, you must be struck by the relative informality of business in the United States compared with Germany, where it is common for colleagues to address each other by their last names and use the formal personal pronoun *Sie*."

This was certainly a good opening remark, allowing me to demonstrate by a casual observation my knowledge of and interest in the business practices of Germany. I hoped and expected that Hans would be impressed. However, I was not expecting the look of amazement that came over his face. His eyes opened wide and his jaw dropped. Before I could follow up with a comment on the workings of the Frankfurt Stock Exchange however, I became aware of a commotion that was taking place behind me. The West Coast salesman who earlier had been trying to take my seat, had somehow lost his balance. He was a very large man. Probably if he had done more to stay in shape, he would have been able to maintain his footing and would not have sat down heavily on one end of the table occupied by Ken and two members of the East Coast sales team. If he had not been so heavy, the other end of the table would not have risen so fast and delivered such a powerful blow to Ken's chin. At the time I was not aware of all this foolishness happening behind my back. I ignored the noise which I took to be some unprofessional horseplay by salesmen abusing the privilege of an open bar. Hans seemed to be momentarily distracted, however. He kind of half stood up and looked over my shoulder for a moment. Then he sat down and fixed me with an intense look, which I assumed must express admiration in Germany, although to us Americans it might appear to be more like amazement.

"No, Herr Dick, things are certainly not dull when you are around."

My remark about the formal personal pronoun had obviously gone down well. Before I could pursue my advantage, however, we were interrupted by a loud groaning sound.

In the interests of accuracy and objectivity, I feel I must put something straight. Some people have tried to suggest that I was in some way responsible for Ken's broken jaw. Anyone who knows me will agree that I have never been one to wriggle out of the blame when something really is my fault. I am always ready to step forward and say "Hey guys, my fault!" if the situation justifies it. If anyone should take management responsibility for this unfortunate accident, it is Ken himself. A Pumpex-SuperPumps salesman represents the company to our customers. A grotesquely overweight salesman is hardly likely to present the desired image. As VP of Sales, Ken should have imposed some maximum weight limit on his staff, which would not only have projected a more professional image but also avoided accidents such as this.

"You shtipid bashtard!" I heard Ken's voice and turned round in my seat to see what had provoked such an outburst. I had never heard language like this from Ken, who is a very cool man, not given to flashes of temper or swearing. I had not been at the dinner to see how much he had drunk, but I assumed it must have been an excessive amount, because he now proceeded to pass out, very unprofessionally I thought at the time, on the floor by the bar.

I turned round again to face Hans. I was worried that Ken's behavior must be creating a negative impression of SuperPumps management, which would reflect badly on us all. Ronnie and Peter had pulled Ken to his feet and were dragging him past the table where we sat. Ken appeared to be regaining consciousness and moaned loudly as they passed on their way to the door. I moved quickly to distract Hans' attention and minimize the damage.

"Of course the single European currency is going to mean big changes in every aspect of the financial markets, Hans. Do you think these changes will be generally positive?"

My remarks succeeded in drawing Hans' attention away from the embarrassing scene which had now moved to the door. He turned and looked at me, his mouth slightly open in astonishment. Despite all the distractions, my international outlook still seemed to be making a big impression on him. He stared at me in silence for a moment, no doubt waiting to hear my opinion. This was something of a setback, as I did not really have anything you could exactly call an opinion on the matter.

"Of course, I think it must be a good thing." This seemed like the best bet. Anything had to be better than having to screw around with all kinds of funny money like Swedish Francs and Italian Pesetas and Greek Dragoons. Hans did not immediately react. He continued to stare at me for a moment, then began slowly to shake his head.

"Well, I mean, must be a good thing in some ways," I said.

He was still shaking his head.

"But not in a lot of important respects, of course. No, not really. Not at all, in fact. No, most certainly not. No." I settled back in my chair, smiling and shaking my head. It seemed that my quick reactions and coolness in a sticky situation had once again saved the day.

Chapter 30

"Scrimping and Saving on a High-Powered Corporate Meeting is a False Economy"

The Seabreeze Inn and Conference Center is not only a top flight hotel and executive resort. It also boasts the very finest conference facilities, making it ideal for a meeting of a world class company such as Pumpex. I had done my research into the resort's facilities during an exploratory visit with Ken three months previously, as part of a two week fact-finding tour of possible National Sales Meeting locations that had taken in potential sites on Hilton Head Island and the Florida Keys. I am considered something of an expert in the planning of events such as these and was only too happy to lend Ken my expertise. Of course, it had not been easy to free myself from my duties back at the office, but the organization of the National Sales Meeting was clearly a top priority project. As I had explained to Grace, Ken was obviously struggling and without my intervention there was a good chance that the meeting would be a dismal failure:

"*Location. Location. Location!*, as the saying goes Darling. There's no more vital key to a successful meeting than its location. I remember once..."

"Oh, for God's sake! Just take off on your two week golfing booze-up on company expenses, T. J." Grace had interrupted, showing a complete lack of understanding of the serious nature of our trip. To be fair to her, this unreasonable outburst can probably be explained by her disappointment at my refusal to let her accompany me. Although I had explained it to her in great detail, Grace had quite failed to grasp the amount of hard work involved and the pressure that Ken and I would be under to complete our research in such a short time. Of course, she was also touchingly upset by the fact that we would have to be apart for so long, including the weekend that I was forced to spend at the Blue Pelican Beach Club in Key West. I am a great admirer of women, but they often exhibit a sad inability to see below the surface. To Grace, a two week tour of the finest resorts in the South-East was just an excuse to "goof off" and play some golf, eat lavish meals washed down with bottles of Chablis and enjoy some early spring sunshine.

Of course, it was necessary to play some golf. A top class sales meeting provides opportunities for the participants to bond on a personal as well as a professional level and a round of golf is an essential and traditional part of this bonding experience. An assessment of the golfing facilities, therefore, was vital to the final determination of the meeting's location. A similar assessment of the cuisine on offer at the various potential sites was, quite naturally, just as important and we did not shirk this duty either. The Seabreeze had come out ahead of the competition on both these counts, and Ken and I had made the reservations in complete confidence that the meeting attendees would have little cause to complain about the recreational facilities.

A National Sales Meeting is, however, first and foremost a working occasion, and Ken and I had been very impressed by the conference facilities at the Seabreeze. We had been equally impressed by the attitude of the staff, who had opened up the meeting rooms for us to have a quick look round after the bar had closed. (The management of the Blue Parrot Inn had not been so accommodating and thus put themselves out of the running for our business.) With my expertise in these matters, a few minutes was enough to make a thorough assessment. I was particularly impressed by the overhead projector, which appeared to be very easy to operate. The chairs were very comfortable, so much so that Ken, who had taken on the responsibility for evaluation of the seating arrangements, had fallen asleep in one of them and had to be roused by one of the friendly and helpful staff.

The first session wasn't scheduled to start until 8 o'clock, but I arrived at 7:30, just to have a quick check on the facilities. The meeting was Ken's department's show, but I thought I would just unobtrusively cast an eye over the arrangements, in case he had missed anything. I was confident that, with my expert eye, I would soon spot anything out of place or not quite right. The first thing I saw when I walked into the room was Ronnie, who certainly fell into both these categories. Of course, I immediately realized why he was there so early—just in case Hans turned up and he could get in some early morning crawling. If he was there before the crowd, he could act as if he was somehow involved in the arrangements and try to take credit for the organization. This was just the kind of thing you could expect from the Ostrich. He would stop at nothing to impress Hans and improve his chances of getting Rich's job. It was just as well I had turned up when I did. Hans would now be just finishing breakfast, and I had had to hurry to make sure I was there before he arrived.

"Ah, T. J." said the Ostrich, with his usual brand of phony friendliness. He was stretched out in a chair in the second row, with his feet on the back of the chair in front. I wished Hans would walk in right then. The sight of the Ostrich lounging around like a slob in a crumpled golf shirt would give him a pretty good indication of the kind of man he was. My book had given me an understanding of the formality of German business life. This was why, although the dress code for the meeting was casual, I was wearing a suit.

"Is that your casual suit?" the Ostrich asked, with that grin that I usually find so irritating. It didn't irritate me this time. The Ostrich, lacking my grasp of the European mind, had totally missed the significance of the suit. There would be two people formally dressed and executive-looking at the meeting—Hans and me. Ronnie would cut a pretty poor figure in his crumpled golf shirt and slacks. I smiled at him with a mixture of pity and condescension. This obviously unsettled him, because he got up and went over to the table at the door to pour himself some coffee.

While Ronnie was getting his coffee, I quickly attended to last minute preparations. I examined the little name cards placed on the desks that were attached to the thirty or so chairs in the room and soon noticed that the seating had been organized in an extremely sloppy manner. In the front row, Rich was seated to one side of Hans, quite naturally, but on the other side was Ronnie, of all people! My own name card was three chairs away, next to Peter Braithwaite, the VP of Engineering. A suspicion flashed into my mind, as I looked over to where Ronnie was filling

177

his coffee cup. So that was why he was so early! He must have switched the name cards around. With a shudder, I realized what a devious and dangerous enemy I was up against. There was no trick too low for the Ostrich. I quickly exchanged my name card with Ronnie's and strolled over to the coffee table.

"Have you any idea how much this lot is costing?" the Ostrich asked between sips.

"What, the coffee?"

"No, this whole thing. The meeting." He seemed irritated, as if it was my fault that he couldn't formulate his questions clearly. Marketeers deal in precision. The Ostrich would not have survived two minutes in the world of marketing.

"Well, uh, about the usual for this kind of thing."

"A ridiculous amount, you mean. Why Ken had to choose such an expensive place, I don't know. I mean, look at this meeting room. It's twice the size we need. And the golf this afternoon. We're playing on a championship course, for God's sake! I bet most of these salesmen don't know one end of a golf club from the other."

It was typical of a bean counter like the Ostrich not to be able to see past his penny-pinching small-mindedness to the real value of a well organized National Sales Meeting. Scrimping and saving on a high-powered corporate meeting is a false economy. Anyone with a broad business perspective and keen understanding of organizational dynamics could see that. But people like the Ostrich, of course, can't see the real value of such things. Their vision is too narrow and restricted. I had heard the Ostrich refer to the finest sales force in the industry as "that amorphous mass of anonymous blubber, none of whom seems to stay for longer than 6 months." This was just the kind of would-be clever remark that he used to try to cover up his own limitations. Such a lack of vision, I noted, hardly suggested that the Ostrich was the kind of person to lead a world class company like Pumpex-SuperPumps into the new millennium. I shook my head sadly as I filled my coffee cup.

"An interesting observation, Herr Straussvogel, about the golf."

I had not noticed Hans entering the room. Europeans have a sneaky way of moving around without making a noise.

"I have a theory about golf, gentlemen. I think that any salesman who is too good at it is spending too much time playing golf and not enough time calling on customers. What are you thinking about that?"

"Perhaps you're right, Hans," said the Ostrich. "What about Vice Presidents of Finance or Marketing?"

"Oh, they should not be too good either. Otherwise they might beat me! Ha, ha!"

The Ostrich chuckled. I was unable to join in the banter due to a momentary confusion. It had nothing to do with Hans' remarks. I certainly had no intention of beating him at golf. What had rendered me temporarily speechless was the sight of Hans himself, who was not wearing a suit as my book indicated he most certainly should have been, but rather a golf shirt and slacks very similar in style to Ronnie's. Even the colors were the same—red shirt and khaki pants.

"Why are you wearing a suit, Herr Dick? Is it not casual clozis that we should be wearing? Must I go to change myself?"

"Don't worry, Hans. You'll do just fine like that," said the Ostrich in his smarmiest tone.

"I must thank you again, Herr Straussvogel, for borrowing to me the shirt and the trouser of your father. I did not think to bring casual clozis with me from Germany. If you had not borrowed me them I would have had to wear a suit like Herr Dick and look like a noodle. Did you forget your casual clozis also, Herr Dick?"

"Yes," I said, and immediately regretted it. Although having forgotten my casual clothes provided a plausible reason for appearing in a suit and looking overdressed, though by no means like a noodle, whatever that meant, I had already decided on a plan to create an excuse to go and change out of my suit. This involved spilling coffee on my pants. I had already started to tip my cup off its saucer, and I did not quite manage to stop myself in time. I had also reckoned without the pain inflicted by the hot coffee and was unable to completely stifle a scream as it landed on my legs.

"My God, T. J! Be careful!" said the Ostrich.

"Ja, Herr Dick. Are you all right?"

"Yes, thanks," I said through gritted teeth. We Dicks are a tough breed, and I maintained my composure despite the agony inflicted by the burning coffee.

"You must take off your pants, Herr Dick. What a pity you have no casual clozis. Perhaps Herr Ronnie can lend you some."

"I think I have something," said the Ostrich. He appeared to be giggling, although what on earth there was to laugh about completely escaped me. He handed me the key to his room. "In the closet. The pants might be a little tight, but I think you can probably squeeze into them."

There was no way around it. I had said quite clearly in front of Hans that I had forgotten my casual clothes, so I could hardly re-appear in them now. The Ostrich would be sure to make some remark. So five minutes later, I was in my room struggling to fit into the Ostrich's pants, while my own new Dockers hung in the closet in front of me. I stood in front of the mirror and winced. The pants were so tight that they were cutting off the circulation to my legs and crushing my private parts. The Ostrich was clearly a lot more compact in that area than I was. But it was not the physical pain that made me wince. It was the sight of the revolting lime green Hawaiian shirt with large, bright yellow pineapples on it. Once again, it seemed, events had conspired against me and, through no fault of my own, I would be forced to arrive late at the meeting looking like a noodle.

Chapter 31

"The Vanity of the Sales Profession Never Fails to Make me Smile"

It took me some considerable time to walk back down to the meeting room in the Ostrich's ridiculously tight pants. By the time I got there, the room was full. Everyone had taken their seats, and Rich was standing next to the overhead projector at the front of the room. As I entered, he examined his watch and said, "Good morning, T. J. Glad you could join us."

I resented the tone of this remark, which suggested that Rich was not aware of the unavoidable reasons for my slight tardiness. I was sure that, if I had had a chance to explain, he would not have made such an inappropriate comment in front of the whole sales force. The high esteem in which I was held by the Pumpex-SuperPumps sales professionals was an essential part of my success in the role of Vice President of Marketing, and such remarks from the company President were, therefore, not only unjust but also organizationally counterproductive. However, there was no chance to explain now, so I smiled apologetically as I made my way to my seat at the front of the room. As I did so, I was aware that the slightly awkward stiffness in my walk caused by the constriction of the Ostrich's pants around the top of my thighs was the cause of some amusement to several of the sillier and more immature members of the sales force, past whom I was forced to move to reach my seat. It occurred to me that Rich would be better employed putting a stop to this foolish tittering than addressing inappropriate remarks to me. However, I retained my dignity and composure until I reached the front of the room. It was only then that I noticed that my seat next to Hans was occupied by the Ostrich, who was looking at me with a particularly moronic smirk. To make matters worse, there were no free seats at all at the front of the room. A less confident man might have been embarrassed in such a situation, stranded there with nowhere to sit and the eyes of thirty sniggering salesmen on him. The only empty seat was at the very back, next to the door through which I had entered. I admit that even I, who am known for my cool head, was momentarily thrown off balance. My frame of mind was not helped by the Ostrich whispering, "Nice shirt, T. J." loud enough for the front two rows to hear. But then the famous Dick coolness under pressure reasserted itself. In front of where Ronnie was sitting, I spotted a pen that someone had dropped. In a flash, I stooped, picked it up and, with a quiet "Ah yes, there it is," placed it in the breast pocket of my shirt, patted the pocket with a show of satisfaction, turned as gracefully as was possible in those pants and started back toward the only empty seat at the back of the room. I am sure I could have carried it off too, had it not been for those pants. If they had been of a looser fit, I would have been able to bend my leg as I turned, and would not have caught the projector table with my foot. The table, a badly designed, unstable structure, swayed momentarily, before toppling over and hurling the projector over the Ostrich's head and into the lap of our sales representative for the New England Region, who was sitting in the row behind. There was a moment of silence before the inevitable silliness began. There were shouts of "Well caught, Larry!" and what I could only describe as hoots of immature laughter. The Ostrich, of course, couldn't resist joining in. He pointed to the trajectory the projector had followed over the people in the front row and screeched:

"So that's why they call it an overhead projector."

The mood of the meeting was now such that even this imbecilic remark was greeted with more raucous hoots. Of course, the irony of the situation was not lost on me. The whole episode had been brought about by the Ostrich's absurdly tight pants, and yet here he was trying to make me look ridiculous with his idiotic jokes. He had reckoned without my lightning wit. I did not get to the top of the marketing profession without an ability to think on my feet. Quick as a flash, and with a devastating smile directed at the Ostrich, I responded:

"Well, if your pants weren't so tight, none of this would have happened."

I was immediately gratified to see how my remark redirected the attention of the meeting to the Ostrich. The laughter died down and was replaced by a roomful of puzzled faces directed at him. Nobody could ever accuse me of being unable to take a joke at my expense, but I drew the line at enduring ridicule for an incident for which I was in no way to blame. Let the Ostrich stew in his own juice! His response was typically moronic. He stood up and danced around like some kind of an idiot, pulling his pant legs out from his thighs and proclaiming, "They seem quite comfortable to me."

Naturally, I could see what he was trying to do—confuse the issue by pretending that he didn't know that when I said his pants were too tight, I meant my pants which were, of course, really his. Obviously, nobody was buying his feeble attempt to wriggle out of the tight corner into which I had so effortlessly maneuvered him. Everyone was laughing at him now, and I joined in. He deserved it. I permitted myself a modest smile of triumph, as I made my way to the empty seat at the back, adding to the Ostrich's embarrassment by comically exaggerating still further the stiffness in my legs, much to the appreciation of everyone in the room.

As I took my seat, not without considerable difficulty in those pants, I glanced at the Ostrich at the front of the room. He had his back turned to me, as he helped Rich pick up his overhead slides which had fallen on the floor when the table toppled over, but I could see his shoulders heaving in forced laughter, with which he hoped to conceal his embarrassment. Had it been anyone but the Ostrich, I might have felt sorry for him. But the Ostrich had brought it upon himself, when he chose to tangle with T. John Dick in a battle of wits.

At last Rich had all his overhead slides back in a neat stack beside the projector. He picked up one of them, and motioned for silence. The last titters died down as he began:

"Well, now that T. J has got us off to a flying start, let's get to work!"

Rich's presentation took longer than the scheduled hour, owing to frequent pauses to find overheads which had somehow been replaced in the wrong order in the pile. No doubt this was the Ostrich's sloppy work, which would not go unnoticed when it came time for Rich to make a recommendation regarding his successor. The frequent pauses gave me time to take stock of the situation and plan my campaign for the Presidency. On the negative side, my failure to put in an appearance at dinner the previous evening had got me off to a bad start. On the other hand, I had certainly sparkled in the bar. I was particularly pleased at the way I had seized the opportunity to demonstrate my international perspective with adroit remarks on the formality of German business practices and the Single European Currency. This could not have failed to make an impression on Hans. Similarly, the incidents brought about by the Ostrich's absurdly tight pants had started out as decidedly negative, but my quick thinking had turned them to my advantage. If Hans was an observant man, he would surely have noticed the speed of my reactions and my coolness under pressure, qualities just as important as an international perspective in a future chief executive. Also in my favor was the Ostrich's striking failure to do anything remotely impressive. Despite this, however, he seemed to have made some headway with Hans by sheer shameless groveling. I would have some work to do to undermine the effects of this disgusting toadying.

Rich finished his presentation, leaving everyone somewhat confused. His last overhead had said *Welcome to the Pumpex-SuperPumps National Sales Meeting*. Those who had been paying attention seemed uncertain of exactly what Rich had been trying to say, although during the five minute coffee break everyone agreed that it had been an inspiring message.

I had plenty of time to continue with my reflections during Ken's presentation. Although unable to speak, owing to his broken jaw, Ken pluckily insisted on going ahead with his presentation, which consisted of a series of overhead slides of charts, lists and diagrams, which he pointed at with one of those telescopic metal pointers. He began logically enough at the top of the slide and moved the pointer down line by line. When he reached the bottom, he looked quizzically at the audience to establish whether they had finished reading the slide. If he judged that they had, he moved on to the next slide and began at the top again. If he felt that more time was needed for everyone to absorb the message on the slide, he waited in silence for a while, raising his eyebrows and looking around at the audience until he was satisfied that the full power of the message had hit home. On a few occasions, he added special emphasis to important points by slapping the screen with his pointer and grunting loudly.

As Ken's presentation proceeded, it suddenly dawned on me why he had insisted on going ahead with it. Absurd though it was, Ken must have thought that he was in with a chance of selection as Rich's successor. The vanity of the sales profession never fails to make me smile. Ken must have regarded his presentation as a chance to shine in front of Hans and now, in a gesture that was as mad as it was courageous, he was going down with guns blazing. I decided there and then that there would certainly be a place for Ken's kind of brave, never-say-die attitude on my team when I was President of Pumpex-SuperPumps.

As Ken continued with his presentation, I turned my thoughts back to my strategy for ensuring that I and not the Ostrich was selected for the post of President. The urgency of my task was brought home to me forcefully as I looked around the room at the fine team of men and women that represented Pumpex-SuperPumps to the world. I could no more allow their future to be directed by a callous and incompetent bean counter than I could that of the splendid workforce back at the factory. They deserved and needed a man of vision and energy to lead them into the next century. These thoughts were surging through my head as I followed the example of most of Ken's audience and fell asleep.

I had just fired the Ostrich and watched him depart my luxurious office in tears, when I woke up to find a rolled up piece of paper balanced on my open mouth. There was no way of determining who had put it there, so I decided to ignore the incident. Ken was emphasizing an exceptionally important point by grunting especially loudly. This was what had woken me, and several others were also shaking their heads groggily.

I returned to my strategizing. I had three important opportunities remaining to make an impression on Hans. There was my presentation that afternoon, the golf match and the team building exercise the next day. I was certain that this exercise had been arranged in order to give Hans an opportunity to observe the leadership qualities of the Senior Management. It could very well be the deciding factor in determining the future leadership of the company. I took my pen and wrote on the pad of paper in front of me:

Presentation
Golf
Team-Building Exercise

I underlined *Team-Building Exercise*. Twice. Then I underlined *Golf* twice also. And *Presentation*. I was leaving nothing to chance.

Chapter 32

"Top Level Executives are as Human as Ordinary People"

As a top level executive, I am, of course, acutely aware of the high esteem in which ordinary people hold those of us whom the media likes to call "captains of industry." I have noticed the extra respect that is accorded me at the gas station, when I pull up to the full service pump in my executive Ford Explorer, the extra second or two that the boy spends washing my windshield, the deference with which the "Have a nice day" is delivered. At Pumpex, although I am never one to stand on ceremony or demand respect simply because I am an important member of Senior Management, I have not failed to notice the high regard in which I am held by the non-salaried workers and Junior Management. This, of course, is as it should be. However, it is important for those aspiring to Senior Management positions, many of whom might be reading this book in search of inspiration, to realize that top level executives are as human as ordinary people and often face the same problems they do. It is the way in which we overcome these problems that provides the real inspiration. To anyone present that afternoon, T. John Dick was seen to deliver the kind of polished presentation for which he is so well known. There was no sign of the turmoil beneath the surface. In fact I could have chosen to gloss over the more uncomfortable aspects of the episode and nobody would have been any the wiser. But this is a no-holds-barred account of executive life and I owe it to the reader to pull no punches and tell it like it is.

The secret of a successful presentation can be summed up in a single word: a powerful message. I was confident that there would certainly be no shortage of power in my message, as I arranged my overheads on the projector table and turned to face my audience. The New England salesman in the second row held up his hands in front of his face and ducked down in his chair—an idiotic piece of carrying on that I chose to ignore.

With an air of superior indifference which I think impressed my audience, I waited for the few silly giggles to die down. In fact I was quite glad of the noisy interruption, as it allowed me discreetly to break wind. I had unwisely eaten shrimp at lunch. It is a weakness of mine that I adore shrimp, although they have a tendency to create a troubling turbulence in my stomach. An ability to recognize and overcome my weaknesses is one of my greatest strengths. However, my craving for shrimp will occasionally overpower even my iron discipline. This had happened at lunch and I had tucked in heartily to a large plateful. I had used the shrimp as an elegant opening conversational gambit with Hans and we had proceeded to a most enjoyable chat about the marine harvest of the North Sea, and in particular the pickled herring so beloved in his native Hamburg. I had by now reached as far as Hamburg in my book. I think Hans had enjoyed the little chat to which my plateful of shrimp had so naturally led us. He had smiled a lot, and jokingly remarked that he had sneaked out to the bar for a couple of what he called *schnapps* before collecting his plateful of cold cuts from the buffet table. I knew what *schnapps* was. I had read about it in a chapter entitled *Food and Drink in Germany*. So, of course, I knew he was joking. The President of a topflight company would hardly drink alcohol during an important National Sales Meeting. I had a good laugh at the suggestion, especially when he quipped that he felt he needed some kind of anesthetic to help him through the afternoon's presentations. I recalled a section in my book which stated that, contrary to all prejudices and stereotypes, Germans were possessed of a lively sense of humor. This was good. After all, my presentation was the first of the afternoon. Hans was sporting with me in the relaxed and jovial way you might expect a respected senior executive to use when talking to a dynamic young mover and shaker on his way to the top.

Marketing is, of course, all about communication. There are no better communicators than marketing professionals, and I think my audience was anticipating something special from my presentation. I make a point of working hand in glove with the sales force, and there were a couple of faces that I was almost sure I recognized from the previous year's National Sales Meeting. Although the dynamic synergy of the marketing/sales interface is the driving force of the company, I can't be expected to remember every salesman I meet from one year to the next. After all, there's not exactly a lot of difference from one salesman to another. However, due to my high profile position in the company and reputation as an incisive and powerful communicator, they would all be very aware of who I was, and would be expecting great things from a presentation by T. John Dick, Vice President of Marketing. Some of them would remember my presentation of last year, shortly after the acquisition, on turning SuperPumps into a marketing-driven organization, and would be expecting the same kind of fireworks today. Others were new with the company, but the older hands would be sure to have told them that T. John Dick's presentation would be a highlight of the meeting and, unlike Ken's, well worth staying awake for.

"Gentlemen," I began. "And Ladies!" I added with a gracious smile, which I directed first at Rachel, sitting with Mike and Harvey at the back of the room, and then at Melissa, our only lady salesman, whom Ken had hired three months previously. Personally, I thought that if Ken had to choose a woman, the company would have been better served by someone a bit prettier and not quite so fat. However, nobody could accuse me of sexism, and to prove it, I went out of my way to make our female colleagues feel at home. "We have two lovely ladies here. Rachel, who is my right hand woman in Marketing Communications and Melissa, who covers Pennsylvania."

"Not literally!"

"What was that, Melissa?" I do not welcome interruptions, but I let this one go, as I hadn't really started yet.

"I may be fat, but even I'm not big enough to cover the whole of Pennsylvania!"

This was, of course, not what I had meant, as she knew very well. Women always seem to have a way of twisting things around, and this kind of thing makes it hard to remain non-sexist, no matter what kind of allowances you make. It was really most unfair that I should be made out to be the kind of man who would make insensitive remarks about a female colleague's weight, when I had intended no such thing. Fortunately, my cool head allowed me to move quickly to repair the damage.

"I didn't mean 'cover' in that sense. And if I had, I would certainly have chosen somewhere much smaller, like Delaware."

My deft compliment did the trick. Melissa gave me a strange look. Then she beamed broadly and started to laugh. Her colleagues joined in. The tension built up by the silly misinterpretation of my remark about covering Pennsylvania had apparently been broken. In the front row, the Ostrich appeared to be choking. I ignored him. I had no time for his nonsense. I had an important presentation to make.

"Many of you," I began, "probably wonder sometimes, what it is that the Marketing Department actually does." I paused long enough to let the effect of my sensational opening sink in, surveying my audience with a look that managed to be both searching and good humoredly ironic. I had often used this look in presentations, always to great effect, and had taken the precaution of practicing it briefly in the bathroom mirror while shaving that morning. Even through a layer of shaving cream, I had been pleased to see that the look had lost none of its power. I am a great believer in the right look to add force to an important point or ironic phrase, and the ability to match just the right look to my words is one of my greatest strengths as a communicator.

"Well, ask yourselves a couple of questions." I laid the first overhead on the projector. It read *New Products*.

"Where do you think that new products come from?"

"The engineers." Some stupid salesman had failed to grasp that my question was rhetorical.

"No, I don't mean the engineers. Peter's troops may actually do the donkey work of product development—and of course we all appreciate their efforts—but I'm talking about the ideas. It's up to Marketing to see the big picture, spot the trends, analyze the needs of the market and develop a broad new product strategy that provides a framework for the company to achieve its growth targets. In a little while, Mike will run you through the new products we have coming down the pike, and I think you're going to be pretty excited."

As I turned back to the projector to lay my next overhead on it, I felt a sudden sharp pain in my gut, and realized to my horror that I urgently needed to get to a bathroom. The shrimps had done their awful work with devastating speed. With my back to my audience I was able to clench my teeth and wait the second or two it took for the immediate pain to pass. I took a deep breath and placed the overhead on the projector. As I turned round, another pain shot through my stomach, causing me to grimace. Before anyone could notice, I was able to turn the grimace into a kind of broad genial smile. I was forced to maintain the smile for quite a few seconds, so I looked around the room, as if surveying the audience with a piercing intelligence before making my next point.

There was nothing else for it. I could hardly stop in the middle of my presentation to go to the bathroom. I would just have to grin and bear it, and get through it as quickly as possible. We Dicks are a resourceful breed and I came up with the idea of fixing my attention on a large pimple on our Pacific Northwest salesman's nose. This had the effect of distracting my thoughts from my painful situation. Gradually, the spasm subsided, and I moved quickly to make my next point before the pain returned. The overhead read *Mission Statement*.

"Marketing has taken a leading role in plotting the course for the company's future." I spoke rapidly, hurrying to make my point in time to turn round for my next overhead before the next spasm hit. Despite my extreme discomfort, my cool head remained with me. I avoided the temptation to panic, and kept my voice almost entirely natural. I am confident that the effect was that of a hard-hitting, quick-fire presentation. "For instance, as Vice President of Marketing, I felt it essential for the company to have a Mission Statement. To make sure that everyone is aware of the company's goals. That we are all singing the same song. Reading from the same page." I had not yet felt another spasm coming on, so I took a tactical decision to keep talking until I did. That way, when the pain returned, I should be able to hide my discomfort, while turning for the next overhead. "Rowing the same boat. On the same bus. Uh..."

"Riding the same bicycle," someone volunteered.

"Singing the same song," somebody else shouted out.

"We've had that one!"

"Oh, sorry."

"I don't think riding the same bicycle really works. It doesn't make sense."

I sensed that the presentation was getting out of my control, but before I could do anything about it, the next spasm shot through my intestines. I span round rapidly and gritted my teeth. This one was worse than the others. I tried to clench my buttocks but realized that, in the Ostrich's absurdly tight pants, they were already as clenched as they could be. There was nothing for it but to strain my whole body to hold it in. I pretended to be looking through my overheads, as if I had lost the one I needed next. This spasm seemed to be going on forever, and it was getting even worse. I held my breath, strained all my muscles and made my body totally rigid in a desperate effort to hold back disaster. Just as it seemed the dam would break, the spasm began to subside. I breathed out again and became aware of the voices in the room.

"What if the bicycle was a tandem? Two people pulling together to, like, reach a common goal."

"That doesn't work because there's more than two of us."

Quickly, I laid my overhead on the projector. It contained the text of the Mission Statement. Fearing another attack, I read it out as quickly as I could:

"Pumpex-SuperPumpsMissionStatement. AtPumpex-SuperPumps thecustomerisnumberone. Bymeetingandexceedingtheveryhigheststand-ardsofcustomerservice,wewillmeetthecompanyobjectivesofmaximizing growthandearnings,whilemaintainingthehighestbusinessandethical stan-dards."

"I am begging your pardon, Herr Dick?"

I stopped and looked at Hans, who was wearing a puzzled expression.

"Of what are you talking? I cannot understand your fastness."

"It's the Mission Statement, Hans. I thought it important to define the direction of the company in broad terms, as the framework in which our business strategy could be determined. So I put together..."

"And how long did it take you to write this?"

This was a difficult question. If I answered too short a time, it would suggest a lack of deep thought, while too long a time would imply a lack of decisiveness and speed of action. Anyone who knows me well is aware that I certainly do not lack a capacity for profound thought, while decisiveness and speed of action are two of my greatest strengths. Hans, however, did not have the benefit of knowing me well, so I would have to weigh my answer carefully. Fortunately, my stomach cramps appeared to have subsided for the moment, and I was able to bring all my concentration to bear on the answer.

"About an hour or so."

I had decided to go for the speed of action. Hans said nothing, but continued to frown at the screen.

"Of course, when I say about an hour, I mean that's how long it took to actually write it. It took me days of deep thought to formulate the ideas. Weeks, actually. I'm always formulating ideas. One of my greatest...."

"Perhaps, if you spent less time formulating Mission Statements, Herr Dick, you might have more time to spend actually doing something."

I was shocked at Hans' suggestion. I am the Vice President of Marketing in a top flight company. I am an ideas man, a leader. I have people to *do* things.

"Do not look so shocked, Herr Dick. I am only pulling your foot."

Of course, I should have known he wasn't serious. I have no first-hand experience of European corporate structures, but I would hardly think that even they would expect top marketing professionals, if they have them, to waste their time doing something. I decided to smile pleasantly, demonstrating that T. John Dick knows how to take a joke, even a stupid one. They must be pretty short on senses of humor in Europe. I toyed with the idea of a good humored belly laugh, but decided that this would carry an unacceptable risk of restarting the pain in my bowels, which had thankfully remained quiet for several moments now. Instead I read out the first part of my Mission Statement again, more slowly for the benefit of Hans and anyone else who had missed it. I then read out the rest of it, pausing for emphasis at the most important parts, such as *innovative product design* and *a dynamic approach to marketing*. I could see that it was well received, and by the time I reached the final *together we can*, I was gratified to see several heads nodding in silent approval.

I was back on top form now. The crisis in my gut appeared to have passed. It was time to move on to the next part of my presentation.

"I mentioned new products earlier. We all know that new products are the life blood of a company like Pumpex-SuperPumps and nobody is more aware of this than I, as Vice President of Marketing." I looked round the room with a serious expression that said, "Here is a man with a mission." I went on, "This is why I took the lead in the drawing up and implementation of a comprehensive New Product Development Procedure. With this procedure, Marketing will be able ensure that a steady stream of winning new products hits the market on time and at the right price."

I looked around at my audience. I could tell they were impressed. Someone said "Ooh!"

"I don't intend to bore you with the details of the procedure." Someone at the back, who I believe is the Salesman for Northern California, cheered. My presentations always stir 'em up and provoke a lively reaction. Smiling, I continued, "What you are interested in are the results, the new products you need to increase your sales. Just the same, I thought you would be anxious to see a few highlights of the procedure, to give you a bit of an insight into how we work back at HQ." I knew they would appreciate this. It can be a lonely life on the road, and it must be a great comfort and inspiration to know that I and my team are working hard to provide the support they need. However, there was another important reason to cover the New Product Development Procedure. Flair for planning and organization would certainly be an important factor in selection of the new Company President, and this would be a good opportunity to give Hans a close-up of my abilities in this area.

One of my strengths as a speaker is my ability to present complex issues in a clear and concise way. I was well prepared and equipped with graphic overheads that allowed me to summarize the whole New Product Development Procedure in a little under twenty minutes. (I had timed myself in my office the previous week). I was moving smoothly and crisply through my explanation of the procedure for presenting the New Product Opportunity Analysis Form (NPOA) to the New Product Review Committee (NPRC), when, to my great surprise, I was struck on the nose by what appeared to be a small paper airplane.

I am well known for my cool head, but this was too much. I immediately directed one of my most penetrating looks at the New England salesman in the second row, who had already shown himself to be a trouble-maker. My initial assumption was that I had correctly identified the culprit, for he appeared unwilling to meet my gaze, preferring to stare guiltily at his desk with his head buried in his arms. I folded my arms and continued to stare at him in a stony silence that said, "Nobody throws paper airplanes at T. John Dick, sonny." I was still staring at him, when I was struck by a second airplane, this time just above the left ear. This was an outrage. Now someone else was throwing paper airplanes at me!

"Who threw that?" I demanded sharply.

"I did, Herr Dick. Better hurry yourself, before they all fall asleep."

This was certainly not the kind of behavior you expect from the President of Pumpex, Inc., even if he is only the *acting* President. In the circumstances, I could not think exactly how to react. I decided to display my good-natured ability to take a joke at my expense, even a stupid and childish one.

"Good shot!" I laughed.

"T. J.," said Rich, looking at his watch, "I think we'd better skip the rest of the New Product Development Procedure."

"OK, Rich. Yes. Got to keep moving along."

Time was running short, and I still had another important topic to cover. I had only got as far as half way in the New Product Development Procedure, but that was certainly enough to give a pretty good idea of my organizational abilities. I was happy to find this confirmed, when I heard Hans whisper to Rich, " I think we have heard enough about the New Product Development Procedure."

The pain in my gut had subsided now. I had felt no cramps for several minutes. I still felt a discomfort in my stomach, but I put this down to the tightness of the Ostrich's pants. I sensed that the presentation was going well. It was time to move on to the dramatic conclusion.

"Of course, as Vice President of Marketing I am responsible for the advertising and promotion plans of the company. I take a keen interest in this aspect of the department's work, knowing how important it is that you soldiers should be given live ammunition by the general before he sends you into battle. I think you'll be impressed with the heavy artillery we've come up with for this year's promotional plan." I was particularly pleased with these military metaphors, which I had thought up while watching the movie *Patton*, starring George C. Scott, a couple of weeks earlier. There are many similarities between myself and the General, despite our different fields of achievement. A dynamic, can-do approach and top class organizational skills are as important in marketing as they were in inflicting crushing defeats on the Nazis in World War Two. As I picked up the next overhead, I glanced at Hans, who was busy folding up small pieces of paper. I placed the overhead on the screen and moved out of range.

There was a murmur of appreciation as the picture of the bikini-clad runner-up in the Miss North Carolina Pageant holding a PX-2 compression unit appeared on the screen. The New England salesman in the second row hooted his approval, and he was soon joined by several other salesmen, who began clapping and stamping their feet. Over the general uproar, I could hear Mike shouting as loud as anyone. Significantly, I noticed Harvey had not joined in the applause. I made a mental note to talk to him about being a team player, but did not let this interfere with my pleasure at the response to my advertisement. I do not need the approval of others to know that I am right. Nevertheless, I was gratified by the enthusiasm of the sales force for my stylish and brilliantly conceived ad and smiled graciously as I waited for the applause to die down. When at last it did, I continued.

"As you know," I said, "pumps don't sell themselves." I pointed at the picture of the runner-up in the Miss North Carolina Pageant. "That's what she does."

"Surely, Herr Dick, you do not mean that?" Hans had put down the paper he was folding and was looking puzzled.

"I do not mean what, Hans?"

"Surely you do not mean that she is a prostitute?"

I was stunned. Was the man mad? "No, of course not," I said. "What gave you..."

"If I am hearing you good, you are saying that pumps do not sell themselves, but she does. In Germany, we call women who sell themselves prostitutes. And we are seldom using them in advertisements. Also, Herr Dick, I do not think it is good to talk of such things in front of ladies."

"No, no!" I said quickly, anxious to correct this misunderstanding immediately. "I mean she sells pumps. Not herself."

"And how does she do that?"

"She's a celebrity."

"Who."

"Her."

"Who is she?"

"She was second in the Miss North Carolina Pageant last year."

"Ah."

"Yes, a very talented young lady. We were lucky to get her. Well, not lucky exactly. It took great negotiating skill on my part to..."

"Her teetz are too big."

"I beg your pardon!"

"Her teetz, Herr Dick, her teetz. Can you not see that they are too big?"

"Well, I suppose that swimsuit kind of pushes them up a bit." I was not comfortable with this kind of talk.

'They look like they want to bite you."

"Umm." For once, even I was lost for words.

"She has a nice smile, but her teetz are too big. They look like they want to bite you."

Beside Hans, the Ostrich appeared to be having some kind of a fit. He had an idiotic grin on his face and was pointing at his teeth. Unnecessarily, of course—I had figured out what Hans meant. I gave a little chuckle at the misunderstanding.

"Ah yes, I see what you mean now, Hans."

"I'm sorry, Herr Dick. What did you think I was meaning?"

"Oh teeth. I knew you meant teeth. Not...um..." I was suddenly aware of how hot it was in the room. Wasn't the air conditioner working? Hans had turned to the Ostrich.

"What does he mean, the swimsuit pushes them up?"

I decided to move on quickly to the next overhead. The stomach cramps were beginning to return. I tried focusing on the pimple on the Pacific Northwest salesman's nose. Only now I noticed that it appeared about to burst, and this realization seemed to emphasize my own predicament. It took all the courage and steely self-control of a top marketing professional to continue.

"As you know, due to a mix-up by Manufacturing, we have an overstock situation affecting the PZ line. In Marketing, we are well aware of the need to move this stock for the good of the company, although if Manufacturing had correctly interpreted our forecast, this would not have been necessary. I have, therefore, come up with a whole new ad concept to help us move the stock. Combined with a strategic decision to cut the price by fifty percent, I am confident that the advertisements will help boost demand for the PZ line to record levels. Indeed, we should be able to liquidate the stock in a very short time."

I surveyed the audience with the look of a man who is quietly confident of the success of his marketing strategy. This look was largely lost on the audience, who had not yet completely settled down after the excitement surrounding the ad featuring the runner-up in the Miss North Carolina Pageant. Melissa, the lady salesman, grinned idiotically and shouted across the room to the New England salesman, "Hey, Larry, do you like my teetz?"

I decided to speak to Ken about her later.

It was becoming increasingly difficult to maintain my quietly confident look, as my stomach cramps increased in intensity. I turned to place the next overhead on the projector and stood with my back turned long enough to take a couple of deep breaths and let a particularly severe spasm subside. When I turned round again, the uproar had died down and everyone was looking at me with expressions of curiosity. My presentations never fail to arouse a lively interest. I pointed at the overhead slide projected on the screen, which showed a picture of a PZ-25 pump against a dramatic background of a starlit sky. Beneath the picture was the text: *The PZ Series from Pumpex. Get them while you can. Pumps this cheap won't last long!*

It was an impressive advertisement and I was expecting a rather more enthusiastic response than the silence with which it was greeted. Indeed, I had been counting on a fairly noisy reaction, as I had an urgent need to break wind again and relieve the pressure on my stomach. Instead, I was thrown back on a closed mouth version of my quietly confident smile, to mask my clenched teeth. At last there was a noise from the far right of the room, where Ken was sitting.

"Shtipid Bashterd."

"I don't think the wording is quite as good as it could be," said the Ostrich, who seemed to have recovered from his earlier fit. I get a little irritated when people who know nothing at all about marketing insist on sticking their oar in and muddying the water. Especially a bean counter like the Ostrich! I have a degree in Marketing from a prestigious university. Still, I maintained my calm. In a voice dripping with irony, though still through clenched teeth, I asked.

"And what is wrong with it, Ronnie? In your expert opinion?"

"Oh, I'm no expert like you, T. J."—that much was certainly true— "Only it seems to me that the words 'Pumps this cheap won't last long' could suggest a deficiency in quality leading to a premature end to their working life, rather than a huge demand resulting in a danger of non-availability."

"Yes, it is hardly the most felicitous combination of words. Ambiguous at best, I would say." I recognized the pompous English voice of Peter Braithwaite. I would have silenced him with a stinging reply about how you would have to be a complete idiot, or an engineer, not to understand what the ad was trying to say, but at that moment I was paralyzed by an especially severe intestinal spasm which forced me to limit my response to a ferocious stare in his direction. The ferocity of this stare was enhanced by a sudden drawing back of the lips to bare my teeth, while emitting a sharp hissing sound. This was in fact a spontaneous reaction to the stabbing pressure in my bowels, but it certainly had a dramatic effect on Peter Braithwaite, who recoiled sharply and shut up at once. I decided to practice this look later and add it to my repertoire.

"T. J.," said Rich. "I can't help feeling that Ronnie and Peter have a point. I think we'd better stop this ad before publication. It could be embarrassing."

"If you say so, Rich." I decided to leave the copy of *Pumps Today* I had in my briefcase where it was. I had intended to pass it around so that everyone could see the ad as it appeared in this month's issue. It was to have been the climax of my presentation. I also made a mental note to make a trip into the plant on Sunday and remove all the copies from the office.

I think that my agreement to go along with the majority of my colleagues certainly showed that I am not only a leader, but also first and foremost a team player. However, I might have been more inclined to display my tenacity and willingness to stick to my guns by arguing the merits of the ad forcefully, had it not been for the latest developments in my stomach. The pressure in my bowels had increased almost to bursting point and disaster was imminent. I could feel the perspiration on my brow, and my fists were so tightly clenched that the nails were digging into my palms. It was imperative that I wrap up my presentation and get to the bathroom. I turned quickly and gathered up my overheads. One of them fell on the floor. I pretended not to notice it.

"Well, if there are nnnnno questions....." I said through my still tightly clenched teeth.

"Herr Dick!"

"Yes, Hans." I could not ignore Hans.

"I think you have let fall one of your overheads."

"Thank you, Hans." I could have wrung his neck. I had no choice but to retrieve the overhead slide from the floor. I started to bend down, but had got no further than 45 degrees, when I found myself prevented from bending any lower by the absurd tightness of the Ostrich's pants. What's more, the pressure of the waistband against my stomach was unbearable. I remained in that position, half bent over, for a couple of seconds, while I struggled for control of my bowels.

"Let me help you, Herr Dick."

Hans stood up and walked over to where I was standing in my painful stooping position. He picked up the overhead slide and handed it to me. As I stretched out my hand to take it from him, I failed to take into account the change that this would cause in my center of gravity. Still bent double, I began to topple forward. Due to the constraints on my movement caused by the Ostrich's dangerously tight pants, I was unable to straighten up in time to avoid a fall. However, where others might have panicked, I was able to call on my steady nerves in a crisis. I stretched out both arms and managed to balance myself on my hands and the balls of my feet, so that only my head hit the floor and I came to rest in a kind of jackknife position.

"Herr Dick, are you all right?"

"Yes thank you, Hans," I said with a degree of composure under difficult circumstances which must have impressed him. In fact this was not strictly true. I was not all right. I was vaguely aware of a pain in my head where it had struck the floor, but I paid it little attention. In my new position, the pressure on my bowels was even greater, and I was straining every muscle in my stomach to hold in their contents. It was imperative that I get to a bathroom immediately. Unfortunately, due to the constriction of the Ostrich's pants, I was unable to bend my legs enough to get up from the awkward pose in which I found myself. In these circumstances, it is hardly surprising that I grabbed the first thing I saw that might help me get back up from the floor. It was typical of my luck that this happened to be the electrical cord attached to the overhead projector, and that the projector was, as previously noted, balanced on a table of an irresponsibly unstable design. The table, of course, overbalanced, launching the projector through the same trajectory as it had previously taken toward the New England sales representative in the second row. Had he been paying attention, instead of indulging in some ill-mannered and inappropriate carrying on with Melissa, our lady salesman, he would have seen it coming and an unnecessary hospital stay could have been avoided. The table, meanwhile, landed on the small of my back with considerable force, causing me to jerk sharply backwards and upwards. To my surprise and relief, I found myself in an upright position again.

"Thank you for your attention," I said, and immediately walked back toward my seat at the back of the room. Everybody's attention now seemed to be on the New England sales representative, who was holding his head and moaning loudly. I continued past my seat and made toward the door.

"Great presentation, boss! I thought...."

I didn't hear the rest of Mike's comments. I was already outside the door and making my way toward the men's room a few yards along the hall. I burst in and made straight for the first stall. A moment later, I was inside and struggling with my belt. I was about to burst, but relief was close at hand. But when I tried to take down the Ostrich's pants, I found they were stuck fast. No matter how hard I pulled, they wouldn't move. My bowels, meanwhile, had slackened in anticipation of relief, and I knew that I could hold them back no longer. Just then, something gave. There was a slight ripping sound, and the Ostrich's pants finally moved down my legs. I sat down just in time and found relief at last. As I sat there, able once again to think clearly, I reflected that it would have served the Ostrich and his absurdly tight pants right if I hadn't made it.

Chapter 33

"It's a Jungle out there with Dog Eating Dog"

One of my greatest strengths is an ability to assess a situation, to see it from all angles and plot a winning course of action. This is what I set about doing as I sat in the bathroom stall and felt my constricted stomach muscles return to normal. My usual clear head also returned, and I began to weigh up the position.

There was no doubt that my presentation had not gone as well as it might. An unwise plate of shrimp and sheer bad luck had combined to hamper my performance. Distracted by my physical discomfort, I had not been able to deliver my message with the customary power. I had to admit to myself that I had missed a chance to cement my position as the next President of Pumpex-SuperPumps. It was a cruel blow.

I was at a low ebb, when my thoughts were disturbed by the slamming of a door and a tuneless whistling, which I recognized as belonging to the Ostrich. To judge by the jaunty melody he was attempting to whistle, he was feeling pretty good about things. My self control slipped for a moment, and I let out an involuntary snort of annoyance.

"Ah, T. J. That's where you are. You seemed to leave in a bit of a hurry. Wondered where you'd got to." The Ostrich's voice had that irritatingly supercilious tone that rubs me up the wrong way at the best of times. In my present frame of mind, it was too much. I snorted again, and it was a snort that would have made it clear to anyone with even an ounce of sensitivity that I wished to be left alone.

"You missed all the excitement, T. J. The ambulance has just left. Only concussion probably. Damned good shot though! You got him right between the eyes. Rich and I had a bit of a disagreement about your technique. He thinks you were aiming for him with your first shot, while I'm convinced that it was a kind of warning. Firing over his head. And then, when he still wouldn't behave himself, you let him have it. Bang. You nailed him with your overhead projectile."

I could tell he was pleased with his idiotic pun. I heard him chuckle. I decided to go out there and give him a good talking to, but when I tried to pull up his infuriatingly tight pants, I found myself unable to force them over my hips. I was obliged to listen to his demented ravings as I continued the struggle.

"Better not be too long, T. J. That young puppy of yours is making a presentation now. It kind of defeats the point if his boss isn't there for him to impress."

At last I managed to pull up the pants and, by breathing in deeply, fasten the button of the waistband. I pulled up the zipper, and the button flew off and landed in the toilet. I flushed with satisfaction and watched as the Ostrich's button disappeared down the pipe. Of course, I had no need of the button. The pants were so tight that there was no question of them falling down for want of a button. The next time that the Ostrich tried to wear them though, he would be in for an unpleasant surprise.

"I think those pants of mine helped your presentation, you know, T. J. Gave it more style."

I am not a violent man, but I was about ready to go out there and punch the Ostrich on the nose, when I heard the door of the stall next to mine close. He was safe for the moment in his cubicle. I took a deep breath, and decided that this was probably just as well. We Dicks are not what you would call big in the conventional sense, but we are wiry and powerful and, in the mood I was in, there was no way of saying what I might have done to a weedy geek like the Ostrich. I opened the door and walked over to the sink.

We Dicks are not only *wiry* but also *wily*. I did not get to be a senior executive in a top company just by being a first rate marketeer. It's a jungle out there with dog eating dog, and you have to have your wits about you and be ready for any opportunity. A grasp of this reality is essential to understanding why an executive of high professional and personal integrity would lock a colleague in the toilet.

Beside the sink was a cupboard containing mops, detergent and other cleaning supplies. And in the handle of the cupboard was a padlock with the key still in it. I looked over at the door of the stall. On the outside of the door was a small metal fixture with a hole in it, matched by a similar one on the frame. I assumed that this arrangement was for locking the door from the outside when the toilet was out of order. It was the work of a moment to remove the padlock from the cupboard and slip it through the holes in the two fixtures. My assumption was correct. I snapped the padlock shut, slipped the key into my pocket and quietly left the bathroom.

I do not generally whistle. It is an annoying habit for which I have little time, my mind usually being too occupied by far more important matters. However, I believe I was whistling, as I made my way back along the corridor to the Meeting Room. I took my seat at the back, folded my arms and leaned back in my chair. I am not the kind of person who smirks, but I came close to doing so, as I thought of the Ostrich's face when he realized he had been outwitted in the bathroom by T. John Dick.

Mike was making his presentation.

"So, as you can see, we have really come up with a winner this time," he said.

I was impressed. He spoke with confidence and was wearing a red tie.

"The new PZ-3 includes a whole list of new features, which are different and ..uh..new."

I really was impressed by Mike's tie. He wasn't wearing a suit, of course, since the dress code was casual, but that red power tie gave him an air of authority which was really quite impressive. As he spoke, I reflected on my own presentation. There was no actual harm done, of course. My form had been affected by my stomach problems, but I had carried it off well, and was pretty sure nobody had noticed anything amiss. The foolish incident with the overhead projector was certainly unfortunate, but it could hardly be said to be my fault. I had not been the one who had placed the projector on such an unstable and badly-designed table. No, I might have lost a chance to excel, but there was still all to play for. And when Hans noticed that the Ostrich had not returned from the men's room to hear the rest of Mike's presentation, exhibiting a lack of commitment and team spirit, the Dick star would shine still more brightly in comparison. I turned my attention back to Mike's presentation, noting approvingly his impressive pile of overhead slides. Somebody asked a question.

"What is it about these features that make the PZ-3 better than the PZ-2?"

"Yes," said Mike, rubbing his chin in a way that was reminiscent of myself in a thoughtful moment. "A good question. I'm glad you asked. Well, they're newer, of course. And a lot of them are features that the other whatsit didn't have."

There was a murmur of approval. Mike's answer seemed to go down well.

"Aren't these the same new products that Harvey introduced last year?" asked the Ostrich.

This was a typical smart-assed question of the kind you'd expect from him. Of course, Harvey might have touched on the PZ-3 at last year's meeting and probably even tried to take credit for it. But Mike was the one who had prepared the New Product Opportunity Analysis Form, without which the PZ-3 would just have been a thing we sold and not officially a product at all. I was so irritated that it took a moment to dawn on me that the Ostrich should not have been in any position to be asking questions. At least, not one that we could hear. I leaned to the side to get a better look at the front of the room past the rows of salesmen who were inconveniently blocking my view. There he was, large as life! The smug face. The moronic grin. If he was there, who was locked in the bathroom? I scanned the rows. All the seats seemed to be occupied. Then I noticed to my horror that the seat next to the Ostrich was empty. Hans! With an unpleasant sinking feeling, I realized the shocking truth. Through sheer bad luck and no fault of my own, I had locked the President of the company in the toilet.

A calm head in a crisis is, of course, one of my greatest strengths, but even I was taken aback by this realization. As calmly as I could, I thought through the probable chain of events. The Ostrich must have left the bathroom immediately following his stupid remark about his pants adding style to my presentation. I was so preoccupied with fighting the desire to punch him on the nose, that I had failed to hear him leave and Hans enter. The whole thing was typical of my luck. There could be no doubt that locking Hans in the toilet would threaten to undo much of the positive impression I had made on him in the preceding days. I had to figure out a way to get him out without him realizing that I had locked him in there in the first place.

I barely heard Mike's presentation, and for the next few minutes I was so deep in thought that at first it didn't register when Rich called my name.

"T. J."

"What?" I recovered quickly. "Yes, Rich?"

"Tell us when, then."

"When what?"

"When will the PZ-3 be in stock? When can they start taking orders? Mike says they should be available soon."

"Oh. Well, we're going to load up out front on this one and hit the ground running."

This seemed to satisfy everyone. There were more murmurs of approval, and I noticed a couple of the more dedicated and organized salesmen taking notes. I returned to the more urgent question of how to get Hans out of the bathroom. I would have to sneak out of the meeting room. This shouldn't be too difficult from my seat at the back. My departure would only be noticed by a couple of salesmen, nobody that mattered. I decided that my only chance would then be to slip quietly into the bathroom, remove the padlock and run before Hans could open the door and see me. It was risky of course, but I could see no other way out of this unfortunate situation. If I just left him in there until someone found him, the Ostrich, who had spoken to me in the bathroom just before Hans entered, would put two and two together and figure out who must have put the padlock on the door. If I was successful in carrying out my plan, on the other hand, Hans would probably assume that the door had somehow been jammed.

At moments of crisis like these, I am grateful for my nerves of steel. I am known as a man of action. Once I have formulated a plan, I waste no time in putting it into operation. At that moment, there was some lively discussion going on. Harvey had made the totally unhelpful remark that the PZ-3 had, in fact, been in stock for almost six months, directly contradicting Mike. Normally I would have had something to say about this lack of team spirit, but for now I was glad of the distraction, which I used to slip unobtrusively from the room. Once outside, I walked quickly along the corridor to the bathroom.

The door to the bathroom creaked slightly as I pushed it open. I froze in the doorway, half expecting to hear Hans call out. There was no noise from the stall. I let out a great sigh of relief.

"Hello. Is someone without?"

It was Hans' voice all right. I remained quite still, barely breathing.

"Please. My passage is blocked. Can you make me to come out?"

I stood rooted to the spot for what seemed like an age. The stall fell silent. I caught sight of myself in the mirror above the sinks. This was the first time I had ever had an opportunity to actually observe myself in a moment of crisis. I noted with some satisfaction that I looked calm and determined. At last I started to move forward in a catlike manner, slowly and stealthily. I reached the padlocked door and stuck my hand into my pocket to take out the key. Unfortunately, the unnatural tightness of the Ostrich's pants once again worked against me. I could not reach further than a couple of inches into the pocket. I tried to force my fingers down between my thigh and the stretched fabric, but it was no use. The key remained tantalizingly out of reach. I barely suppressed a cry of annoyance. I thought quickly. It was clear what I had to do. I unzipped the Ostrich's pants, and took a deep breath. It took a great deal of skill to lower the pants in silence, but with a lot of tugging and wriggling, I eventually succeeded in pulling them down to my knees.

What happened next was typical of my bad luck. I am convinced that I could have completed the operation as planned, if events had not conspired to prevent me from doing so. Hans would have been freed from his temporary confinement with no harm done and the blame put on a faulty door. We could all have gone about our business as if nothing had happened and the whole silly incident would have been forgotten, instead of being blown out of proportion and being used as an excuse for a lot of pointless discussion, distracting attention from the important business of the Sales Meeting.

I had just turned the key and silently removed the padlock, when the door to the bathroom swung open and the Ostrich walked in.

"T. J!" he said, with a look of astonishment on his silly face.

I have often thought it a great injustice that cruel luck and circumstances outside my control can, on occasion, conspire to make me look a little foolish, even when there is a perfectly rational explanation for the situation in which I find myself. I was immediately aware that this was one of those occasions, made worse by the fact that, although there was a rational explanation, it was not one I could easily use to explain why I was standing in the middle of the bathroom with my pants down around my knees and a padlock in my hand. I would have to do some quick thinking.

I have already mentioned my ability to keep a cool head in a crisis, which this certainly was, and I am sure that I would have come up with a convincing explanation, had I been given the chance. As things turned out, however, I had little opportunity to say anything.

"T. J!" the Ostrich repeated stupidly.

"Ah, Ronnie," I replied. "I'm glad you're here."

At that moment the door of the stall containing Hans flew open and struck me very hard on the head. The Seabreeze Inn is a high class luxury resort, constructed of the finest materials throughout. The toilet door, being made of solid oak, delivered an extremely powerful blow. I started to fall backwards, and then everything went black.

Chapter 34

"In Marketing we have to Take a Long Term View"

I am not the kind of person who makes a habit of remembering dreams. My mind is far too busy with business insights to have time for such things. I must have been dreaming particularly vividly because of the blow to my head. I was in the Ostrich's office, only it wasn't his office. It was bigger, with a bigger desk, more comfortable chairs. It was Rich's office, but the Ostrich was sitting in Rich's chair. His eyes had a penetrating intensity, as he looked down on me from behind his desk. I was not occupying one of the comfortable chairs. I was sitting on a tiny little stool in front of his desk. I tried to avoid his stare by looking past him at the wall, but everywhere were pictures of the Ostrich, shaking hands with the President of the Pumpex Group, opening a new building, accepting a Nobel Prize, setting foot on Mars. All the pictures seemed to stare at me. My pants were very tight.

"Well, T. J. Sales are down again." His voice was deeper than usual.

"Yes. The market's very weak right now. If you care to look at these charts I...."

"Damn your charts, T. J."

"Yes, Ronnie. Of course."

"Of course what?"

"Damn my charts, Ronnie."

"Yes. I was talking to the President of International Pumps yesterday. His sales are up.

"Ah yes, but...."

"Clayton Sipe says his sales are up on everything except our pumps. Why is that T. J.?"

"Well, as you know, we inherited a sorry situation, when we bought SuperPumps. In a turnaround situation, there is always..."

"Damn it, T. J. SuperPumps was making money when we bought it."

"In the short term, yes. But in Marketing we have to take a long term view."

"Nice pants."

"Thank you, Ronnie."

"You're fired."

I awoke with a start to find myself in my room, with no recollection of how I had got there. It was dark. My head was spinning and I had a loud ringing in my ears. I turned and rolled toward the edge of the bed. The ringing got louder. I swung my legs over the side of the bed in an effort to get up, and in doing so knocked the telephone off the bedside table. To my relief the ringing in my ears stopped. I sat on the edge of the bed holding my head. It hurt a lot. And now I was hearing voices in the dark. Very faint.

"T. J."

"Yes" I said as boldly as I could manage. We Dicks are not the kind of people to be scared of voices in the dark. If there was any unsteadiness in my voice, it was due to the pain in my head.

"T. J." The voice was a little louder but still very faint. It sounded agitated, as if it had been trying to communicate for some time.

"Yes. Who's there. Show yourself."

"Pick up the damn phone, you idiot."

I picked up the phone.

"Hello."

"Are you OK, T. J? You still sound a bit groggy."

"What?"

"You sound like you're still a bit dazed. You were out cold, you know."

"You can't fire me."

"I wouldn't dream of it."

Dream of it. Of course! It had all been a terrible dream. In a second it all came back to me. The incident in the bathroom. The blow to the head. The Ostrich continued:

"We thought we'd better leave you to sleep it off. You know, T. J., that head of yours comes in for a staggering amount of wear and tear in the course of an average month."

I had no time for idle chit-chat. My senses had returned, and I knew I had to find out what had happened after my unfortunate blow to the head. Of course, the Ostrich wasted no time in telling me, although, as usual with him, I had considerable difficulty following his drift.

"You gave rise to quite a vigorous debate, you know, T. J. It's like one of those lateral thinking puzzles. You know, like the one about the man who lives on the twenty-fifth floor of an apartment building, and every morning he gets into the elevator and presses the button for the first floor, but when he comes home in the evening he hits the button for the twentieth floor, gets out there and walks the last five flights of stairs. You have to say why he does this, and it turns out he's a midget. Can't reach the button for the twenty-fifth floor."

Listening to the Ostrich's ravings was not helping the pain in my head.

"Or the one where Romeo and Juliet are found dead in the middle of the room with a pool of water and some broken glass. Turns out they're goldfish and someone knocked their bowl over. You know the kind of thing. Only this time, there's a Vice President of Marketing standing in the middle of the bathroom with his pants down. I guessed that a very style-conscious thief had taken a fancy to my pants, followed you to the bathroom and tried to take them from you at gunpoint. He must have heard me opening the door and made a lightning fast exit through the window. Rich pointed out a few flaws in this theory though. For one thing, there was no window. He reckoned you had discovered a deadly spider, which had somehow got inside your pants. Hans wondered if you were mad, but we assured him that this was quite normal, and there was bound to be a rational explanation. "With T. J. there's always a rational explanation," we said."

There was a pause. I was thinking.

"Well?" said the Ostrich.

"Well what?"

"What's the explanation?"

"I've forgotten."

"Forgotten?"

"The blow to my head. It's made me forget. Amnesia."

"Oh come on, T. J!"

"No really. I have no memory of the incident. Probably only temporary memory loss. It'll come back to me."

This was, of course, a clever stratagem on my part, allowing me to buy time to come up with a convincing explanation.

"Well, if you say so, T. J. By the way, have you any idea how Hans came to be stuck in the bathroom?"

"No." I immediately realized that this meant that nobody had found the padlock. It must have rolled away into a corner when I dropped it after being hit on the head. For once Fortune was on my side. "The door must have jammed."

"Hmm, yes. I suppose so. Anyway, get a good night's sleep. Maybe your memory will come back in the morning."

I had laid back on the bed, but now I sat up with a start. I must have been asleep for hours. It was night time. I had missed the golf.

"It's night time. I've missed the golf!"

"Right and wrong there, T. J."

"What?" I said in a voice that must have made clear my exasperation at his silly word games. With his inability to come quickly to the point, the Ostrich would certainly never have made it in marketing.

"Right on the first count. It is night time. Ten thirty-seven to be precise. Wrong on the second count. The golf was canceled. We had a bit of a downpour this afternoon. Completely rained out."

"So, I didn't miss the golf."

"As usual, T. J., you have a brilliant grasp of the situation."

I let this feeble attempt at sarcasm go. The Ostrich continued:

"And if you're feeling up to it, you get to plow up the course tomorrow morning instead."

"But what about the Team-Building Exercise? Pratt and Poziemski?"

"Oh, that's been canceled. It seems that the facilitators had a bit of a falling out. I understand it had something to do with royalties for their latest book, *Pulling Together*. Have you read it?"

"No."

"A load of crap apparently. Anyway, Pratt reckoned he had contributed more to the book than Poziemski and deserved a larger share of the royalties. This didn't go down too well with Poziemski, who figured that Pratt's contributions were a lot of hot air and only served to get in the way of the reader's understanding of his concise and hard-hitting ideas. Anyway, the upshot of it all was that they got together in the bar tonight to iron out their differences, and Pratt punched Poziemski on the nose."

"What?"

"Yes. Rich was there. Saw the whole thing."

This was staggering news. I was a great admirer of Pratt and Poziemski. I had bought a copy of their latest book and, although I had not yet found time in my busy schedule to read it, I had been inspired by their two previous works, *Together We Can Do It, You Know.* and *Teamwork—The Key to Organizational Success.* I had recommended Pratt and Poziemski to Ken, when he was looking for some way to fill the afternoon of the second day of the Sales Meeting. This was certainly a blow. I had been depending on the Team Building Exercise as a chance to show my leadership skills. During a similar exercise at a gathering of key staff at Pumpex Corporate H.Q., my team of senior executives had devised the most efficient means of lowering an egg to the ground from the top of a ladder without breaking it, using only paper, a strictly limited supply of tape, two rubber bands, a length of twine and our own ingenuity and teamwork. It was an inspiring experience, and we all bonded, learned to respect each other's talents and developed a team spirit, which would certainly have made us a formidable force for advancing the company's goals if we had ever seen each other again.

Marketing is a discipline that constantly demands vision and ingenuity, and I have often had occasion to call upon the lessons I learned in lowering that egg safely to the ground with the help of my peers. Just in case they made us do the same exercise again, I had dug out the notes and sketches my team had made the last time. I had been confident of shining and displaying my leadership qualities. The Ostrich had not been at the exercise at H.Q.

"It's probably a good thing it's canceled," said the Ostrich. "They'd probably just have made us do that egg thing."

"What! How do you know about that?"

"The egg thing? Oh, they all make you do that. Jerry in Human Resources told me. They don't have a lot of imagination, these motivational consultants. It's a bit of a shame though. I went to the trouble of obtaining a hard boiled egg, just in case. Needn't have bothered, as it turns out."

I sucked my breath in sharply to indicate my disapproval of the Ostrich's underhand tactics. If he noticed, he gave no indication.

"I'll see you on the first tee at 8:30 sharp, T. J."

"What do you mean? You're not in my group."

"Well actually I am, as it turns out. After you took out that guy with one blow of your deadly overhead projector, we had to make a few changes. You're playing with Hans, Ken and me. See you tomorrow. Sleep well."

As I hung up the phone, my mind was awhirl with conflicting thoughts and feelings. On the positive side, luck had for once been with me. If I had not dropped the padlock when I fell, I would have had a very hard time coming up with a convincing explanation for the afternoon's incident. It was one thing to have to explain why you were standing in the bathroom with your pants down, and quite another to have to explain why you were standing in the bathroom with your pants down and a padlock in your hand when the President of the company had been stuck in the toilet for half an hour. The padlock was the key, or the lack of it. Without it, there was nothing to connect me with my pants down to Hans' confinement in the cubicle. They could be treated as two separate matters. I lay back on the bed and smiled. Explaining the pants situation would not be difficult for a man with my imagination. You don't get to be a senior marketing executive without a keenly inventive mind. In fact, I already had an explanation that was beautiful in its simplicity. The tightness of the Ostrich's pants having become unbearable, I had sought relief by retiring to the privacy of the bathroom to take them down for a moment. That was what I would tell the Ostrich, Rich and the others. That would put a stop to their ridiculous speculation and tittle-tattle. I snorted contemptuously at the thought of the Ostrich's theory. What kind of a thief would take a fancy to *those pants*?

There would be no reason why Hans should doubt my explanation either. And that was the most important thing. My dream had shaken me, and I shuddered now to think of it. I couldn't let the Ostrich beat me. I had to become the next President of Pumpex-SuperPumps. And if I was to do this, I would have to pull out all the stops tomorrow. I went through to the bathroom and spread toothpaste onto my toothbrush. As I did this, I caught sight of myself in the mirror. I was encouraged to see a steely glint in my eyes.

Chapter 35

"My Ability to Take Command and Get Things Done"

I recently read an article in a women's magazine about the difficulties of being a woman married to a successful man. I am not in the habit of reading women's magazines, but I happened to be at the hairdresser's for my weekly trim and it was the only reading material provided for waiting customers. Since then, I have always made it a habit to bring with me a copy of *Marketing Magazine* when I visit the hairdresser's. I am a very busy man and do not have time to waste reading about dieting or orgasms. On this occasion however, I was faced with the choice of staring at photographs on the wall of people with hairstyles or leafing through the magazine. I chose the magazine.

One of the strengths of our marriage is my sensitivity to Grace's feelings and needs. I firmly believe that a modern husband should take his wife's concerns seriously, no matter how trivial they may actually be. So, naturally, I read the article carefully and was surprised by its striking relevance to Grace and me. The author gave the example of Tony, a successful senior executive, and his wife, Angela, who had problems dealing with her husband's success. The article was a revelation. Grace has often commented that it is not easy being married to someone like me. I had never really understood these remarks before and had shrugged them off as her just being silly again. Suddenly, they made sense. It cannot be easy to be in the shadow of an over-achieving husband. Like Angela, she was bound sometimes to feel inadequate. Angela also envied what she saw as Tony's glamorous lifestyle of important meetings, vital business trips and crucial working lunches. This, of course, was symptomatic of her failure to understand the pressures faced every day by top-flight executives like Tony and me. Her inability to deal rationally with her feelings was driving a wedge between her and Tony and threatening to break up their marriage. The article suggested several ways to overcome Tony and Angela's problems. In my opinion, the author could have placed more emphasis on Angela's need not to be so damn silly, stop nagging and clean the house occasionally. A word or two about laying off the booze wouldn't have been a bad idea, either. And a bit more gratitude for the tasteful executive house in an exclusive upscale neighborhood wouldn't have been out of place. However, one tip that I took on board was that, while on business trips, Tony should always take time to call home as often as his schedule would allow, and listen sensitively to Angela's concerns. This was what I decided to do when I woke early the next morning.

"Hello."

"It's me, honey."

"What?"

"How are you?"

"T. J. It's half past four in the morning."

I had not realized how early it was. The blow to my head and subsequent period of unconsciousness had caused a malfunction of my biological clock.

"Oh, sorry. Were you asleep?"

"Of course I was asleep." Her voice had an unnecessary sharpness about it.

"I was just calling to ask you if you had any concerns you wanted to talk to me about."

"Oh for God's sake, T. J.! What's all this about?"

Angela had not reacted like this. Her reaction to Tony's thoughtfulness and consideration had been a lot more positive.

"I thought maybe you might want to discuss some domestic problem or other. Something that's cropped up while I've been away."

"No."

"Nothing at all?"

"No, nothing."

"Oh, well that's good then."

"Yes."

"Yes. What's that noise?" I could hear a kind of rhythmic rasping sound. A bit like somebody snoring.

"What noise?"

"I don't know. Sounds a bit like someone snoring."

"Oh, that. It's the ceiling fan. I have the ceiling fan on, and it must need oiling or something. It makes a funny kind of a noise."

"Hmm, yes. I see what you mean," I said. "It seemed to change to more of a grunt just there. And now it seems to have stopped."

"I've turned it off. So that I can hear you better."

I was silent for a moment. I often find that a well placed moment of silence adds weight to your words when you have something important that has to be said. I sighed and said:

"You could have told me, you know. I would have understood."

"Told you what, T. J?"

"About the fan. This is precisely the kind of thing I want you to tell me about. It's a concern, isn't it? A problem?"

"Well, yes."

"It may need more than just oiling. A screw may have worked loose. Maybe too short. That's what it sounded like."

As it happened, I was a bit of an expert on fans. I continued:

"The secret with these babies is to make sure they're well oiled and have a good long screw."

"It always works for me," she giggled.

"What?"

"Oh nothing."

"If they're not well oiled, they can make a really irritating squealing sound."

"Mmf!" It sounded like her face was buried in the pillow.

"It's not funny, Grace. The arms could fly off and cause serious injury."

"Mmmffagh!"

"Are you all right?"

"Yes, yes. Fine."

For some reason, she appeared to be crying. I applied some of the sensitivity that had worked so well for Tony.

"I'll be back soon, honey. And I'll fix the fan. Don't worry. Then you'll be able to get a good night's sleep, undisturbed."

"I know."

"In the meantime, if you get hot, just turn up the air conditioning."

"Yes, T. J. I know what to do when I get hot. How's your little meeting going?"

It irritated me that she should refer to something as important as the National Sales Meeting as "your little meeting," but I was being sensitive.

"Just fine." There was no need to worry her with details about my concussion.

"Any serious injuries?"

"No." This was not a lie. At the time I had no indication that the New England salesman's injury was anything more than a minor bump.

"Good."

"What's that noise?" I asked.

"What noise?"

"It sounded like somebody flushing the commode."

"That? Oh that's the air conditioning. It's started making these strange noises."

I was beginning to be very glad I had called. It seemed that Grace had some real concerns for me to be sensitive to.

"I'll take a look at it when I get home," I said. Then I added with a sensitivity that I think she appreciated:

"In the meantime, if you get too hot, get somebody in to see to it."

"I will, T. J. Don't you worry."

I hung up the phone with some satisfaction. Sensitivity, I realized, was one of my greatest strengths. I looked at the clock. Ten past five. I had almost three and a half hours before I was due to tee off. I wasn't tired. There was no point in going back to bed. I decided to get dressed and take a walk before breakfast. This would give me a chance to prepare myself psychologically for the game ahead. As I removed my golfing outfit from the wardrobe, I reflected that I had not got to be a successful top executive in a dynamic marketing-oriented company without preparation.

I had spared no expense in my golfing wardrobe. The golf match was one of my best chances to catch Hans' eye, and it seemed to me that it would be to my advantage to do so in classy attire. Everything was new, from the Arnold Palmer cap to the shiny white Foot-Joys. I looked in the mirror. I certainly looked like the kind of man you would want to head up a subsidiary of a top class international company. The sharp crease in my pants, the muted pink of my shirt—everything was casual, understated elegance. I walked over to the window and watched the sun rise over the ocean. It was a beautiful morning, and my instinct told me that soon a new day would dawn for Pumpex-SuperPumps too. I felt the old confidence return. Things may not have gone as well as planned yesterday but this was a new day full of new opportunities. It was up to me to seize them for the good of everyone at SuperPumps.

I took off my golf shoes, slipped on my sneakers, also brand new, and walked out into the cool air of the morning. The Seabreeze consists of a collection of what they call cottages along the shore on either side of the main building. Each is named after a bird. My room was in Puffin Cottage. I chuckled as I walked down to the shore, wondering if there was an Ostrich Cottage.

Those who know me well are aware that there are many sides to my character. I am what you might call a Renaissance Man. The pressures and responsibilities of executive life leave me little time to indulge my more spiritual side, although a glance at the impressionist prints in my home would leave little doubt of my cultured mind. Anyone who knew T. John Dick only as a razor sharp executive and top class marketeer might have been surprised to see me walking along the shore in the early morning responding to nature. The breeze ruffled my hair. The smell of the sea filled my nostrils. Some kind of big white birds made squawking sounds overhead. I was alone on the shore with my thoughts.

There would certainly be some changes at SuperPumps under a Dick regime. Far reaching changes that would set the company on the right track for the twenty-first century. For a start there would be a greater emphasis on quality and teamwork. I had in mind a T-shirt to be given to all employees with *Pumpex-SuperPumps—The Quality Team* written on it. And everyone would soon learn that I ran a tighter ship than Rich. No more ignoring the Meeting Room Procedure. And I would need a bigger desk. The one in Rich's office would have to go. There would have to be some personnel changes of course. I was just reflecting on the words I would use to the Ostrich while leaning back in my new leather executive chair and explaining to him that his services were no longer required, when something landed on my head. I reached up and touched what felt

219

like a raw egg. I looked at my fingers and then up at the big white birds circling above me.

Luckily I had plenty of time before breakfast. I would just have to go back to my room and have a shower. I walked quickly in the direction of Puffin Cottage. The bird dropping was beginning to run down my forehead and onto my face. In less than a minute I was standing at my door feeling for my key.

"Good morning, Herr Dick."

"Ah, Hans!"

"Herr Dick, you appear to be shitfaced!"

"What? Oh, yes, I see what you mean. I just got dive bombed down on the beach. Not that I mean anything offensive to you as a German, by referring to dive bombing," I added sensitively.

"You mean a bird has shitten on your head?"

"Yes."

"You should go and wash your hair."

"I'm going to right now, Hans. Thank you."

"How is your head? Apart of course from the shitting on it."

"Fine, thanks. A bit of bruising. Nothing to worry about."

"I am glad. I am sorry that I hit it. The door was stuck. If I had known that you were standing behind it with your trouser down, I would not have pushed so hard."

"Yes, I should explain about that. The pants were too tight, you see."

"That makes no sense, Herr Dick. Too loose they fall down. Too tight they stay up. Is it not?"

"No, you don't understand. They were too tight, so I took them down."

"Ah."

"Yes, I couldn't breathe properly."

"I thought that you looked strange during your presentation. Was that because you could not breathe?"

"Ah, yes. Yes, it was." Who would have believed that my intestinal troubles would turn out to my advantage. I had been sure that nobody had noticed anything wrong. "That's what it was. Yes."

"At the time, I had been thinking you were needing to go to the bathroom."

"Ha, ha, ha!" I laughed airily. "Ha, ha! That's very funny Hans. That German sense of humor again. No, it was the pants. Absurdly tight!"

"So you were standing in the bathroom breathing, when I hit you on the head?"

"Yes."

"With your trouser down?"

"Yes."

"I still do not understand why it was so stiff."

"What?"

"The door. It was stiff. Then suddenly it opens."

"Ah yes. Those doors do that sometimes. I noticed it earlier. Had a hell of a job getting out."

"But I went last night with no difficulty."

"It only does it sometimes you see. Other times it's fine."

"We must complain to the manager, Herr Dick."

"Yes. I'll go and see him after breakfast."

"No, I mean now. Here he is now."

Hans was pointing to a tall, thin balding man walking up the beach toward us. He was wearing swimming trunks and was rubbing what there was of his hair with a towel."

"Good morning, gentlemen," he said when he came within range.

"Good morning," said Hans.

"I have a serious complaint to make," I said. Here was a chance to show Hans that I knew how to deal with people and take control of a situation presidentially.

"Oh. I'm sorry to hear that. What seems to be the problem?"

"Nothing *seems* to be the problem. I'll tell you what *is* the problem! A sticking door, that's what."

The manager reached in front of me and pushed open the door to my room. He swung it to and fro a couple of times. "Seems OK to me."

"Not that door." This man was exasperating. "The one in the bathroom."

"Oh, I'll get someone to fix it right away."

"Good. See that you do."

"I will. Have a pleasant day, gentlemen."

"Thank you. I will see you later, Herr Dick."

"Yes, Hans. Can't wait to get out on the course!"

In my room, I undressed quickly, taking care not to get any of the bird dropping on my shirt as I pulled it over my head. A moment later I was in the shower, whistling *Deutschland Über Alles* as I washed my hair. Despite the inconvenience of the bird dropping (a top class hotel really ought to be able to do something about birds), the day had started remarkably well. I had cleared up any misunderstanding in Hans' mind regarding the previous day's incident. *He* had apologized to *me*! And I had had a chance to show my ability to take command and get things done. And we hadn't even had breakfast yet! By the time I emerged from the shower, I was singing *Oh What a Beautiful Morning* at the top of my voice. I had just reached the part about everything going my way, and was standing naked by the bed, when I noticed a large black man in overalls in the middle of the room. I was somewhat taken aback by the sight and naturally took him for an intruder, being aware of no other satisfactory explanation for the presence of a large black man where previously there had been none. I soon recovered my composure however, and spoke boldly.

"Who are you?"

"Sam, sir."

I was not expecting a polite intruder. Still, polite or not, there was nothing to be gained by unnecessary heroics. I am not lacking in courage, as anyone who knows me well can tell you. But there were too many people depending on me for me to risk my life foolishly.

"Here, take it," I said, lifting my wallet from the bedside table, pulling out three hundred dollars and handing it to him. "It's all I have."

As he took it, his eyes opened wide with surprise. I guessed he hadn't expected such a rich haul and was thanking his luck that he had stumbled into a top executive's room. If only he knew that I had another three hundred in my wallet! You have to get up pretty early to get the better of T. John Dick!

"Thank you, sir."

"Now get out."

"But what about the door?"

"The door?"

"Yes. I came to fix the door. The manager said there was a guy in room four in Puffin with shit on his head that couldn't get into his bathroom. Said the door was stuck."

"What?"

"Yes. He said I'd better get over here right away, 'cos the guy needed to shower."

"You're not an intruder."

"No sir. I'm Maintenance."

"Maintenance?"

"Yes sir. Let's have a look at the door."

"There's nothing wrong with the door."

"So I see. Did you fix it yourself?"

"No, there wasn't anything wrong with it."

"The Manager said you told him it was stuck."

"Not this door, you fool! The one in the Conference Center."

"Well, why did you say this one was?"

"I didn't, you idiot."

"The Manger said you did. And I don't think there's any need for name calling, sir."

This guy was too much to take. The cheek of a maintenance man talking to an executive like that!

"Give me back my three hundred dollars."

"No, sir."

"What do you mean, 'No, sir?'"

"You gave it to me." After a moment he added "Sir".

"That was when....Oh, never mind. Just give it back you big ape!"

"No sir. You gave it to me and I'm keeping it. And I don't have to stick around to listen to you calling me names. Good-bye sir."

He opened the door to my room and stepped out, closing the door behind him. In a flash I was out the door after him. He saw me and began running along the path toward the main building of the hotel. I started after him and would certainly have caught him, for we Dicks are noted for our speed, and the maintenance man was carrying a lot of extra pounds. However, just as I was closing on him I collided with somebody carelessly coming out from his room. I fell heavily on top of him and we ended up in a tangle of limbs on the footpath.

"What the....Ah, T. J. Of course."

Just what the Ostrich meant by 'Ah, T. J. Of course' I didn't know. What I did know was that by not looking where he was going he had allowed the maintenance man to escape.

"You let him get away," I said angrily.

223

"Did I? Oh, sorry." He watched the maintenance man disappearing into the distance. "I hope you don't mind me asking, T. J., but why are you chasing a black man naked around the neighborhood."

"He came to my room and I gave him three hundred dollars and he just took off."

"I see," said the Ostrich, in a tone of voice that suggested he didn't. "Well, T. J., I'm not one to judge, but surely there's a time and place for everything."

"What?"

"Well, if you want to pay men to come to your room and ....well that's none of my business. But at 6 o'clock in the morning, at the National Sales Meeting. Hardly the time or place."

This was an outrageous insinuation. It was typical of someone like the Ostrich to leap to such a ridiculous conclusion.

"No, no, no!" I said emphatically. "I didn't pay him to come to my room. He turned up there to fix the bathroom door."

"What was wrong with it?"

"Nothing."

"Well why did he have to fix it then?"

"He didn't. It was all a mistake."

"So you gave him three hundred dollars."

"I thought he was an intruder. I was taking a shower and when I came out, he was there in the room."

"Was it a cold shower?"

"No. Why?"

"Oh, nothing. I was just wondering. If I were you, I'd go back and get some pants on. I can lend you some if you need them. I'm not sure of the dress code at this golf course, but it's a fair bet they'd draw the line at bare-assed naked."

In all the excitement of the chase I had forgotten that I was completely naked.

"Oh my God!" I said and scrambled to my feet. I hurried off toward Puffin Cottage. As I ran I heard the Ostrich yell:

"Good for you, T. J. Keep practicing that swing!" It was, I thought, exactly the kind of remark you would expect from a man like the Ostrich.

Chapter 36

"The Business of Being Leaders"

We Dicks are known for our indomitable spirit. When my illustrious forebear Henry Dick, known as the Navigator, was negotiating a route through the ice floes of Hudson Bay, he remained steadfast and undaunted by the cold and the danger. It is recorded that while passengers and crew huddled below, he remained on deck, plotting a course by the stars. Nor was he deflected by the constant complaints of the passengers who had paid for a passage from England to Boston, and although the Northern Route, as he named it, is seldom used today, there is no denying him his place amongst the great pioneering seafarers. When he was discovered frozen to the wheel that January morning in 1837, the symbolism was not lost on those present. Even in death he clung to leadership, ready to guide the ship to its destination.

"See how the great Dick clings to the wheel!" the first mate was heard to cry. It was not until they were sailing along the coast of Maine that my ancestor thawed out enough to separate him from the wheel. Until then he was always there next to the helmsman, an ever present inspiration, his face frozen in an encouraging smile.

I tell this story not to boast of my ancestry but because I think some of the Navigator's indomitable spirit has come down to me through the generations, and this will make it easier to understand how I was able to take the incident with the Ostrich and the maintenance man in my stride. Leaders like Henry and myself just seem to have this ability to shake off stuff like this, put it in perspective and get on with the business of being leaders. If I was to take the helm of SuperPumps, I could not allow myself to be distracted by trivial incidents like this. Besides, there was no real harm done. I would talk to the manager later and have the maintenance man fired after returning my three hundred dollars. I had been forced to put up with the Ostrich's silly jokes and I had no doubt that I would have to listen to more of them before he tired of the whole business, but just as Henry had put up with the whining passengers, I could put up with a few stupid jokes, consoled by the thought of the Ostrich trying to be nice to me before I fired him.

It was in the best of spirits, then, that I walked into the restaurant for breakfast. There was no sign of Hans or Rich, so I decided to sit with Mike, Harvey and Rachel who were occupying a table by the window. It would certainly do no harm, should Hans walk in later, to be seen surrounded by my team, as at home amongst the Product Managers of the world as I am amongst Vice Presidents. The common touch has always been a key part of my management style.

"Good morning, team!" I said sharing a friendly smile with everyone. "Beautiful day for golf. Are you all looking forward to playing?"

"You bet, chief!" said Mike. I noticed he was wearing a muted pink shirt just like mine.

"Pass the coffee please, Harvey," said Rachel.

"You know, Rachel," I smiled at her. "I've seen some pretty good lady golfers. Girls that really didn't embarrass themselves at all. And anyway, it doesn't really matter. It's all just for fun."

Rachel gave me one of those peculiar looks she has, which I can never quite figure out. I decided that it was a look of gratitude for my easing her fears about looking foolish on the course compared to the men. It really was becoming apparent that sensitivity was one of my greatest strengths.

"What about you, Harvey?" I noticed that Harvey didn't appear to be dressed for golf at all. Perhaps he didn't know any better. Probably he wasn't familiar with the standard of dress expected at the better clubs. Still, even Harvey should have realized that a T-shirt would hardly do.

"I'm not playing," he said.

"What do you mean? Everyone's got to play."

"I can't."

"I don't care if you can't play. You'll play anyway. It's an opportunity to bond with the sales force. Who's he playing with Mike?"

"Who are you playing with, Harvey?" asked Mike.

"No, you don't understand...."

"I think we'll be the judges of whether we understand or not, thank you, Harvey," said Mike with an authority that left no doubt that he was settling into his managerial role well.

"It's not that I can't play. It's that I can't play *today*."

"Oh really?" I said with just the right level of sarcasm to indicate who would decide who in the Marketing Department could and could not play today. "And why not?"

"Yes, why not?" said Mike.

"There's been a bit of a problem with those PXs we sold to Pumps-R-Us. Someone's got to go down there, calm down Clayton Sipe and get them working."

"And I suppose you think that's more important than bonding with the sales force?" I said.

"Yes."

This was not the answer I had expected. It was pure insolence. Before I could respond, he went on:

"Anyway it doesn't matter what I think...."

"You're damned right it doesn't matter what you think," I said, controlling my fury.

"Everything all right here?"

I had not seen Rich approach the table.

"Yes, Rich. Just fine." I saw no reason to give Rich the idea that I didn't have my department under control.

"Are you ready to go, Harvey?"

"Yes, right after breakfast. I just need to change."

"Good. Well good luck then, and we'll see you this evening."

Rich headed off in the direction of the buffet. Harvey got to his feet.

"See you later," he said and started toward the door.

"Just you see that you do." I said. It wasn't the greatest parting shot, but I felt that it was important to leave Harvey in no doubt who was in command here.

"Yes," said Mike. "See that you do."

"It really didn't matter what he thought," said Rachel unnecessarily. "Rich and Hans told him to go. Seems he's the only one the customer trusts."

"Yes, yes." I said, jabbing my fork into a sausage, as I watched Harvey go. He had his back to me, so I couldn't see his expression. But I could imagine it, and I didn't like it one bit.

Chapter 37

"We Always Like to Promote from Within the Company"

I soon put the incident with Harvey behind me. The only thing that bothered me was Rich's readiness to take Harvey's side against his Department Head in what I considered a most unprofessional way. Not that it really mattered, of course. When Rich moved back to Corporate, there would be nobody for Harvey to shelter behind and he would soon learn the consequences of crossing swords with T. John Dick. I imagined him and the Ostrich together taking that long last walk across the parking lot with arms full of the personal items from their desks, as I watched through the window of my office, before swinging my executive chair round to face the future. Still Rich's attitude did bother me just a little, so I decided to take the bull by the horns and mention it to him over breakfast. I excused myself from Mike and Rachel and strolled over to where Rich had just taken a seat by himself.

"Mind if I join you, Rich?"

"Not at all, T. J. Pull up a seat. Ronnie and Ken should be here in a few minutes."

The prospect of taking breakfast with the Ostrich did not appeal to me. I reflected that it probably didn't appeal much to Rich either, which was why he was anxious for me to join him. I sat down, but before I could even begin to explain my concerns about the Harvey incident, Rich said:

"Sorry about the thing with Harvey just now. This whole problem with Clayton Sipe just blew up yesterday and I didn't like to bother you with it at the time, as you were unconscious. I tried to get in touch with you this morning, but I met Ronnie on my way to your room and he suggested I shouldn't disturb you as you had some private business to attend to with Sam the maintenance man."

"He would!" I muttered.

"Yes, I didn't quite grasp the whole story. As far as I could gather you had devised some kind of fitness routine which involved giving the maintenance man three hundred dollars and then running after him in an attempt to get it back. I confess I couldn't understand the bit about being naked. Do you give the maintenance man your clothes too?"

I was about to explain to Rich that the whole thing was a silly misunderstanding, blown out of all proportion by the Ostrich, as usual, but before I could do so, he continued:

"Anyway, I didn't mean to keep you in the dark about it. It seemed that sending Harvey was the best thing to do. After all, we could hardly send you."

It was true that Harvey would hardly be missed, while I was a vital part of the National Sales Meeting.

"No, of course not," I said.

"The man threatened to set his dogs on you, remember?"

I took a gulp of my coffee. Rich continued:

"By the way, T. J., I take it you've heard the rumors about me going back up to Corporate?"

"Well, yes. I had heard something."

"Yes. It seems to be all round the company. Well, you might as well know it's true."

He paused. He seemed to be waiting for something.

"We'll all miss you Rich. You'll be a hard man to replace."

"Thank you, T. J. I suppose you know that Hans has been asked to nominate a successor."

"Really? I hadn't given it much thought."

"Hmm, well he's going to have to make up his mind soon. I'll be leaving in three weeks. I'll be announcing my departure at the Awards Dinner tonight."

"Any idea who he might have in mind?" I asked casually.

"I don't know if he's made a decision yet, but you know we always like to promote from within the company."

I did not know this, but I didn't say anything. I nodded in agreement. If this was the policy, it suited me just fine. At that moment I spotted the

Ostrich and Ken at the door to the restaurant. The Ostrich waved with that irritating cheerfulness of his. I was sure that he would be just bursting with stupid remarks about the incident with the maintenance man. When people like the Ostrich get hold of something like this, they don't bother with any perfectly rational explanation behind it. They just blow it out of all proportion and use it as an excuse to try to make somebody look foolish, no matter how unjustified this may be.

"Good morning, Rich," said the Ostrich. "And greetings to our modern Olympian."

I did not look up, but continued to concentrate on the piece of toast on which I was spreading grape jelly.

"I apologize, T. J., for not recognizing the significance of your nude athleticism. It could, of course only have been a tribute to the great sportsmen of Ancient Greece."

I sighed. I don't think the significance of the sigh was lost on Rich. He could identify it as the kind of sigh of resignation you might hear from someone about to have to listen a foolish and immature joke from a small child. Of course, the sigh had no effect on the Ostrich.

"Do you have Greek blood in you, T. J.?"

"Of course not," I said, continuing to spread the grape jelly.

"Ha-aargh!" said Ken suddenly and loudly, making us all jump.

"What the hell was that?" asked Rich.

"Oh, don't worry," said the Ostrich. "It's just that it hurts his jaw to laugh. You really must try not to be so funny, T. J. It's not fair."

"I fail to see anything funny," I said coolly. With that, I rose from the table and said, "I'll see you later, Rich."

"See you on the first tee, T. J.," said the Ostrich. "Don't be late."

I ignored him and walked out of the restaurant with what must have been impressive dignity.

Chapter 38

"People Should Have More Respect for the National Sales Meeting"

The weather forecast called for a very hot day and it was already beginning to warm up when I arrived at the golf course after a pleasant ten minute stroll from the hotel. I was the first of our foursome to arrive, and the previous foursome comprising two salesmen, Rich and Peter Braithwaite was just getting ready to tee off. There were twenty minutes or so before we were due to start, but I was glad of the chance to reflect on Rich's words. *We always like to promote from within the company.* So my analysis had been accurate. It could only be between the Ostrich and myself. I took out my seven iron and executed a few warm up swings, before stopping to stand still as they tee-ed off.

I smiled as I watched Peter Braithwaite tee up his ball, reflecting on how sometimes you can tell just by looking at someone whether he's got what it takes to get to the top. I shook my head sadly. I felt almost sorry for Peter despite his pompous English ways. Looking at him you could see why America was top dog these days, while England was just a crummy little third-rate power. His pants were too short, exposing plain gray socks. His shirt didn't even look like a proper golf shirt. The English have no sense of style. Of course, he was also an engineer. Enough said! It was obvious that someone like Peter was hardly likely to catch Hans' eye as a potential President for a dynamic company like Pumpex-SuperPumps. Two other things counted against him. He hadn't been with the company long enough, and anyway who's ever heard of an engineer as President of a company? As Peter addressed the ball, I wondered if he was still smarting from his defeat in the battle of the New Product Development Procedures. I decided that in a Dick regime Peter could stay. After all, he would hardly be a threat, and how difficult can it be to run an Engineering Department, even for a loser? No, Peter could stay. Unless that limey accent got too annoying, in which case I'd have to fire him.

Peter drove his golf ball. His swing too seemed to have no style, very loose and untidy, just like his clothes. It must have been a lucky hit, because his ball went a long way down the fairway.

"Not a bad shot."

The Ostrich has a way of just appearing without warning, which I find very irritating.

"Did you think so? I didn't think much of his swing," I replied.

"Oh, well at least it went a lot further than I ever hit it."

I smiled and took a slow stylish practice swing, which made it quite clear that I didn't share the Ostrich's reservations about my own game. I had not played a lot of golf. In fact, I had only been out on the course a couple of times, one of which was at the last Sales Meeting. But we Dicks are natural athletes, and I had taken several very expensive lessons, which had equipped me with what Jock McPherson, the professional at the Falling Rock Country Club, assured me was a classic swing. My clubs were the last word in golfing technology. I was quietly confident of putting in a pretty good performance.

"Have you seen his golf bag?" asked the Ostrich.

"What? Whose golf bag?"

"Peter's. It looks like it's about fifty years old."

I had not noticed Peter's bag on the back of his golf cart. It was a disgrace. An old brown thing, all battered and torn. It looked like it might fall apart if he were to drive the cart over a couple of bumps.

"It's a disgrace," I said, walking over to my own brand new bright red leather and canvas bag and slipping my club back into it. "People should have more respect for the National Sales Meeting. Just look at his clothes."

"Oh, they're not that bad, T. J. A little lacking in flair perhaps. Not as dapper as you. But he is an engineer, after all. Which reminds me of a joke."

I groaned. I was not interested in the Ostrich's jokes, which I have never found amusing.

"How do you know when an engineer is dead?"

I sighed. "I don't know."

"His clothes match."

I didn't laugh. This didn't seem to discourage the Ostrich.

"Or what about this one? You'll like this one. What does an engineer use as a contraceptive?"

"I don't know."

"His personality."

The Ostrich seemed to find this hilarious. Nothing shows a lack of class so much as laughing at your own jokes. I tell many excellent jokes, but never laugh at them.

"Oh, I laughed myself silly when I first heard that one," the Ostrich spluttered. "He's got lots of them, you know."

"Who?"

"Peter."

Braithwaite was obviously a fool. You won't hear me telling stupid jokes about marketeers. Marketing is a serious business. The whole success of a company depends on it. I didn't say anything. Rich was about to hit his ball. His swing was certainly much better than Peter Braithwaite's, although his ball didn't go as far.

"Good morning, gentlemen."

"Ngah."

I turned to greet Hans and Ken, who had arrived together and were stepping out of a cart. I was not pleased. I had intended to share my own cart with Hans. It seemed, however, that I had been outmaneuvered by Ken, who was obviously playing a spoiling game. Unable even to talk, never mind impress Hans with his personality, he seemed to be intent on getting in the way of anyone else. I wouldn't forget this. There was nothing to be done now, of course. Ken's and Hans' golf bags were both strapped on to the cart. Behind me I heard the Ostrich loading his clubs onto my cart.

"Looks like you and me then, T. J."

I glowered at Ken, who grinned back at me as best he could. I promised myself that I'd find a way to wipe that stupid smile off his face.

Ken was first to tee off. He removed his driver from his bag with a great flourish and held it aloft. It was then that I saw what a dangerous rival Ken could still be, despite his inability to speak. The driver wore a little hat. There was, of course, nothing unusual in that. My own woods were protected by little hats too. They were bobbly woolen hats, which I had thoughtfully selected in red, gold and black, the colors of the German flag, as a gesture of welcome which I thought Hans might appreciate. The hat on Ken's driver was not the conventional woolen type. The club wore a little Tyrolean hat, complete with that kind of shaving brush thing at the side. Clearly I had underestimated Ken as a rival. He grinned at me again as he pulled off the hat. Hans looked at him.

"Why is your club wearing an Austrian hat?"

"Nnghah mmm?" said Ken.

It was my turn to grin. An *Austrian* hat! Ken's great gesture had fallen flat on its face, owing to sloppy research that a true sales professional would never have been guilty of. I saw Ken's triumphant grin turn to a bad tempered look of frustration.

"Mmngya!" he said, as he pushed in his tee and placed the ball on top of it. "Mmngyoo gnnah!" He took a mighty swing and the ball flew off at about a forty-five degree angle into a great clump of trees.

"Nnngghaa!" he said.

I gave him a smile which said: "There's more to this game than just crawling up to Hans!"

The Ostrich was up next. His swing had even less style than Peter Braithwaite's, and in my opinion he was lucky to hit the ball at all. It bounced along the fairway about 150 yards.

"Oh well. At least I hit it," he said.

I took out my driver and walked onto the tee. The driver was brand new, with a titanium head and graphite shaft. I always like to have the very best tools for whatever I undertake. You don't reach the top in a dynamic field like marketing without the best tools.

"That is a very nice stick, Herr Dick."

"Thank you, Hans."

"Very shiny."

I placed my ball and took up my stance. I was about to swing, when I noticed one of the salesmen in the group in front of us emerging from the trees about two hundred and fifty yards ahead. I stepped back and stood waiting until he had walked on about another fifty yards. There was no point in taking any chances with a classic swing and a club like this.

"I think you're probably safe to go now, T. J." said the Ostrich.

I walked forward again and addressed the ball. I flexed the massive club head a couple of times, then drew it back slowly, keeping my left arm straight and my shoulder square to the ball. I brought the club swinging down fast and connected.

A club takes some getting used to, of course, as anyone knowledgeable about golf is only too well aware. Someone without my classic swing would almost certainly have missed the ball altogether with his first shot with a brand new club. As it turned out, the balance of the club was possibly not quite right and certainly must have been different from what I was used to. As a result, I did not make a perfect connection with the ball and it spun off the tee, running forward about fifteen feet. It was straighter than Ken's shot, but still very disappointing.

"Ngggh," said Ken with an unsportsmanlike grin.

"Hard luck, T. J." said the Ostrich.

"Herr Dick, might I make a suggestion?"

"Of course, Hans," I said.

"I think that you are standing too close to the ball."

"Do you really, Hans? I thought I was just the right distance away when I swung."

"No, Herr Dick, I do not mean before you hit the ball. I mean now."

The Ostrich laughed and Ken made a kind of choking noise.

"Forgive me, Herr Dick. It is only a joke."

"Ha, ha. Yes, very good, Hans," I said, impressing him with my sense of humor.

Hans stepped forward and placed his tee. He took a couple of practice swings, then quickly slashed at the ball.

"Great shot, Hans!" I said.

The ball trickled forward and landed a foot beyond mine.

"Ach! I am afraid that I am not good. I have not played often."

"Yes, well, it was a pretty good shot in the circumstances, I thought. With the sun in your eyes, you know. I had the same problem."

Hans grabbed his three wood and walked to where his ball lay. I did the same.

"You first, Herr Dick," said Hans, pointing at my ball.

I removed the little hat from my three wood, making sure that Hans saw its red black and gold colors. Once again I addressed the ball and executed my classic swing. This time I connected much better and the ball went a good distance up the fairway.

"Good shot, Herr Dick!"

"Thank you, Hans. I model my game on Bernhard Langer, you know."

Hans walked up to his ball and wasted no time in playing his second shot. He too made better contact this time. The ball went flying up the fairway and straight into a bunker about a hundred yards away from where we stood.

"Hard luck, Hans. I think the wind took it."

"Scheisse!" he said.

"Yes indeed."

Over to our left there was a great crash and the sound of a ball ricocheting off several trees. A voice cried, "Gnnghaffug!" We started walking toward the bunker. Meanwhile the Ostrich walked up ahead of us to his ball and played a mediocre shot which took several lucky bounces to just short of the green. He parked our cart and joined Hans and me at the bunker where Hans' ball lay almost buried in the sand.

"That's a tough looking shot," said the Ostrich, displaying his talent for stating the obvious.

"Very tough," I said, staring at the ball, "but with the right attitude by no means impossible."

I wondered if Hans was perceptive enough to pick up on the contrast between the Ostrich's negative attitude and my positive, can-do approach. His face gave no clue, as he stepped into the bunker still holding his three wood. This was obviously the wrong club. I wondered if I should tell him. I didn't want to risk making the acting President of the Pumpex Group feel foolish. But what if it was a test? To see if I would have the strength of character to tell him he was wrong. The next President of Pumpex-SuperPumps should certainly be someone with the courage to speak his mind. This, as it happens, is one of my greatest strengths.

"Shouldn't you have a sand wedge, Hans?"

"I have just had breakfast, Herr Dick."

"I don't quite follow you," I said.

"I have just had breakfast. Why would I want a sandwich?"

"No Hans," I laughed pleasantly at the misunderstanding. "Not a *sandwich*. It's a club. *Sand wedge*."

"A club sandwich? But I tell you, Herr Dick. I am not hungry."

"He means one of these," said the Ostrich, pulling the sand wedge from his bag and handing it to Hans. "You'd better borrow mine. I think Ken is going to be some time over there and he has your clubs on the cart." From the trees came the sound of a ball crashing into a tree, followed by a strangled yell.

"Thank you," said Hans, taking the club. He walked down into the bunker and took up position beside the ball. He swung hard and a great cloud of sand flew up into the air, much of it landing in my face. When it settled, we could see that the ball had not moved.

"Hard luck, Hans," said the Ostrich.

"Yes, hard luck," I said through the sand that coated my teeth and gums.

"Scheisse!"

I decided I must look up what this word meant in my German-English dictionary back at the hotel. I wondered if it was a German golfing term. Hans took another swing. This time the ball moved a few inches closer to the lip of the bunker, giving him an even more difficult shot.

"Scheisse!" I said.

The look Hans gave me was not what I had hoped for. It was already becoming very hot, and I could see that he was perspiring heavily. I was also feeling the heat. I took off my glasses and stuck them in my back pocket so that I could mop the sweat from my face. Hans took another mighty swing. The ball flew up, hit the lip of the bunker and bounced back to approximately its original location.

"Verdammte Scheisse!"

This time I said nothing. I took a few steps back under the shade of a large oak tree and waited for Hans to play his next shot. The Ostrich joined me under the tree.

"You know, T. J," he said. "I reckon you could read a hundred books on golf etiquette and another hundred on business etiquette and still not come up with just the right way to behave in a situation like this."

Hans played another shot. Another cloud of sand flew out of the bunker, but his ball remained where it was.

"I mean," he continued, "these books don't contain chapters on correct behavior when your boss is up to his neck in sand and apparently destined to remain there for some considerable time in the blazing sun, running up a basketball score on the very first hole. Do you keep saying 'hard luck' every shot? Bound to get on his nerves."

Another great cloud of smoke flew up from the bunker bringing no ball with it.

"Scheisse! Scheisse! Scheisse!"

"But you can't just not say anything. That suggests a lack of sympathy. Do you give advice? That might just make him angrier."

It was then that something very unexpected happened. Ken ran across the fairway some distance ahead of us, pursued by an alligator.

For a moment, none of us spoke. Hans, down in his bunker, had not seen anything. Then the Ostrich broke the silence.

"Hans, I think you may want to take a look at this."

We both stepped out from under the tree to get a clearer view of the chase. Hans joined us from inside the bunker and together we watched as the alligator, showing surprising speed and agility, gained on Ken, who, to be fair, was limping somewhat due to a heavy bruise on his right knee, sustained during the previous night's incident in the bar.

The scene we were witnessing was certainly unusual, but not as totally implausible as it might seem. "Wakiah" is an old Indian word for "alligator," and the island is so named because of the large number of the creatures to be found there. As I had left the hotel that morning, the desk clerk had called out cheerfully:

"Enjoy the game! Watch out for those 'gators!"

I had taken his remark for some kind of joke and had responded with a pleasant smile and an 'I will'. Now, as we watched the grim spectacle unfolding ahead of us, the clerk's remark took on a deadly significance.

It was a moment before any of us were able to react.

"Come on!" said the Ostrich. We started to run in the direction of the lake on the right of the fairway, toward which Ken and the pursuing alligator appeared to be headed. Being a natural athlete, I soon found myself ahead of the others. The Ostrich was in poor physical condition and soon fell behind, while Hans had to stop and stood wheezing in the middle of the fairway. I was not altogether happy about this. I was rapidly converging on Ken and the alligator with no clear plan regarding what to do when I met up with them. Marketing is based on sound planning and I always try to bring this principle to everything I do. For the moment, however, I had no plan, and was drawing very close to an extremely dangerous reptile that was obviously annoyed.

When I was only about twenty feet away, the alligator finally caught up with Ken at the edge of the lake. With a loud snapping sound, the brute closed its powerful jaws on the closest part of Ken. This happened to be his bottom. Ken let out a great piteous yell of pain and tried to pull away, but he remained in the grip of those massive jaws. I was still carrying my three wood and began waving it and shouting in an effort to scare off the alligator. It was no use. The animal was not to be distracted. I was at a loss for what to do.

"Nggggaaahh!" screamed Ken. He was clearly very upset.

The situation was extremely serious. Coolness under pressure is one of my greatest strengths, and I have no doubt that I would soon have hit on a plan and taken decisive action. Instead, my pants caught fire.

I mentioned earlier that I had removed my glasses in order to mop my brow, as I stood watching Hans toiling in the bunker. I had placed the glasses in my back pocket. More accurately, I had placed one of the legs of the glasses inside my pocket, leaving the lenses dangling outside. We Dicks have a tendency toward short-sightedness and the lenses of my glasses are designed to provide quite a powerful magnification. Although I didn't realize it at the time, a combination of this magnification and the strong sunlight was responsible for the flames that now leapt from the seat of my Dockers.

I had been aware of a warm glow in this region for a few seconds now, but in the emergency I had paid it no attention. Now the whole of my pants was on fire in what must have been to the onlooker a quite spectacular blaze. The effect on the alligator was dramatic and immediate. It released Ken's bottom from its jaws, turned and dived into the lake. This presented me with a dilemma. On the one hand, I had no desire to get any closer to the alligator. On the other hand, I was on fire. I weighed the options and took the only viable course of action. I jumped into the lake. A great cloud of steam rose from my pants, which seemed to scare the alligator even more than the flames of a second earlier. The brute took off swimming across the lake at great speed, as I sat gasping in two feet of muddy water.

"Are you OK, T. J?" It was the Ostrich, who had arrived at the side of the lake.

"Not really," I said. This was true. Although my quick thinking in jumping into the lake had extinguished the flames before they could cause more serious injury, I was feeling considerable pain where they had singed my buttocks.

"Just hang on, while we check on Ken. Boil me up a catfish or two."

"Oh, shut up!" I said.

He didn't hear me. He had already started running over to where Ken was lying face down in the rough. Hans arrived at about the same time. I wanted to get up and join them. They would certainly need my input in a situation as serious as this one. However, in the circumstances I felt it best to remain in the cool water of the lake. Besides, I was still trying to figure out why my pants had caught fire. It was only when I shifted my weight and heard the crack as the frames of my glasses snapped that I realized what had happened.

Hans and the Ostrich remained bent over Ken for a moment or two. Then the Ostrich shouted to me.

"Hey, T. J. Have you got your cellular phone with you?"

This was a stupid question. I was Vice President of Marketing. People might need to reach me urgently at any time. The Ostrich knew this very well.

"It's in my bag." I shouted back.

The Ostrich ran off in the direction of the cart. A minute later he was back with the cart, holding my phone.

"I've called for an ambulance," he said. "Ken'll be OK. You should see the size of the teethmarks on his ass, though. And, boy, is he mad! I reckon if his jaw wasn't broken, he'd have bitten the damn alligator back, right in the ass. That's if alligators have asses. Bit difficult to tell exactly where an alligator's ass would be."

I was glad Ken was OK. Despite his underhand attempts to undermine me, I did not wish to see him seriously injured by an alligator, especially in the middle of the National Sales Meeting. The pain in my own buttocks appeared to be subsiding a little. I rose to my feet and waded to the edge of the lake. The Ostrich held out his arm and helped me up the bank.

"That was quite a stunt there, T. J. How the hell did you manage it? Some sort of spontaneous human combustion?"

"It was a simple case of magnification of the sun's rays through the lenses of my glasses."

"I see. Just as well you were wearing them on your ass."

I ignored him. Even in moments of crisis, it seemed the Ostrich could not refrain from idiotic and inappropriate remarks. I walked over to where Ken was still lying face down on the grass. The Ostrich had not exaggerated the size of the teethmarks on Ken's buttocks. The seat of his pants had been completely ripped away, and you could see where each tooth had made a deep cut in the flesh.

"Herr Dick, you are a hero!" said Hans. He slapped me on the back. "You saved his life. How did you make the flaming trouser?"

"With the lens of my glasses. It's a simple matter of magnification of the sun's rays."

"Amazing!"

"Oh, it was nothing really. A little something I picked up in the Scouts."

"Does it hurt?"

"A bit." I said bravely.

Just then we heard a siren and the ambulance came racing across the fairway. Two paramedics jumped out and ran toward Ken.

"Now what seems to be the trouble?" said one.

"He was bitten by an alligator," said the Ostrich.

"You're sure it was an alligator?"

"Of course it was an alligator. Either that or a huge, long, scaly green dog. Perhaps a dachshund in a Halloween costume."

"Looks like an alligator sure enough, Roy," said the other paramedic, examining the tooth marks on Ken's bottom.

"You weren't over in those trees were you?" Roy asked Ken, bending down.

"Nnnghagh!"

Roy stood up again.

"Did it bite him in the face too?"

"No," said Hans. "That was Herr Dick."

"Whose dick?"

"He means *Mr.* Dick, our friend here."

"Why did he bite him in the face?"

"He didn't. It was an accident in the bar."

"It was not my fault." I insisted on putting the record straight. "It was that West Coast salesman who..."

"Because if he did go into those trees, he's only got himself to blame. That's where they lay their eggs."

"Look, shouldn't we be getting him into the ambulance?" said the Ostrich. "He's losing blood."

"They're OK unless you make a lot of noise," said Roy, as they lifted Ken, still face down, onto a stretcher. "That spooks them."

They carried Ken into the ambulance. The one named Roy started unrolling some bandages.

"Do you think I might borrow one of those bandages?" I asked.

"Why. Did it bite you too?"

"No. I need it to patch my pants. I burnt a hole in them."

"Why?"

"It scared the alligator."

"The alligator was scared of a hole in your pants?"

"He is a hero," said Hans.

"You'd better rub some cream on there," said Roy, looking at my singed skin. He reached back into the ambulance and handed me a tube. "Here. Try this."

I rubbed some cream carefully over the affected area. It was cool and soothing and must have contained some kind of local anesthetic because I soon felt much better.

"You'll never patch those pants up" said the Ostrich. "There's hardly anything left of them. Why not try these?"

He went over to his golf bag, unzipped a side pocket and produced a pair of bright orange plastic rain pants. I was not enthusiastic about putting on another pair of the Ostrich's pants. However, these were designed to go over a pair of normal pants to protect them from the rain and were consequently very loose. It seemed safe to accept the Ostrich's offer. I pulled on the pants as Roy closed the doors. We watched the ambulance disappear across the fairway toward the first tee.

"Well, gentlemen. Shall we continue our game?" said Hans.

"Certainly," I said.

Ken was in good hands. There was nothing more we could do for him. I sat down in the cart and immediately stood up again, stifling a cry of pain. Hans had already started walking back to his cart, which was still parked next to the bunker. I decided to walk too. As we approached the bunker, I noticed a ball about fifty yards up the fairway.

"I wonder whose ball that is," I said.

"It is mine, Herr Dick. I got it out with my last shot."

"Great shot, Hans."

Hans played his next shot about fifty yards, just beyond my own ball, and a couple of shots later he was on the green. His first putt was short of the hole. The next one went just past. The next one went in. The Ostrich and I each three-putted.

"A six for me," said the Ostrich.

"Six for me too," I said.

"Five for me," said Hans.

"Well played, Hans," I said.

Chapter *39*

"In Life There are Only Winners and Losers"

In life there are only winners and losers, and I, of course, have always been a winner. You don't get to be Vice President of Marketing in a top company like Pumpex-SuperPumps without the winning instinct, and you don't find losers in executive homes in Regal Pointe. However, I have learned to assign priorities and concentrate on winning where it counts. In the great scheme of things a little thing like a game of golf is not really important and, in my opinion, those who think it is are obviously pathetic losers, trying desperately to make up for disappointments and inadequacies in their real lives. It's hardly surprising that people like Peter Braithwaite shoot a seventy-four, when you think what losers they are.

Of course, if it hadn't been for some appalling luck and the effect on my balance of unfamiliar pants, I would certainly have shot a far better round, despite the new clubs and the damned wind always seeming to come up just as I hit the ball and always blowing in the worst possible direction. A lesser man might make excuses for a poor score. I am not that kind of man, of course, although for the record I am a far better golfer than a score of one hundred and twenty-one suggests. I also categorically deny any suggestion from anyone that I broke my eight iron in a fit of anger after my fourth shot in the woods at the fifteenth. Firstly, it was only my third shot, and secondly, I did not intentionally snap the club, even though its poor design was responsible for my ball being in the woods in the first place. I happened to hit a particularly powerful shot and the club obviously had some sort of a structural flaw because it broke under the force of the impact. What the Ostrich stupidly called

245

a temper tantrum was no more than a small cry of astonishment that the idiot McPherson would sell me such a piece of junk.

In the absence of Ken, it was natural that I should be called upon to present the trophies in the clubhouse after the match. Everyone gathered round in the bar, as I announced the winners. Peter accepted his trophy for first place with a broad smile which was quite inappropriate in the circumstances. After all, it was Ken who had organized the whole thing, and now he was lying in a hospital bed in Charleston while Peter grinned like a jack-ass in his awful pants that were too short and exposed his plain gray socks. I have had my disagreements with Ken, and, indeed, had not appreciated his embarrassing toadying to Hans a few hours earlier, but I still felt a little less grinning like a jack-ass and a little more respect for a seriously injured colleague would not have been out of place. And I couldn't help feeling that if Braithwaite had thought he had any chance of winning, he might have dressed a bit better. I let my disapproving frown say it all as I handed him the handsome trophy with a figure of a golfer swinging at the ball.

"Congratulations, Peter," I said.

"Thanks, T. J." Peter took the trophy and looked at it. "Isn't that a baseball player?"

"No, it's a golfer."

As a favor to Ken, I had bought the trophies a few weeks earlier. I had spent an entire Wednesday afternoon in Frank's Trophies and Fishing Supplies in downtown Falling Rock selecting the prizes. As I have mentioned before, attention to detail is one of my greatest strengths, which is why Ken entrusted me with this task in the first place. It was therefore obvious that, as the one who picked it out, I should know better than anyone what the figure on the trophy was.

"Oh," said Peter Braithwaite. "Only it looks more like a baseball player to me."

This was outrageous. The guy wasn't even a real American and here he was telling me what a baseball player looked like.

"He's right," said some idiot, who may have been a salesman for someplace in the Mid-West. "It does look more like a baseball player."

"Look," I said, "any fool can see it's a golfer. Look at the way he's holding the bat."

"Aha!" said Braithwaite. "You said bat."

"I meant club. Look at how he's holding the club."

"Bat! It's a bat."

"Look, I don't go telling you what croquet bats look like. Why don't you leave baseball to us Americans who invented it. And golf too."

"You tell him, T. J.!" said the Ostrich.

"Cricket. And I think you'll find that golf was invented in...."

"Look, do you want the damned trophy or not?"

I had had enough of this. Braithwaite obviously sensed that he had pushed me far enough. He took the trophy and sat down muttering something about Scotland or some other god-forsaken town in England where they played golf or cricket, as if anyone cared!

I moved on quickly and called up Rich to receive the runner-up trophy, which was a smaller version of the winner's one. He thanked me and made a remark that his little trophy looked a bit like Babe Ruth, which made Peter's larger trophy a Daddy Ruth. Not only was this remark not very funny, it also seemed to me to be a bit of a stab in the back, but he slapped me on the shoulder and said "Just kidding!" I have always been known for being able to take a joke at my expense and I joined in the laughter with a good humor that must have impressed Hans.

Rich called for silence.

"I'd just like to bring you up to date on Ken's condition," he said when the laughter had died down. "I've just spoken to the hospital. It seems that he's going to be OK, despite some pretty severe injuries to his...ah...buttocks."

"I suppose that means he won't be able to speak out that end either now," whispered the Ostrich, who was standing next to me. I ignored his tasteless remark.

"I guess after this," Rich went on, "he'll never complain again about getting his ass chewed by *me* when sales are down!"

Everyone laughed. I laughed too. Rich has a very sharp wit. I felt that if Ken had been there, he would have appreciated the joke too.

"Anyway, the important thing is that he's going to be OK," Rich concluded, as he walked off with his trophy.

The last award was to Hans. It was a special category, which Ken had created for top European player. Obviously he had intended to score points with Hans by presenting him with the trophy. In a dramatic twist of irony, it was now me that handed him his prize.

"Congratulations, Hans" I said.

"Thank you, Herr Dick."

"A round of 82. Well done."

Behind me I heard the Ostrich whisper to Rich, "Must have been using the metric system!" Unfortunately, Hans didn't seem to hear.

"What about the booby prize?" someone shouted.

I had been hoping that nobody would remember the booby prize. It was a tradition that at each National Sales Meeting the person with the worst score received a humorous trophy and had to buy a beer for all the other players. Given the rapid turnover of salesmen, it seemed reasonable to hope that the whole thing would have been forgotten. But someone had remembered, and now everyone was looking at me expectantly. The trophy, which consisted of some sort of a troll-like figure carrying a battered golf bag, rather like Peter Braithwaite, was sitting on the table beside me. It had a particularly obnoxious facial expression which bordered on hostility. Not the kind of thing you would want on your mantelpiece, or even in your attic, come to that.

In a purely technical sense, and seen from a particular viewpoint, my hundred and twenty-one was the highest score. However, I had no intention of awarding myself the booby prize. I had analyzed the situation objectively and concluded that in all fairness, the booby prize belonged to Tab Masterson, the coach of the 1984 South Carolina Water Polo Championship-winning Charleston Penguins. Tab, who was due to deliver an address entitled *The Winning Instinct* that evening had joined us for golf, forming a foursome with Mike and the Texas and Florida salesmen. He had quit after nine holes however, blaming the heat for a very poor start to the round, and spent the rest of the morning in the bar with Melissa, our lady salesman. He was now stretched across a bench at the back of the room with his head back, snoring loudly. Clearly, his failure to complete the round qualified him for the booby prize. I was just trying to figure out how best to wake him up, in order to call him forward to receive the trophy, when Rich appeared by my side.

"Well now, we can hardly expect you to present the trophy to yourself, T. J.," he said. "Let me do the honors."

"Actually Rich, I believe Tab Masterson should really be the one..."

"Don't be ridiculous, T. J. Tab's...ah...resting. Look at him. How's he going to present the trophy?"

Rich thrust the troll into my left hand, shaking the right one vigorously. There was loud applause. I could do little but accept the horrid little figurine with a gracious smile.

"Thank you, Rich. Although I don't really deserve this...."

"Yes you do!" someone shouted.

"Don't be so modest!" said the Ostrich above the spontaneous applause that had broken out. "You earned it."

I found myself moved by this display of affectionate admiration from my colleagues. Surely Hans could not fail to see the leadership potential.

"Beers for everyone!" I cried.

"Way to go, T. J!"

"You're the man!"

"Why don't you all shut the hell up? I'm trying to get some sleep back here!"

Chapter 40

"Leading the Company into the Twenty-First Century"

I was disappointed in Tab Masterson's presentation on *The Winning Instinct*. He made several good points in his description of his many personal qualities which had enabled him to lead the Charleston Penguins to success in 1984. These included courage, wisdom, perseverance, faith, dedication, leadership, a never-say-die attitude, a can-do mentality, enthusiasm, will-to-win, refusal to accept defeat, refusal to accept anything but the best, a couple of other refusals, courage again, and, strangely, kindness to animals. I made detailed notes and was gratified to notice how many of these qualities were among my greatest strengths.

The weakness was in his presentation. His diction was slurred, making it hard to follow him sometimes, and he had a tendency to wander from the point. He spent several minutes describing how the same qualities that had made him a winner were conspicuously lacking in Chuck Towlin, who had taken over at the Penguins after Tab's dismissal in 1986, and whose six championship successes were due to one of the most amazing lucky streaks in the history of sport.

When Tab asked for questions, the Ostrich, of course, just had to have his say.

"Which of your many qualities most contributed to your last place in 1985?"

"You want a fight, wise guy?"

"No. No thanks. I'll shut up, will I?"

"Yeah"

"OK then."

"What is water polo Herr Mustardsauce?"

The rest of the presentation was spent in a description of the rules of water polo, which it turns out is about as well known in Germany as it is in the US. By this time, I noticed, several people were asleep, while others had drifted away to the bar. I remained behind, although I was no longer really listening. My mind was on other things.

We like to promote from within the company. It certainly seemed like a pretty heavy hint. I wondered if Rich had made the same remark to the Ostrich. I doubted it. It was the kind of thing that you would only say to somebody if you were pretty sure that that person from within the company was the person you were talking to. And if Rich was going to announce his intention to leave in three weeks tonight at the Awards Dinner, this would be a perfect time to announce his successor. I was preoccupied with these thoughts, when I realized suddenly that Tab Masterson had finished and everyone else had left except Hans, who came over and sat beside me.

"Herr Dick. I would like to talk to you tonight after dinner."

"Yes, Hans."

"As you are knowing, Rich is leaving, and the company will need a new President. This will mean a lot of changes and reorganization at SuperPumps, but I am sure that we can achieve a smooth transmission."

"Yes, of course. Smooth transition. Yes."

"I will be making an important announcement tonight."

"Yes."

"There will be much to talk about."

"Yes."

Just then, Harvey came into the room, with typically insubordinate timing.

"Not now, Harvey," I said. "Hans and I are having an important discussion."

"No, no Harvey. Come on in. I want to hear how you got on at Pumps-R-Us," said Hans.

I looked at my watch. Five-fifteen.

"Yes, Harvey. You've been away long enough."

"It went very well," said Harvey.

"Yes, well we can hear all about it back at the office next week. I want a full written report, of course. Ask Jill for a Customer Visit Report Form."

"I want to talk to you about it now, Harvey," said Hans. "Herr Dick, I will see you at dinner."

I watched Hans and Harvey walk off in the direction of the bar, then headed to Puffin Cottage to change for dinner.

The Awards Dinner is the only formal occasion at the National Sales Meeting. The meeting is very much a working session, during which we roll up our sleeves and get down to the serious business of planning our sales successes for the coming year. Vice presidents mingle with ordinary salesmen and product managers, with no time for standing on ceremony. The Awards Dinner is an exception, however. Its purpose is to honor the outstanding achievements of our best salesmen, and it is a gala occasion at which suits are worn.

As I straightened my red silk tie in front of the mirror in my room, I reflected on my conversation with Hans. It seemed that my plans were about to come to fruition. I was glad for Pumpex-SuperPumps. The company needed a man of vision at this critical time. I spent a few extra minutes making sure that my tie was just right. It was possible that I might have to make a short inspiring speech, and I certainly wanted to get off on the right foot. I thought about what I might say and noted down a few headings on a page of my personal organizer. *Building on past successes... Exciting times ahead... Leading company into 21st century... A vision for the future... Everyone pulling together to achieve aims of Mission Statement.* I tore out the page, put it in the breast pocket of my jacket and paused to take another quick look in the mirror. My suit was crisply pressed and neatly creased. My shoes shone. My hair was impeccable, combed over the slightly thinning area on top. I am not a vain man, but a dynamic young leader was what the company needed and impressions do count for a lot. I looked at my watch. Six-fifteen. Time to go.

People were already gathered in the bar when I arrived. Some of them looked like they had been there for some time.

"Would you like a drink, T. J?" The Ostrich was at the bar.

I thought for a moment. "Scotch on the rocks." I was in a celebratory mood.

The Ostrich brought me over my drink and three others on a tray. I noticed his suit was crumpled and there was a spot on his tie, which was dark blue. The tie, not the spot.

"Shall we go in, T. J? It's half past six."

I looked around. There was no sign of Hans or Rich.

"They've already gone in," said the Ostrich. "I just came out to get these drinks for them."

We went into the dining room, and I followed the Ostrich to a large circular table at the back of the room. Hans and Rich were already there.

"Here you are, Rich. Scotch on the rocks." The Ostrich turned to Hans. "And here's your schnapps Hans. I would never have thought you could get that here. They've got a very well stocked bar."

"Schnapps is a very popular brandy-like drink that can be flavored with a variety of fruits," I said.

"Have a seat, T. J." said Rich.

I sat down on the empty chair to the left of Hans. Rich was on his right. The Ostrich sat down on my left. A few seconds later Peter arrived and sat down opposite us. There was one extra chair next to him, which had presumably been intended for Ken. I looked around the room. There were six circular tables, each seating six people. They were rapidly filling up as the salesmen appeared from the bar. I caught sight of Mike at the table next to ours, where there was some small commotion, caused by Rachel slapping the Florida salesman in the face. The commotion soon died down. I thought of asking Mike to join us. It seemed silly to have an empty chair at our table, while the future Vice President of Marketing sat with a bunch of salesmen. Before I could do so, however, I heard Hans call out:

"Harvey. Come please and sit by us at our table."

I had not noticed Harvey. I wondered if he had been late. It was now six-thirty-three. I certainly could see no reason for him to sit at our table. I glared at him and looked pointedly at my watch, as he pulled out a chair and sat down. I don't think he noticed, which was typical of him. He certainly didn't look like somebody who belonged at the Senior Management table. I am not one to attach much importance to rank, and an unpretentious informal approach to management is one of my greatest strengths. I am quite at home rubbing shoulders with product managers and even Production people. Still, Harvey simply didn't look right sitting with top executives. His hair was untidy and could have benefited from a trim. His suit was obviously a couple of years old and his tie was dark blue like the Ostrich's. In fact, come to that, the Ostrich didn't look like he belonged at a table of top executives either. However, he *was* a top executive, so there wasn't much that could be done about it, at least not yet. Harvey, on the other hand was a Product Manager. All in all, I considered Hans' invitation inappropriate.

The first course arrived. Shrimp. I decided not to risk a repeat of the previous day and waved the waiter away. Everyone else began to eat.

"It's a pity Ken couldn't be here to present the awards," said Rich. "He's such an inspiration to the sales force. It would have meant a lot to them to receive their rewards from him. He couldn't have spoken, of course, but at least he could have handed over the plaques."

"Are you going to do it all yourself, then?" asked the Ostrich.

"I guess I'll have to."

I found my attention wandering. I was not really interested in the details of the awards ceremony. I was trying to decide between a solid mahogany desk for my new office and one of those modern ones with lots of chrome. I decided on mahogany. Its traditional solidity would provide a reassuring counterbalance to my dynamic up-to-the-minute management style.

The main course arrived. It was Beef Wellington, which prompted Peter Braithwaite to launch into a long boring story about the Duke of Wellington's horse. Why he should think anyone would be interested in some limey lordship's nag was beyond me. I didn't catch the end of the story, or the middle actually, as I was still working out the final details of my desk. I also decided to have some modern art on the walls. Probably by a local artist, to highlight my involvement in the community. This kind of thing would be expected of me as a leading figure in the local economy.

When I tuned into the conversation again the Ostrich had taken up Peter Braithwaite's ridiculous theme and was telling some sort of pointless story about Alexander the Great and his horse. Personally I have no great liking for either horses or Frenchmen, so I had little interest in the story. I could see that Hans was bored too, so I decided to involve him tactfully in the conversation.

"Did Bismarck have a horse, Hans?"

"What was that, Herr Dick?"

"I was wondering if Bismarck had a horse."

"Who was Bismarck?" asked Rich.

"Bismarck," said Peter," was a great German statesman of the nineteenth century."

I could have strangled that limey know-it-all. He had obviously invested in a book too.

"I thought it was a battleship," said the Ostrich.

"Ha, ha. A battleship. That's ridiculous," I said, giving the Ostrich a pitying look.

"It *was* a battleship," said Hans.

I wondered if Hans was having another of his unfunny German jokes. My book had said nothing about a battleship. Come to think of it, it had had very little to say on the subject of the war.

"And a statesman," Hans continued. "The battleship was named after the statesman. And I am not sure whether the statesman had a horse."

"He must have," said the Ostrich. "It was a hundred years ago. If he didn't have a horse, how would he have got to meetings with other statesmen."

"I think you are right of course, Herr Ronnie."

"Yes, it would be a pretty lonely life for a statesman without a horse."

I sensed that I had lost control of the conversation. I had wanted to drop a couple of other famous Germans into the discussion, but, before I could say anything to steer the subject in that direction, there was a sharp rapping sound, such as is made by a table being struck by a spoon.

"Ladies and Gentlemen," said Rich, who had risen to his feet holding a spoon, "it's time to turn to the main business of the evening."

There was a lot of shuffling and scraping of chairs, as everyone turned to look at the top table. Rich cleared his throat and continued.

"I know that Ken is very upset that he can't be here tonight. The Awards Dinner is always very special for him. It is his chance to pay tribute to the finest sales force in the American pump industry."

There was enthusiastic applause. The Ostrich leaned across in my direction and said in a loud whisper "Poor old Captain Hook!" This was a typically stupid remark as anyone familiar with "Peter Pan" knows very well that the animal pursuing Captain Hook was a crocodile and not an alligator. The Ostrich was never known for precision. Before I had time to point out his mistake, Rich continued:

"I am very proud to be able to step into his shoes and present the awards here this evening." He paused and cleared his throat again. "The award for Salesman of the Year, based on total sales as a percentage of quota....."

I didn't pay much attention to the presentation of the awards. The Salesman of the Year award went to Melissa, our lady salesman. I am not sure whether, as a woman, she had received a lower quota to make it fair, but if she had, nobody seemed to mind too much, and there was very chivalrous applause. After she had accepted her award, Rich moved on to the Runner-Up Award, and then the Most Improved Sales Performance Award.

"It seems that everyone gets an award," whispered Hans.

Rich had just presented the Perseverance Award and was delivering a short speech about the importance of integrity, as a build-up to the presentation of the Integrity Award.

"Only those who have shown special merit are recognized," I said.

"I do not recognize any of them, Herr Dick."

"No, I mean only those who have shown special merit get awards."

"Moving onto the next award," said Rich, "the Cleanest Car Award..."

"I see," said Hans. "It is of course, coincidence that everyone has shown special merit."

"It's supposed to keep them motivated, I suppose," said the Ostrich. "Although I personally would not feel spurred to greater things in the year ahead by a cheesy plaque with the word *Perseverance* on it. I guess that's why I'm not a salesman."

"One of the reasons!" I thought to myself, wondering what made the Ostrich think he knew anything about motivating people. His department was just a bunch of bean counters, who didn't really need to be motivated, and nobody would notice if they were. However, despite my more progressive view of awards ceremonies, I found myself wishing this particular one were over, so that we could get down the main item on the night's agenda. Hans was going to have to get a move on, if I was going to have the opportunity to make my inspiring speech over coffee. Dessert had already been served, and Rich was still presenting the awards.

"And the award for neatest presentation of expense reports goes to Lance Boyle of Detroit. Congratulations, Lance!"

Normally I would have paid special attention to this award, which Ken had introduced at my suggestion. I applauded with everybody else, but I hardly heard Lance's words of acceptance. The future of Pumpex-SuperPumps was about to be revealed and it was hard to concentrate on anything else, even expense reports.

At last Rich called for a round of applause for all the award winners and sat down, just as coffee was being served. Hans had ordered another schnapps, which he downed quickly before taking a sip of his coffee.

"Gentlemen," he said.

The conversation at the table stopped. There was something in the way that Hans said "Gentlemen" that told you he was about to say something very important. Everyone sensed that a crucial moment had arrived. I looked at the Ostrich. He had stopped talking and was looking at Hans. If he was nervous, he was hiding it well. I wondered if he had already given up and accepted defeat. Or was it a sign of misplaced confidence?

"Gentlemen," said Hans, "I have been in the pump industry since 40 years. In that time I have seen many changes. Just-in Time Inventory, Total Quality Management, Customer Care Programs, even Mission Statements." At this point, he looked at me. I smiled modestly. "But one thing remains the same. If you make a good pump and treat your customers as people who know a good pump when they see one, you will do well. Gentlemen, the man to lead SuperPumps must be a man who *knows pumps*."

The waiter delivered another schnapps. Hans drank it down and continued:

"That is why I have decided on a little experiment."

Hans reached into his jacket pocket and brought out a short fat cylindrical object with two pipes attached to it, which he laid on the table. From his other pocket, he produced two more pipes and several pieces of metal and rubber in varying shapes and sizes.

"Does anyone recognize this?" asked Hans.

There was a moment of silence, before Peter said: "It appears to be some kind of hydraulic assembly."

"Its a PX-2," said Harvey.

"That's right," said Hans, "our best selling product."

"Well done, Harvey," I said. "You and I were probably the only ones who knew!"

Hans picked up the pieces of metal and rubber and placed them in front of me.

"Do you know how the pieces fit together, Herr Dick?"

I looked at him in astonishment.

"Do you know how it works?"

I continued to look at him in astonishment. Nobody had ever asked me a question like that before. I am a top marketing executive.

"What about you, Herr Ronnie?"

"I have to admit I don't. I know how much it costs of course, and what kind of margin we make on it. I don't really know how it works, though."

"Harvey, do you know?"

"Yes, Hans. Let me show you."

Harvey took the pieces of metal and rubber and assembled them into something that looked very much like the object held by the runner up in the Miss North Carolina Pageant in our advertisement. He then moved part of it up and down so that air was blown out the end, making ripples in my coffee and spilling some of it onto my saucer. I gave him a look that said, "You'd better not be doing that deliberately, my boy, if you value your job!"

Hans took the assembly from Harvey and held it up to his eyes.

"Gentlemen, is not that a thing of beauty?"

"Yes, Hans," I nodded. "I've always admired the PX-2."

"But only Harvey knew what it was and knew how to put it together. I should make Harvey President of SuperPumps. He *knows* pumps."

I laughed. Hans looked at me for a moment. Then he too started to laugh.

"You are right, Herr Dick. I was only joking. You cannot choose the next President because he can put together again taken apart pumps."

It took me a moment to figure out what he was saying. The man spoke like a crossword puzzle. As the Ostrich later remarked, the darned pump was easier to put together than one of Hans' sentences.

"Ha, ha," I said. "That German sense of humor again."

I wished he would stop messing around and get on with it. People would be finishing their coffee soon and would start heading for the bar. I didn't want to make a speech in the bar. It would not be easy to be inspiring in there. Hans took a sip of his coffee and continued:

"However, I have made a selection for the next President of Pumpex-SuperPumps, and I would like to tell you all, as Senior Management, before I announce it to everyone else."

"At last," I thought. There might still be time to make a short speech before everyone finished their coffee.

"I spoke to the concerned person earlier this evening and I am sure he will make a fine President. In my short visit, I have noticed how he holds the Marketing Department together despite many difficulties."

I tried to look modest.

"But that is not the only reason that I am selecting this fine fellow to be President. There are practical and immediate reasons why he must be my choose."

He paused to take another sip of coffee. The waiter removed two empty glasses from the table in front of him.

"One more schnapps please, my friend," he said. The waiter glided off toward the bar. Hans put down his cup and looked round the table. "As you all know, in the time since Pumpex bought SuperPumps, you have somehow managed to lose almost every customer the company had. Only Pumps-R-Us continues to buy."

"That's not strictly speaking true, Hans," I said. "There's a company in Kansas that just last month...."

"Walnuts!" said Hans.

"I beg your pardon."

"Walnuts, it's all just walnuts compared to sales before the buyout."

"It's true that sales are way down," said the Ostrich.

"Anyway," Hans continued, "the fact is, if we lose Pumps-R-Us, we might as well close down when the insurance for the fire runs out. We have only one factory for Herr Dick to burn down. Today I spoke to Clayton Sipe, the owner of Pumps-R-Us. He is a nice man who knows pumps. He told me his company has bought its pumps from SuperPumps since many years. He said that he will continue to buy from us, on one condition."

The waiter arrived with Hans' schnapps. He drank it down and gave a sigh of satisfaction. "Very good schnapps. It reminds me of home, where I hope to be very soon. Have you ever been to Germany, Herr Ronnie? You must visit me. I live in Hamburg."

"What is it?" asked Rich.

"A city, Herr Rich."

"No, the condition. What was Clayton Sipe's condition?"

"Ah yes, the condition. The condition, gentlemen, is that the next President of the company should be Harvey."

"Ha, ha," I said.

Nobody else seemed to be laughing. Hans' features showed no trace of amusement.

"Ha, ha, ha," I repeated.

"You *are* joking, aren't you, Hans?" asked Rich.

"It is no joke, Herr Rich."

"But we can't let customers, of all people, tell us how to run our business!"

"It's ridiculous," I said. "If we went around listening to customers, where would we be?"

"Perhaps you would have more of them, Herr Dick."

"But Harvey is a Product Manager," said Rich.

"Yes, he lacks the vision of a Senior Executive," I added.

"You do not need a lot of vision to see where this company is headed under its current men of vision," said Hans, finishing his schnapps.

For some reason, the Ostrich found this funny. Out of the corner of my eye I saw him fighting to suppress a smile. I could see nothing amusing in the situation.

"But what about qualifications?" said Rich.

"Yes," I said. "You can't have just anyone as President. It has to be someone with a degree in Business from a top rank college."

"Have you ever asked Harvey what his qualifications are, Herr Dick?"

"Well, no." It had never occurred to me to ask Harvey about qualifications. I had not hired him after all. I had inherited him from the pre-takeover management. I assumed that they couldn't be very impressive, if indeed he had any at all. He certainly didn't look or behave like somebody with qualifications.

"Well, Herr Dick, Harvey has an MBA from a top college. I am surprised that you did not know that."

"Good God, does he really? I just always assumed, seeing him sitting there...well you know. Looking at pumps. Knowing about how they work and things. That's not the kind of thing you expect from somebody with that kind of qualification."

"Perhaps he should have been writing Mission Statements, Herr Dick."

"Yes, exactly."

"But surely you can see, Hans," said Rich pointing at the PX-2 that was still lying on the table," that somebody who knows how to put that thing together can hardly be the kind of guy that's going to be able to see the big picture."

"Yes," I nodded, looking at the pump with disdain. "Harvey may be OK with details, but what about the big picture? An ability to see the big picture. Vision. That's what the company needs."

"And just what is the big picture, Herr Dick? What is vision?"

"Well, it's....you know....um...."

"Yes, Herr Dick?"

"Well it's not being able to put pumps together."

"I see. So the definition of vision is not being able to put pumps together."

"Exactly."

"Hmm. If that is so, I must compliment you on your vision. But do you know what I think the big picture is, Herr Dick?"

"No, Hans."

"Details. What is the big picture, if it is not a collection of many details?"

I didn't get it. Was this some weird kind of German logic?

"I don't get it, Hans."

"I know, Herr Dick. I know. And now, if you will excuse us, Rich and I have some announcements to make."

I hardly heard Rich's announcement and was only vaguely aware of the applause when he finished. I clapped mechanically, but my mind was numb. Hans started speaking, but I couldn't bring myself to listen. I had been passed over in favor of *a Product Manager*. A Product Manager in a blue tie and a two year old suit. It was, I decided, the treachery and ingratitude of it all that hurt the most. I had taken Harvey under my wing, nurtured him in my department. And all the time he was treacherously harboring an MBA. And now some podgy Kraut with absolutely no vision had picked this nobody as the next President of Pumpex-SuperPumps. All because he *knows about pumps*. It was absurd.

Suddenly everyone was clapping again. The Ostrich was thumping Harvey on the back, and saying, "Congratulations, Harvey. I'll admit it was a bit of a surprise. But you know, I don't see any reason why you shouldn't be a really good President."

I could think of lots of reasons, but there was little to be gained by mentioning them. A crowd of people had gathered round Harvey now, shaking his hand and making sycophantic comments. I watched the disgusting spectacle for a moment. There was, I realized, only one course open to me. I knew what I had to do. I pushed my way through the crowd of people until I reached Harvey.

"Harvey," I said.

"Yes, T. J."

"I was wondering if you'd like a drink from the bar."

"No thanks, T. J. Mike's already getting me one."

EPILOGUE

Strategic planning, leadership and teamwork have always been three of my greatest strengths, so my new position as leader of the Corporate Strategy Development and Long Range Planning Team is a natural fit. It allows me to continue my own career development while making telling contributions toward meeting corporate goals. My Corporate Mission Statement seems likely to be a great success.

Grace is glad of the move back to Boston. We bought a home in a prestigious executive development and, on her insistence, are having extensive work done on it. This means a constant stream of construction workers filling the house for days on end, but I must give credit where it is due and say that she has never complained. It was her idea that I should offer Randy the position of Assistant Team Leader. To be honest, I didn't think he would come, which is why I asked him in the first place. I would have preferred Mike, but that young thruster had already accepted a post as Corporate Director of Systems Development, which lets him do things with his prodigious computer skills.

I see Rich occasionally, and we always find time for a chat. It came as a great surprise to me that he and Liz have split up. He seems to be bearing up remarkably well and has lost none of his sharp sense of humor.

I try not to worry too much about SuperPumps. In my new position, I have to take a more global view and keep focused on the big picture. Of course, Harvey is destroying everything we built in the name of short term growth. It is typical of him to let his personal feelings influence his decisions, at the cost of the company's future. I have it on good authority that the New Product Development procedure is not being followed. The Mission Statement has been removed from the notice boards, leaving the company essentially rudderless and the promotional campaign centered on the runner-up in the Miss North Carolina Pageant, which had promised so much, has been shelved. I had occasion to go down there a couple of weeks ago to make a presentation on the Corporate Strategic Plan, and everything was a shambles. As far as I could see, there was no viable Meeting Room Reservation Procedure and I could only assume that it was through sheer luck that there was a meeting room available for us at all. I pointed this out to Harvey, of course, but he just made some pointless observation about being too busy cutting costs and growing the company's sales by 30% in six months to enforce unnecessary procedures. Unnecessary procedures! I told him there was more to running a successful company than turning a loss into a profit and expanding the business. You need procedures or it will all collapse like a house of cards. I started to ask him what he was going to do about a Mission Statement, but I could see he wasn't listening. Let him stew in his own juice!

The trouble with Harvey is that he's not really executive material. He doesn't see the big picture. What they really need down there is a first class marketing professional running things. Not that I would want the job now, of course, when I am in such a vital corporate role, where the real action is. In fact, Harvey is so short sighted that he has not even replaced me yet. How he hopes to be successful without being able to draw on the strengths of a top class marketeer is completely beyond me. I can only assume that he has tried and failed to find someone with my skill set and personal drive.

I saw Ken when I was down there. I don't think he will last long in the Harvey regime. Like me, Ken is the kind of man who thrives in a thoroughly professional environment. His injuries had healed, but he was a bit depressed when I spoke to him. He had hoped to set up his own consulting business on the money his lawyers promised to extract from the Seabreeze Inn for their negligence in the alligator incident. However, the Seabreeze people had a better lawyer and were held not to be liable, owing to the fact that Ken should have dropped his ball two club lengths from the alligator. All he got was a complimentary round of golf and a rather nice golf shirt, which he happened to be wearing that night at a party thrown by Peter Braithwaite, which, as a representative of Corporate, I felt compelled to attend.

Of course I couldn't avoid bumping into the Ostrich. He cornered me at the party and brought me up to date with what he called "all the latest developments." It turns out that *he* sent Ken the golf shirt, which Ken had assumed to have come from the Seabreeze Inn. He kept telling me it was a Lacoste shirt, pointing to the logo and chuckling to himself in that strange way of his. As usual with the Ostrich, I couldn't figure out what it was he found so funny. We did agree on one thing. Harvey will not last long as President of Pumpex-SuperPumps. Our reasons for believing this are quite different however. The Ostrich has some absurd conspiracy theory that what he calls "the old boys club of talentless, self-important gnomes at Corporate" will find a way to stab him in the back because he's not one of them. I disagree. I think his own inadequacies and lack of vision will be disastrous for the company and eventually he will have to be removed and replaced with someone of vision. Rich and I happened to mention this to the new Group President over lunch the other day and he seemed most concerned.

I may also have happened to mention that I have not yet sold my house in Falling Rock.

READERS' GROUP GUIDE AND DISCUSSION TOPICS

1. Augustus Gump has been called "the greatest living exponent of the English language." How many beers do you think Mr. Gump had had when he made this claim?

2. "The character of T. John Dick is so troubling because the pathos of his situation contrasts starkly with the bathos of his character. Within the parameters of his corporate microcosm, he achieves the status of a contemporary tragic hero, destined to fail by the very flaws which drive his aspirations for success."
Which of these two sentences is the more patently absurd?

3. T. J.'s obsession with trivial details, such as the Meeting Room Reservation Procedure might be described as a serious personality defect. Discuss some of your own personality defects. Bet you've got some real doozies! You might like to help your co-members by pointing out some of theirs.

4. The Management Secrets of T. John Dick contains strikingly few references to fish—yet water covers 70% of the earth's surface. Coincidence?

5. Augustus Gump is considering the purchase of a pipe in the belief that being observed to smoke one will enhance his profile as an important literary voice. Do you think this will be a waste of money?

6. What is it about "The Management Secrets of T. John Dick" which gives it its power to fascinate the reader to the extent that he/she would prefer to sit around in someone's living room or a bookstore coffee shop dicussing its nuances, rather than to head on down to the bar on the corner for a couple of swift ones and maybe some buffalo wings? Hey, come back! Where are you going? Hey!